all
eyes
on
her

all eyes on her

L.E. FLYNN

{Imprint}
MAKE YOUR MARK
NEW YORK

SQUARE FISH

An imprint of Macmillan Publishing Group, LLC
120 Broadway, New York, NY 10271
fiercereads.com

Our books may be purchased in bulk for promotional, educational, or business
use. Please contact your local bookseller or the Macmillan Corporate and
Premium Sales Department at (800) 221-7945 ext. 5442 or by email
at MacmillanSpecialMarkets@macmillan.com.

Library of Congress Control Number: 2019941053

[Imprint]
MAKE YOUR MARK

Originally published in the United States by Imprint
First Square Fish edition, 2022
Book designed by Elynn Cohen
Square Fish logo designed by Filomena Tuosto
Imprint logo designed by Amanda Spielman
Printed in the United States of America.

ISBN 978-1-250-76283-2 (paperback)
1 3 5 7 9 10 8 6 4 2

Never forget whose book this is.
If it isn't yours, return it to its rightful owner.
Or else you might find all eyes are on you.

For my dad—
I'm forever proud to call you
my father, hero, and friend

all
eyes
on
her

PART I

Jack and Jill went up the hill
To fetch a pail of water

HER

THE LIGHTS ARE HARSH, more white than yellow, like nothing found in nature, even though nature harbors so many harsh things. The girl sitting under the lights is still a teenager. Most of the time, she looks older, but today, she looks young and scared, blue eyes blinking like a doll.

The host asked her to tell her side of the story. She told it, with her chin raised. It was the first time she could really be sure people were listening. Now it's the final question.

The host—the one who secured the interview, the one who wanted it badly enough to be the highest bidder—looks at the girl, serious. Maybe she sees something she didn't at first. How the girl is a bit rough around the edges, if you look closely. Her skirt a bit too short, her legs bare, no pantyhose. Her lips too red. And those eyes, like the lights. Like nothing found in nature.

"What do you want people around the world to know about you that they don't already? What's the one thing you'd like to tell everyone who has followed your story?"

The girl sucks in a breath, holds it there. It's something she must have thought about so many times, the words rolling in her head, sometimes calm, sometimes a tidal wave. When she answers, her voice is a crescendo, getting louder. She looks straight into the camera. She gets the last word.

"Don't believe everything you read," she says. "Don't believe everything you hear. Make up your own mind about me."

Princeton student dead after hiking accident
By Julie Kerr

The body of Mark Forrester, a 20-year-old Princeton student, was found in Claymore Creek on Saturday morning. Forrester had been hiking the Mayflower Trail with his girlfriend, Tabitha Cousins, 17, late Friday afternoon. Cousins stated that Forrester wanted to hike to the trail's renowned but dangerous lookout point, popularly known as "the Split," to see the sunset. But once at the top, he lost his footing and fell, plummeting almost 40 feet down.

"It was terrifying," Cousins said. "One second he was looking over the edge, then he was just gone."

Neither Cousins nor Forrester were experienced hikers. The Mayflower Trail, extending eight miles, is marked with signs warning hikers about the dangers of ascending to the lookout point. It is advised that only experienced hikers make the attempt.

Cousins was the first to report the incident in the early hours of Saturday morning, after she found her way out of the woods in the dark. "I kept calling for help," she said. "But nobody was around to hear me. I was so scared."

Forrester's death brings the death toll in Queen Anne's Woods to seven since the first was recorded in 1916. The Split was referred to as "Suicide Sledge" during the 1960s, when three female cult members jumped as part of a suicide pact. The last death to occur at the Split before now was in October 1989, when teenagers Ernest Malling and Desiree Hind went into the woods for a camping trip. Hind reported Malling missing the next day, after she claimed he went off on his own, but his body wasn't found until two days later. No foul play could be proven, but Malling's family maintained that they were certain Hind was involved.

A team of police divers found Forrester's body. He is survived by his mother and father, longtime Coldcliff residents, and his older brother.

YOU

YOU HEARD THE STORY ON THE NEWS. A girl and a boy went into the woods. The girl carried a picnic basket. The boy wore bright yellow running shoes. They weren't planning to be out past dark, but the sky was pitch black when the girl found her way back, without the picnic basket and without the boy. The boy was discovered the next morning, floating facedown in Claymore Creek, his yellow running shoes obscured by hazy water.

You heard that it was a tragedy, that the boy had his entire life in front of him. That he was returning to Princeton on a swimming scholarship. *Mark the Shark*, his pool nickname. Soon enough, you'll be going to his funeral with everybody else.

You've been following her online. Maybe you knew the suspicion was bound to trail her like a cape. After all, there are plenty of holes in her story. But there are holes in everyone else's version, too.

Maybe you know her—you might have gone to a party with her. She liked those. Or maybe you just stalked her on Instagram and saw all the selfies, her #nofilter face, all lipstick and electric-blue eyes. Maybe she was a bitch to you once. (She probably was a bitch to you once, and maybe you deserved it.)

But now you're going to learn all sides of this story. You'll find out what really happened, from the people who know and love her, and from those who know her but wish they didn't. Here lie the facts. Once you have them, you'll be equipped to decide for yourself. Guilty or not guilty. If you think she did it, you'll wonder if she's going to get away with it.

If you think she didn't, you'll wonder why she was in the woods that late at all.

1

ELLE

"ELLE, IT'S ABOUT MARK."

I barely recognize her voice. This isn't the first time she has called at 2 a.m.—she's nocturnal, awake when the rest of us are drooling into our pillowcases. This isn't the first time she has called and sounded scared. This isn't the first time she has started with *Elle, it's about Mark*. The fights are getting more intense, the days between an argument getting shorter. She never used to call—it was always a text. But lately she needs to hear my voice. Or needs me to hear hers.

"What did he do now?" I snap up in my bed, pushing sweaty hair out of my face. "Where are you?"

"He fell."

"What? Fell where?"

"In the woods, Elle."

"On what? Is he okay?" Hopefully, he didn't break anything. Mark the Shark needs all body parts intact for his illustrious swimming career. Even though that isn't going so well anymore—*You ruined my life*, I heard him tell Tabby at my last party. A conversation she denied ever happened when I asked her about it later.

Tabby never lied to me before Mark came along. Even though I didn't pay her the same courtesy.

"This is serious, Elle." Her voice trails off. "He's not okay. He's . . ."

I know it before she says it, by the weight of her silence. I know it.

"He's dead."

And for a terrible few seconds, or maybe longer, I'm relieved.

2

BRIDGET

SHE SAYS SHE'LL BE HOME LATE, but that maybe we can watch something on Netflix later. "Your choice," she says, which is rare, because usually it's the two of us arguing about what to watch for longer than it takes to watch an actual movie.

She's at her desk before she leaves, looking at the map I drew her. I would have recognized it anywhere. The Split, tall and menacing.

"I can't believe he's taking you there," I say. "It's going to take hours. It's super hilly, you know, and getting to the top is a real struggle. In this heat, it'll be brutal."

"That's why I'm getting prepared," she says. "I'm taking your map with me, like a good little Girl Scout. That way, if anything happens, I won't get lost."

"Okayyyyy." I drag out the word, pulling it through my mouth like taffy.

"What are you so afraid of?" Tabby swivels around. "That the woods are going to swallow me whole? I'm the big sister. I'm supposed to be the overprotective one."

I do the math in my head. Even if they manage to hike three miles an hour, they won't reach the Split until after seven. It makes me feel better, somehow, knowing where she'll be, when to expect her home.

"I'd text you to let you know I'm okay, but there isn't cell reception that deep in the woods," she says. "At least, I bet there isn't. Just don't worry about me, okay?"

Later, I watch her jump into Mark's car, picnic basket

9

swinging from her arm. She has my shoes on, pink Nikes. I can't describe it, but I feel like I'm being haunted as soon as she's gone. It's like I'm sure I'll never see her again.

She doesn't come home in time for a movie, and she never messages to let me know where she is. Mom and Dad start getting worried around eleven, when they haven't heard from her. They're oblivious. They should have been worried before she even left.

She's dead, my brain screams. I picture Mark's big hands, Mark's cocky grin. We'll have to identify her body.

"Don't go out again." Dad wags his finger at me. "I want you where I can see you."

I forgot I even went out. I went for a run, my phone in the palm of my hand, my fingers clutching it tightly, like it could be a weapon if I needed it to, something hard enough to crack a skull. But that was hours ago. I forgot to shower. It was like I blacked out.

At midnight, Mom and Dad are pacing, and I'm upstairs with my face pressed against the window, like a little kid waiting for Santa.

They call Elle, but she doesn't answer. Maybe I'm imagining it, but things seem to have changed a bit between them lately. Tabby doesn't spend as much time with Elle. I know this because she's spending that time with me instead.

By twelve thirty, Mom and Dad convince themselves Tabby lost track of the time. They say that she'll be eighteen soon enough, and they have to loosen the leash before next year anyway, before college.

(What leash? There is no leash. There isn't even a collar. Tabby belongs to nobody.)

They go to bed. I stay up, my nerves frayed like wires, fidgety with electricity splitting my body. I know something happened. I know it and it must be my sister intuition. Or maybe I don't even need sister intuition, because anyone could see that it was wrong, Mark wanting to take Tabby to the Split. I imagine her eyes, big and panicked. Her head, smashed against rock, cracking in two like the Split itself.

The door doesn't open until after one. Me at the kitchen table, on my phone, scrolling through her Instagram, trying to find a clue: Tabby's syrupy smile, all summer long. Mark's arm, a permanent fixture around her. A caption underneath one of her photos, the two of them looking slightly away from the camera. A *prayer for the wild at heart kept in cages.*

The door opens so quietly I barely hear it. Almost like she's trying to sneak in, like she has done a thousand times before. Her face is a mess of the makeup I teased her for putting on before the hike, and her hands are shaking. Actually, her whole body is shaking, its own earthquake.

"What happened?" I say. "Where were you?"

Her hair isn't straight like it was this morning but curly, bordering on frizzy, the way it gets after she showers and leaves it alone. Then I notice her legs. Dirt-stained, streaks of brown crosshatching every inch of bare space. My Nikes are soaked, more red than pink.

"Bridge," she says. "Something happened. He—he—he fell."

Then she collapses on the kitchen floor, and I know Mark is gone.

3

KEEGAN

HOW DO YOU THINK I FEEL? I get a call telling me my best friend is dead. The same guy I just saw in the morning, and now he's gone.

And right away I know why.

4

BRIDGET

WHAT THEY DON'T TELL YOU is that death doesn't kill a golden boy. Death will only make him immortal. Maybe I didn't fully understand that before, but I do now that Mark's funeral has become this year's defining event in Coldcliff.

Here's something to understand about our community. We have something like eight thousand residents, so we're called "cozy" in tourism brochures. If you haven't heard of our little pocket of Colorado, you're not alone. We're about thirty miles from Boulder and our nearest mountain is Longs Peak, so we get overlooked. We tend to disappear. Sure, people come to hike the trails, but they usually don't stay. Every town has its thing. Some are famous for a huge ball of twine or the world's best hot dog. We have the Split. Suicide Sledge. The Giant's Thumb. Whatever you want to call it. Basically, we have a piece of rock where a bunch of people have died, and for some reason other people want to see it in person.

Especially now.

Now, when I run in the woods, there are memorials for Mark. A bunch of guys from the swim team at our high school, Coldcliff Heights, put swim caps and goggles on the path leading up to the Split. It's their version of flowers. Today on my run, I stepped on one of the pairs of goggles and enjoyed how the wet ground sucked them up.

Here's something else to understand about our community. We protect our own. We curl in like a leaf, blocking out intruders. We're small and sheltered and when one of us gets

13

hurt, everyone rallies together. The owner of Reid's Ice Cream, Mickey, got in a car accident a couple years back and someone set up a GoFundMe page to pay for his hospital bills, and everyone donated. My parents gave something like five hundred bucks. So of course, someone set one up for Mark's funeral, and it raised a ridiculous amount of money.

My parents donated.

My parents are at the funeral today. We all are. We're in a church and it's way too hot and crowded, and I'm making awkward eye contact with a guy with blond curls who keeps staring at me. Boys usually stare at Tabby, but this one seems almost determined not to notice her.

He's the only one. Everyone else notices her. I don't blame them. She's in black, like the rest of us, but it looks different on her, less dead and more alive. "Your dress is too short," Mom told her before we left the house.

"Mark liked this dress," Tabby shot back. "He would have wanted me to wear it."

Mom didn't argue with that. That's another thing about dead golden boys. They always get the last word.

The service is what you'd expect from a funeral, stuffy and smothered with tears. A priest reads from the Bible. Everyone bows their heads. When I glance over at Tabby, her eyes are cast down like the rest of us, but she's staring at something in her hand. Her phone. Then she knows I'm looking, and she sneaks me a little smile.

People deal with grief in weird ways. But sometimes it's like my sister isn't sad at all. And I honestly don't blame her, because I'm not either.

The blond guy gets up now and stands behind the podium. "Most of you don't know me. I'm Mark's older brother, Alexander. I've been living in Australia for the past year. I was supposed to protect Mark, but he never needed protection. If you knew Mark, you knew he would give you the shirt off his back. He'd do anything for anyone."

Then a loud sob from a lady in the front row. Mark's mom. She had stiffly embraced Tabby on the way in. I know for a fact that it was the first time they'd ever met. *It's like I'm a secret*, Tabby once told me. *Like I only exist when he wants me to.*

Alexander continues. "My parents asked me to say a few words today, and a few words is all I have. I just want everyone to remember Mark as he was. Smart and strong and good to everybody. He would have gone on to do great things, but let's not think about what he didn't get to do. Let's think about what he accomplished when he was here, and live how he would have liked us to. Bold and honest and grateful."

He goes on for a bit, shares some memories of his childhood with Mark. Beside me, Tabby yawns. She hasn't been sleeping well. When we were little, we insisted on sharing the same bedroom, even though we each had our own in the Rochester two-story. We would fall asleep cocooned on the floor under a sleeping bag. Then Tabby grew up, and the two years between us reared its head. Tabby had her own private life, a fabric that was too slippery for me to grip on to. When we moved to Coldcliff, Tabby put caution tape on her door, the kind you see at crime scenes on TV. It was a joke, but it wasn't. She was guarding her new life, crouching in front of it like a dragon. She still is.

Elle is a few rows behind us with her parents; Elle's mom is watching the back of Tabby's head. She loves Tabby, and I know she's worried about her. My sister is the kind of person you either love or hate. Nobody ever seems to be in the middle about her. Meanwhile, everyone is in the middle about me, stuck in the center of some invisible hammock, making it sag under their collective weight. I don't have any enemies, but I don't have anyone professing their love either.

When the service is finally over, we all start to shuffle out of church into the hot pocket of humidity Coldcliff has turned into. I guess they're going to bury Mark's body now at the graveyard, but it's just the family—they're doing some private interment. No Tabby. I'm grateful to have her to myself. The same way I'm grateful there wasn't an open casket. I heard rumors about his head being caved in, and no amount of funeral makeup would be able to cover that up.

Alexander approaches us when we're almost outside. My parents have already wandered ahead, holding hands, looking all disoriented, suburban zombies. They don't know how to act around Tabby anymore. They haven't for a while.

"Hey," he says to Tabby. His eyes dart to me, but it's more like a warning. *You're not part of this conversation.* I pretend to be interested in the crucifix on the wall, the too-realistic Jesus nailed to it, blood surrounding the nails in his hands.

"You shouldn't have come here," Alexander says to Tabby. "You're not welcome. I don't want to make a scene in front of my parents, but stay the hell away from us."

"Come on," Tabby says, all candy-sweet. "You don't seriously believe—"

I don't get to hear the last part, because Coach Taylor comes up to me and asks how I'm doing, as if I suffered some kind of loss.

As if this isn't more of a win.

Don't take that the wrong way—I'm not a psychopath. I didn't fantasize about Mark falling off a cliff and ending up dead. But it's really no secret that I imagined him just *going away*. He didn't bring out the best in my sister. He brought out something else entirely, and I still don't understand what it was. What exactly he woke up.

"Hey," Tabby says, swinging her hip into mine. "Hi, Coach. Isn't my sister such a superstar? I can't wait to see her kick ass again this year."

16

Coach smiles. "Bridget is very talented. We're excited for cross-country season."

"I'll be at every race," Tabby says. "Your own personal cheerleader."

I bark out a laugh. I swear, Coach blushes. He's probably not that much older than Mark was—early twenties, baby face. Tabby has a way of making people react, of making their hearts beat just a little bit faster. Maybe it's how she says things. She meant she would be my personal cheerleader, but now Coach is probably picturing her as his.

"What did Mark's brother say to you?" I ask when we're walking across the parking lot toward Dad's Toyota Camry.

"He just said thanks for coming," Tabby says. "It meant a lot to his mom."

But I know what I heard. She's lying, and I don't know what else she has lied about.

Mark is everywhere on our drive home. Someone erected a billboard with his face on it, a picture of him in the pool after one of his swim meets, those giant fists churning up the water. He looks practically feral. REMEMBER MARK FORRESTER it says. Gold wreaths ring the streetlamps that line Main Street, downtown. Gold, because that's what he would have won at the Olympics one day. Gold, because he still holds a bunch of high school swim records and Colorado state championships, his name immortal. Gold because Mark was golden, and now he'll never tarnish.

Tabby looks out the window and dabs at her eyes, even though I don't think she has been crying at all.

New evidence in Princeton hiker's death
By Julie Kerr

Following an autopsy, the cause of death for Mark Forrester, 20, has been named as drowning. Initial reports pointed to his fall from the Split, the lookout point on the Mayflower Trail, being the likely reason for his death, but the autopsy shows that Forrester was alive when he landed in the water, despite a severe head injury. His time of death has been recorded as approximately 9:36 p.m., several hours after he and his girlfriend, Tabitha Cousins, had been spotted by another hiker on the Mayflower Trail.

Police divers have also been spotted in Claymore Creek. At this point, the police will not verify whether foul play is suspected, although online chatter continues to swirl around Cousins and her behavior in the days leading up to the hike.

5

ELLE

I'M NOT THE GOOD FRIEND everyone thinks I am.

Tabby and I are at the Forest Glen Mall today, shopping for new school clothes, which is a normal thing we do together, except nothing is normal after Mark. She says she needs to get on with her life and not think about death. "It's what he would have wanted," she says.

My stomach is flat again. Tabby comments on it when I try on a crop top. "You're so skinny. You should definitely buy that. You're going to have the best body at school this year."

"Yeah, right," I say. "That'll be you." As usual. Tabby's body is the stuff of locker room legend, somehow both tight and soft.

"We'll see," she says. "So, have you talked to him yet?"

"Who?"

"Elle," she says, putting her thumb against my chin like my mom does. "You know who I'm talking about. Have you honestly not talked to him?"

"There's nothing to talk about."

"Okay," she says, drawing the word out. "But you pretending it never happened won't make it go away."

She's wrong. I look the same as I did before—better now, actually. I'm fitter and tanned from the past couple weeks, from the time since Mark died, when Tabby and I have been going to Crest Beach almost every day. She claims that's the only place she feels normal, staring at the water.

Tabby thinks she knows my whole story. And she knows most

of it. But her version is missing a giant chapter, and I'll make sure she never gets to read that chapter. Because it would destroy us.

When we're in the food court having lunch—salad for me, no dressing—I can tell people are staring at us. No, not at us. At Tabby. That part isn't unusual. She gets a lot of second looks—it's her eyes, I think, how ridiculously blue they are. People stop and comment and ask if they're real.

"Of course they're real," she always says. "They're in my face, aren't they?"

But this is different. Nobody comes up to us. They're keeping their distance, whispering behind their hands. Judgmental, disapproving. I know that look well. I've been looked at like that myself very recently.

"Why is everyone staring?" I ask. "Is it because you're the dead guy's widow?"

You probably think that's rude. Insensitive. Or maybe you just think I'm a bitch—that's okay. People have thought worse about me. But I have nothing to hide. I wasn't sad to see Mark go. I didn't cry at his funeral. I went to his funeral only because Mom dragged me, and Mom dragged me only because she loves Tabby, thinks of her as a second daughter. Mom wanted us to be there for Tabby.

(I lied—I do have things to hide. But not about my feelings toward Mark. Everyone is mourning a guy who didn't exist. I didn't like the real version, and I'm really not sorry he's gone.)

"Must be," Tabby says between bites of her sandwich. Ever since Mark died, her appetite is back. When they were together, he was always on her about what she ate. *Mark wants me to cut out junk food. Mark said I would tone up fast if I stopped eating sugar. Mark said hiking would be a great workout for my legs and ass.*

Mark wanted. Mark said.

People keep staring the rest of the day. When Tabby drives

20

us home, I give a gaggle of middle-aged women in cardigans the finger out the car window. They look familiar. They've judged me. Let them talk.

It's when I log on to Facebook after dinner that I see it. A link to a *Coldcliff Tribune* article about Mark's cause of death. Lou Chamberlain posted it. She hates Tabby.

Drowning. My chest constricts, like my skin is too small. Everyone assumed he was dead when he hit the rocks. There's a horrible, twisted irony to it. Mark the Shark, felled by a shallow, muddy creek.

But it's not the article that plucks at my skin, making goose bumps rise up. It's the comments under it, the ones about Tabby.

Something isn't adding up here—why wouldn't she check if he was OK? That's what Lou wrote.

They were fighting at Elle's party—everyone saw it.

I bet she knew he was going to break up with her and she lost it. You know she has a temper right? She flipped off Mr. Mancini once.

They were arguing about their baby!!!

I stop reading. I don't need to see any more. Maybe it was inevitable, and I knew this was going to happen. The world is choosing sides. Tabby was never just going to be Mark's widow.

She would also be his executioner.

Excerpt from Tabby's Diary

July 23, 2018

I met a boy, and I already love him. How is that even possible? I'm not even sure why I'm writing this down. I guess because I should be writing everything down if I want to become a writer someday. Most people don't even know that about me—that I want to become a writer. It's the kind of dream that's too big to share.

Anyway, Mark Forrester. I know he loves me too. He might be the one. Elle told me it's too soon to know, but she has never been in love, so she wouldn't understand. Mark is everything the other boys weren't. He's not afraid to show me how much he cares. He actually brought me flowers on a date—these red roses. I'm going to dry one to show our kids one day.

I guess this is why I'm writing this down. Because it's another dream that's too big to share, and I need it to be real. I can't describe it to anyone out loud. Nobody likes anyone this happy.

6

ELLE

IT'S IMPORTANT FOR ME to give you some context about Tabby. You need to know how she met Mark. It was because of me, so this is all partially my fault. I forced her to go mini-golfing last summer since my dad had a Groupon he didn't want to waste.

"I hate mini golf," Tabby said. "You have to wear those ugly shoes that a thousand people's feet have been in."

"That's bowling. I promise that if you go with me, I'll get you ice cream after."

We never did get the ice cream, though. We took so long mini-golfing that the group behind us—a bunch of boys who looked a few years older—caught up. Tabby had grown frustrated at that point and went to kick the ball in with her foot.

One of the boys laughed. Tabby spun around. "Is something funny?"

"Your, uh, technique. It's interesting." He leaned on his golf club.

"And you can do better?"

He shrugged. "Well, I don't need to use my foot."

"What can I say? When there's a problem, I fix it. I don't need some guy to mansplain something to me."

"Mansplain?" He was laughing, but she wasn't.

"Yeah. When some asshole guy tells a girl how to do something better."

And that was the start of them. Tabby was always obsessed with the idea of having someone to argue with. Her parents were

23

still together, but they were more like placeholders than actual people. They didn't bicker or disagree, because neither of them had any fight left.

Tabby loved Mark. He wasn't a perfect boyfriend, and she wasn't a perfect girlfriend. They hurt each other by accident. They hurt each other on purpose. Sometimes there's such a fine line between the two that you barely notice it until you're jamming the proverbial knife in deep enough to graze bone.

Now, here's something about me and Tabby. We've been friends since the first week of eighth grade, and it was blood that brought us together. Specifically, I was bleeding, and she was there. Me, staring at my underwear in a school bathroom stall, frantically pinching the ruined pink of my skirt between a wad of toilet paper, willing the stain to disappear. I had waited until it was totally quiet before leaving the stall, where I tried pulling the skirt away from my ass and sticking it under the sink tap. That was how Tabby found me. She was the new girl, and stories had already circulated about her. How she came from New York, how her dad was a musician who had a big hit in the nineties, how she was a child model, how she wasn't a virgin. How that big black cross necklace she sometimes wore was really filled with cocaine.

I knew I would cry when she laughed at me, standing there with my bloody underwear and wet skirt. I braced myself for the impact. But she just reached into her purse and pulled out a tampon.

"Here," she said. "I always carry extra."

I didn't want to tell her that it was my first time bleeding, a moment I knew Mom would want to celebrate with me when I got home from school. I had no idea how to use a tampon, but it was too embarrassing to admit that to Tabby. I somehow didn't have to.

"The first time I got mine, I was at a pool party. Wearing a white bikini. That was when I knew there was no God." She laughed, which was more like a bark. "These ones have plastic applicators. As far as I'm concerned, there is no other kind. Just kind of squat and push it in. I'm here if you need help."

I really fucking hoped I didn't, and luckily, it only took me a couple minutes of trying in the stall before it went in without much resistance. By the time I came out and washed my hands, Tabby had shrugged out of her oversized plaid shirt, which she proceeded to tie around my waist.

"There. Now nobody will ever know what happened. Plus, your outfit looks cooler now."

I laughed, and so did she. I wanted to hug her, but I didn't. I spent the entire night totally paranoid that she had told everyone about me and my period, about the mess she covered up. The next day, I figured it would be awkward to see her in the halls, but it wasn't. She came over to my locker and started talking to me, and after that, we never really stopped talking. She meant it when she said nobody would ever know what had happened.

Tabby and I have things in common. We were both named after our grandmothers—Tabitha and Eleanor—and we both hate our names, so when high school started, we ditched them for the nicknames they had the decency to lend themselves to. She became Tabby and I became Elle, and we became different with the loss of those extra letters, girls who wanted to lose more.

We both like to be the center of attention. Sometimes it's like we're fighting for a spotlight that doesn't even exist. I'm not content to orbit her sun, nor she mine. Usually with girls there's one friend who is okay with being behind the scenes, propping the other one up, always the sidekick, loyal and a bit shy. We're unbalanced that way, both outspoken, clamoring to get everyone else to notice us. Sometimes they notice too much.

We both like *Real Housewives* and karaoke and jalapeños. We love Halloween because it means we can dress up without being judged for wanting to show skin (at least, not as much). We spend

25

too much time on Snapchat, filtering the shit out of our faces. We want to travel somewhere together after high school is over, even though we never did agree where. Tabby says Australia, and I say Thailand. Somewhere we can work as waitresses and live in hostels and chew through boys like candy.

And then there's the other thing we have in common: Beck Rutherford. But I'll tell you more about him later. I don't want you to hate me right away.

You know I'd do anything for you, right? Whatever you asked. Because I love you.

Text message from Tabitha Cousins to Mark Forrester,
July 23, 2018 10:18pm

7

BRIDGET

I CHANGED MY MORNING ROUTE. Not to avoid Mark's parents' house, but to purposely run past it. I know his brother is still in town, and there's a shrine on the porch with all sorts of candles and flowers. The flowers are browning with each passing day. I know this because I'm here, the house a blur in my vision as I run by. It's my own vigil, although I'm not sure why.

Maybe I'm afraid of what they'll find out, if they know where to look.

My friends keep asking me about Tabby. *Do you think she was involved?* Honestly, I'm tired of talking about my sister. I've been talking about her my entire life. Literally. Mom loves to tell people that my first word was *Tabby*. Not *Mama* or *Dada* like other babies. I wasn't attached to either of the parental units, but I was attached to my sister, grabbing on to one of her chubby legs, pulling on the back of her T-shirt, tugging on her braids.

If you've heard about me before now and didn't think of me as Tabby Cousins's little sister (you'd be in the minority), you know me as the runner. The Silent Knife. When we lived in Rochester, my parents tried to shove me into the same group sports they made Tabby do: soccer and baseball and basketball. *Being involved in sports is good for young girls* was adopted as their mantra. *It gives you self-confidence.* They made confidence sound like something that just appeared, a gift sent in the mail from a relative you saw once a year.

Anyway, I sucked at sports. I couldn't kick a ball into a net.

28

I couldn't hit a ball or sink one into a basket. But I was fast and I didn't seem to get tired, so it was decided that I would become a distance runner. This was around the same time Tabby started behaving badly, so I glommed on to my newfound calling, grateful to it for setting me apart, giving me something my sister didn't have. Suddenly my parents took an interest in me. Dad came to all my cross-country meets with his stopwatch. He'd be there at the start of the course, then halfway through, then again at the end, red-faced and screaming. I'm pretty sure he ran as many miles as I did.

You're wondering what all this has to do with Tabby, and specifically with Tabby and Mark. I'm getting there.

Tabby and I have turned on each other so many times that we've spent the equivalent of years back-to-back with our arms crossed. We've had big fights and little fights and fights about nothing and fights about something. The same eleven-year-old sister who once chopped my hair off while I was sleeping also punched Teresa Morgan, who had bullied me about my newly shorn hair, in the stomach at recess and got suspended. Tabby was allowed to do bad things to me, but nobody else was. It was some kind of sister code.

Nothing can stop Tabby when she wants something. I think that's part of her problem. She doesn't know how to not want too much.

Tabby has a work ethic. "Bridge, my best advice is to make it look like you're not trying," she once said when she put my hair in French braids before one of my meets. "Because it's when you try that people can break into you." She made it sound like we were some kind of bank that could be robbed, a vault with weak defenses.

What I will give you is this. I can't say with total certainty that Tabby would never hurt anyone, because I've seen her do it. Mostly it's a joke to her, but I've been around for the times it wasn't. And those times all had something in common. She was doing it for somebody else. Tabby is a lot of things: impulsive, vain, moody, proud, sarcastic, fun. But she's also loyal. It's her trademark, if you really know her. Yes, she sucks up the sunshine, but she'll find a way to warm you with it.

"Did you go to the woods today?" Tabby asks when I'm back from my run. She's standing in the kitchen with a mug of coffee, her hair impossibly shiny down her back.

"Yeah," I say. "The caution tape is still there."

She nods, like she isn't surprised. I don't know what the cops expect to find.

I'm sure of one thing. If Tabby hurt Mark, it was because he did something to really deserve it.

Anonymous tip to police hotline
September 4, 2019, 10:02 a.m.

"Hello? Yeah, I just wanted to report something I saw. That story about the guy and girl in the woods—the guy who died. I was coming out of the woods on a different trail, the Cider Creek one, when they were going in. So anyway, he was yelling at her to hurry up, which I thought was really rude, you know? She was lugging this picnic basket, and it looked like it weighed about a hundred pounds. Then he kind of walked ahead of her like he was irate. She had to run to catch up. And she kept saying 'I don't know about this, I really don't know,' and he told her to shut up and follow him.

They never even looked up and probably had no idea I was there, but she just looked so upset, and he seemed really mean. And the other thing was his hands. They were clenched into fists. I don't know; for some reason I just pictured him using them on her.

I didn't say anything. I didn't want to draw attention to myself. It wasn't my place. I just got the hell out of there as fast as I could. But I kept thinking about that girl, and when I saw the headline a few days later—well, I was just surprised it wasn't her body they found.

Anyway. I don't know if any of this is important, but I couldn't sleep at night until I said something to defend that poor girl. He looked dangerous, and she looked sad. And I know, well, I know from experience that sometimes sad is what you feel right before you finally fight back."

8

BECK

Coldcliff Police Station, September 5, 2:18 p.m.

OFFICER OLDMAN: Thanks for coming to meet with us.

BECK: Well, you made me. It didn't exactly sound like an invitation.

OFFICER OLDMAN: Beck Rutherford. Is Beck short for something?

BECK: It's my name. Are you going to arrest me for something, or can I get back to school now?

OFFICER OLDMAN: Don't lash out at me, son. We just want to ask you a few questions.

BECK: I'm not your son.

OFFICER OLDMAN: Sorry. Beck. We have a few questions we hope you can assist us with in the Mark Forrester case.

BECK: Case? I thought he fell off a cliff.

OFFICER OLDMAN: It's not that simple. We're still investigating, and we'd like your help.

BECK: I already told the last guy my statement. I don't know anything about what happened. I heard about it the same as everyone else.

OFFICER OLDMAN: From your girlfriend, right? Louisa Chamberlain?

BECK: No, I saw it online. I guess she called me, but I didn't pick up.

OFFICER OLDMAN: Why didn't you pick up when your girlfriend called?

BECK: She's not my girlfriend, okay? And do you pick up the phone every time your wife calls? I doubt it.

OFFICER OLDMAN: Where were you the evening Mark Forrester died?

BECK: I was riding my bike. I already told the last guy. Don't you share notes?

OFFICER OLDMAN: So you were on your motorcycle. Were you alone?

BECK: Yeah, I was alone.

OFFICER OLDMAN: Where do you ride it?

BECK: Just around. Mostly the roads around town. Not a lot of traffic. Don't worry, I don't go over the speed limit.

OFFICER OLDMAN: Sounds dangerous, being on your own like that. What if something happened?

BECK: Something doesn't.

OFFICER OLDMAN: Did you know that Tabitha and Mark were taking a hike that day?

BECK: Why would I know that? Tabitha and I don't even talk anymore. I really don't care about her weekend plans.

OFFICER OLDMAN: Anymore. You don't talk anymore. But you used to. Looks like you used to do more than talk.

BECK: Yeah, we used to hang out. But not now. She has her life. I have mine.

OFFICER OLDMAN: So you weren't with her the night of Eleanor Ross's party on August tenth?

BECK: No, I wasn't with her. I mean, I saw her there, but I also saw a hundred other people. That's kind of what happens at parties.

OFFICER OLDMAN: Sources say they saw you with Tabitha. We have an account that you left the pool house together.

BECK: Sources. Okay. I seriously doubt it. I wasn't in the pool house that night.

OFFICER OLDMAN: Another witness puts you in the kitchen the same night. Says that you had your arm around her and stuck something in the pocket of her jeans.

BECK: She wasn't even wearing jeans. She had a skirt on.

OFFICER OLDMAN: You remember what Tabitha was wearing the night of a party that took place last month?

BECK: (pauses) I have a good memory.

OFFICER OLDMAN: So maybe you can remember what Tabitha told you about her plans with Mark.

BECK: I can't tell you something I don't know. Look, am I under arrest, or am I free to go now?

9

ELLE

TABBY KNOWS ABOUT DALLAS. She didn't find out because I told her, but because of what came after. Dallas was supposed to be nothing serious, a good excuse to lose my virginity because he was there and willing. But he went and became a defining moment in my life anyway. It's unfair, how I fail spectacularly at not taking something seriously. It's like my body has other plans.

Maybe Tabby knows the feeling.

It's the first day of school, so of course I'm seeing him today, and I won't be able to avoid him like I did all summer. He's a year younger than us—Tabby called me a cougar when she found out—so he won't be in any of my classes, but he'll be everywhere else. I've known him for years. His family lives three doors down from ours, and his mom sometimes comes over and drinks wine with Mom on our deck, their laughter puncturing the sky. Now, every time Mrs. Mackey comes over and says "Hi, Elle," I wonder what she knows. Now, whenever she and Mom are half drunk, voices carrying into the night, I wonder what they're really talking about. If they stumbled onto dangerous ground.

"You're nervous," Tabby says when she picks me up in her dad's blue Camry. "Relax. You don't owe him a goddamn thing, remember?"

Her voice is hard, unflinching. She's back, the girl who had the ability to make me feel both seen and invisible. Mark had done something to her, made her less somehow, turned her from larger-than-life into something scared of its shadow. Her shadow is here now, longer than ever, covering both of us like a tent. I'm used to its shade.

"You're right." I take in what Tabby's wearing, or the lack thereof. Shorts that have ridden up so high that I can't see where they end and a low-cut tank top. It has been three weeks since Mark died, three weeks during which Tabby has vacillated from a state of disaffected calm to a waterlogged mess, shot through with bolts of laughter and girlishness that she apologized for, like she shouldn't be allowed to be happy when he's six feet under. But now here she is, looking more herself than she has in months. Mark never liked her showing too much skin, she told me. I argued that it didn't stop him the night they met.

The truth is, Mark not being around has made things easier. She's easier, looser, more like she used to be. Maybe you're thinking it would have been like that anyway. He doesn't go to Coldcliff Heights. He'd be away at Princeton. But control makes distance evaporate. It shrinks people into specimens, easy to view under a microscope. And Mark's eye was constantly on his microscope, studying Tabby.

I'm not sure how Tabby will act when we walk into the school. If she'll reach for my hand or link her pinkie through mine, like I reached for her months ago, sure I was about to face my own reckoning. I'm not sure if she's nervous, or if she's scared to enter the real-life version of the online gossip minefield. But if she is feeling either, she hasn't shown it. She isn't shrunken anymore. She's her full height, confidence sweeping behind her like the train of a wedding dress.

We shuffle down the hall, our flip-flops thwacking the ground. Pockets of girls are clustered by their lockers, staring. Tabby doesn't seem phased.

"Apparently they have no lives of their own," I say. "Isn't there anything else to talk about?"

Ever since Lou linked to that article and the comments

dogpiled underneath it, everyone has something to say about Tabby. Nobody thinks Mark's death was an accident. There are too many indicators that it wasn't.

SOMEBODY *pushed him*, one of the last comments said. *If it wasn't her, who was it?*

That stuck with me. The image formed of somebody else there, on the Split, with Tabby and Mark.

Sometimes I picture it being me. My hands against his back. Sometimes I imagine how it would feel, his hot skin. How it would sound, his scream.

But that's only sometimes, and I'd never admit that to anyone else. I see what the media does to girls. It drains them, a collective vampire sucking until its mouth is a ruby smear. It drains out every detail, everything they've ever done. It empties the blood and goes for the vital organs. For her lungs, until she can't breathe. Her brain, until she can't think. Her heart, until she can't feel.

"That cop asked me to come in again today after school," Tabby says, as casually as if we were talking about an annoying teacher. "Stewart. The one who hates me. I've already told him everything I know. I mean, whatever. I have nothing to hide."

They haven't gotten to her yet. Maybe they've feasted on a bit of her blood, but she can make more. Tabby has thick skin.

I don't get a chance to respond, because a few guys from our grade stop in front of us. Connor Lawson and Brian Hull as well as Lance Peterson, who Tabby made out with during freshman year. He told all his friends that she gave him a blow job and didn't know what she was doing. She shrugged off the rumors like a too-big coat, but a week later, Lance got suspended for having weed in his locker. I never asked Tabby if she was responsible for putting it there.

"There she is," Connor says. "I just have to ask. Did you do it?"

We keep walking. I give him the middle finger. Tabby laughs.

"You don't seem too torn up about it," Brian shouts after us. "I saw you at his funeral. You were smiling the whole time."

They don't know Tabby, and I do. Tabby's mouth betrays her in little ways—not even what she says but what she doesn't say. Her perma-smirk, as I once called it. The way she laughs at inappropriate times. I've seen her do it when she gets in trouble with a teacher, when her mom says *This isn't funny, Tabitha Marie*.

Tabby doesn't dignify the comments with a response. It's not until Lance jumps in that she stops walking.

"I guess we knew what she was capable of doing. She's already lied and cheated. We knew she could be a killer."

She whips around and puts her hand on his chest, pushing him backward. Her nails are painted purple. Most people would say Tabby isn't a patient person. Her temper can be an animal, forever pulling on an invisible leash. But she's patient when it comes to her personal grooming. Her nails are always the same length, always painted, never jagged and bitten like mine.

I focus on her nails. Connor calls her a crazy bitch. A crowd is drawing closer, eager for more. I grab Tabby's hand to tug her down the hall, but she wiggles out of my grip.

"You want a show? Here I am. Instead of hiding behind your fucking computers, say it to my face. Tell me what a terrible person I am. And what a fucking perfect person he was."

But nobody says anything. There are a few laughs. Most people are on their phones, probably taking pictures. They're thinking, *Look. She got mad*. And we all know angry girls are mentally unhinged.

And there, standing behind everyone, is Dallas. He's maybe the only person not looking at Tabby. He's staring at me instead. Asking me a very different question than the one everyone was too afraid to ask Tabby before today.

10

BRIDGET

THE VIDEO HAS ALMOST two thousand views, and it has been up for only three hours. Two thousand views. Nowhere near two thousand students go to Coldcliff Heights, so obviously other people are interested. I'm not sure Tabby knows it exists, and I'm not going to tell her.

It makes her look really bad. That's what my friend Laurel said after she watched it. Laurel immediately texted me in our group WhatsApp—*Have you seen it? It makes her look really bad.*

It does. Her teeth flash, her hair flies. She's a live wire, all instincts. More animal than girl. Because that's what it comes down to, isn't it? They want to strip her down to her barest instincts.

I wish they would stop. They have no idea what they're up against.

Video of Coldcliff girl goes viral
By Michael Dixon

Rumors have been swirling since the hiking death of Mark Forrester, a 20-year-old Princeton student, in August. Now, a profanity-laced video of his girlfriend, Tabitha Cousins, losing her temper at a bunch of her classmates has gone viral, garnering sixty thousand views in less than 24 hours. In the video, posted to a YouTube channel owned by Louisa Chamberlain, another student at Coldcliff Heights High School, Cousins seems to invite people to accuse her of involvement in Forrester's death.

"It was scary," said a classmate who asked to remain anonymous. "It was like she just lost it. And it sounds bad, but she obviously liked the attention."

Lance Peterson, a senior and the swim team captain, said that Cousins physically and verbally attacked him without any provocation. "She came at me. I didn't say a word except that I was sorry about Mark. I mean, the whole swim team looked up to him. He's a legend around here."

Cousins wasn't available for comment, but online chatter surrounding this video implies that there may have been more to her relationship with Forrester than meets the eye.

A link to the video can be found here.

11

LOU

YES, I'M THE ONE who posted the video. You probably think I'm a horrible person for posting it, right? But hear me out. I did it in the heat of the moment. She looked so violent. Tabitha has a temper—I mean, it's no secret—she gets *passionate about things*, as Mr. Lowe, our junior year homeroom teacher, once said. (And the way she looked at him after he said it—gross. She was always flirting with him in these little ways, even though he's, like, forty and married.)

Yeah, so I wanted to show everyone that mean side of Tabitha. Mostly she does a good job of keeping it in check. She disguises it as something else. *Passion*, I guess. But—you've seen the video, right? She's, like, ugly. She's outraged. That's the real Tabitha.

Anyway, now I wish I had never posted the video, because suddenly not just everyone at our school has seen it, but everyone else, too, and some detective actually made me take it down. (If you still want to see it, I have it saved on my phone.) And it's, like, I get the feeling this is what Tabitha wanted the whole time. For people to be talking about her. Maybe she knew someone was going to take a video and she played this perfectly, so that the media would glom on and make a martyr out of her. Or whatever she is.

I hate losing. I especially hate losing to Tabitha.

I suppose I should clarify something else, speaking of losing. Most people think I hate Tabitha because of Beck. Because there was this rumor he slept with her while he was dating me. But I don't believe that crap, because Beck told me it wasn't true. No,

I hate Tabitha because of what happened sophomore year with the play.

(Not everything is about a boy, you know. We're made up of more than the sum of their parts.)

It was *A Streetcar Named Desire*. Of course I was going to be Blanche—everyone knows I'm a good actress, and I've been the lead in, like, every play at Coldcliff Heights. It was important to me, being good at that. Pretty much everyone thinks I'll do acting professionally someday, but I'm not so sure anymore.

So the auditions were on a Tuesday. The usual girls who tried out every year were there—Gina Forsyth and Julia Petersen and Tara Waters and Lexie Roth, who looks horrible with blond hair (I think she was trying to copy me, and just—honey, no). I overheard Tara saying she couldn't remember the lines to her monologue, and Lexie telling her she was planning to "just wing it." I had smiled because I knew none of them were any competition.

Then Tabitha showed up in the auditorium. She looked like white trash, all ripped tights and dark eyeliner and clunky Doc Martens, like she was from the nineties or something.

"What are you doing here?" I asked. Maybe I didn't say it very nicely. Maybe I don't care about being nice.

"Auditioning. My parents want me to get more involved." She popped a bubble with her gum. "Hey, you're always really good in these things. Any tips?"

These things. Like the plays were amateurish, not worthy of her time. She diminished me with those two words, whether she meant to or not. And I think she meant to.

I had prepared one of Blanche's monologues—from Scene Four—*He acts like an animal, has an animal's habits!* It was some of my best work. As soon as I got onstage, my confidence came back. *Fuck Tabitha Cousins. She'll never get a leading role,* I thought.

I didn't see her audition—they're private, just in front of Mr. Mancini, who directed the play, and Mrs. McDougall, who just kind of, like, bosses people around. But when they announced the parts, my name wasn't beside *Blanche*. Hers was. I was *Stella*.

So I got a bit pissed off and told a few people she must have done something for Mr. Mancini to get the role. That rumor gained traction for a while, and the infuriating part was that Tabitha never even denied it. I think she liked it.

(By the way, she sucked as Blanche. She barely showed up for rehearsals. It was like she only wanted it because I did. She only ever wants what other people have. And to this day, the name *Stella* makes me want to scream.)

Anyway, when we were getting our stage makeup done on closing night, Tabby leaned over and whispered something: "I heard there's some kind of scout in the audience."

That made me snap to attention. "Scout? How do you know?"

Tabby smiled, like she really enjoyed having a piece of information I didn't. "I heard her talking to Mancini. She has bright red hair. You can't miss her."

My whole body basically thundered. I never get nervous when I act—it wasn't like that. I was electrified. I knew I had to give my best performance yet, even though I wasn't Blanche. I needed to be the one everybody saw first.

Oh my God, I acted the hell out of that role. I *was* Stella. And I don't know if it was the adrenaline or heightened emotions or just pure bravery, but after the show, when I saw a red-haired woman with Mr. Mancini backstage, I went up and introduced myself.

"I'm Louisa Chamberlain," I said. "I hope you liked the play."

"You were terrific," she said, clutching her program. "I was just telling Bruce how wonderful the entire show was."

I could have just moved on and left it at that, but I'm not

a girl who just leaves an opportunity. So I gave her my biggest smile. "I really believe acting is my future. If you have the time, I'd love to talk to you about what that might look like."

It was super bold, but it just felt right. Until she looked at me, then at Mr. Mancini, with this totally confused expression. Ugh—I still see it so clearly. It's, like, permanent decor in my brain. A shameful throw rug.

"Um—" she started, but Mr. Mancini cut in, placing his hand over hers.

"Louisa," he said. "This is my wife, Melinda."

His wife. His *wife*. And if that's not horrifying enough for you, picture the rest of the cast scattered around, within earshot, trying really hard not to laugh. And picture Tabby, *beaming*.

"You told me she was a scout," I hissed later, when Tabby was sitting on a bench, pulling on her Docs.

"Sorry," she said. "It was a different red-haired woman I saw. She must have left."

What a little liar! *Bravo*, Tabby. That was your best performance. Until now.

"That was beyond embarrassing," I said. "Everyone thinks I'm a joke." Closing night was supposed to be a celebration—we always went out and partied. But I wasn't going anywhere but home. Tabby took away what I had achieved and replaced it with the hot burn of humiliation.

"Oh, come on," she said. "It wasn't so bad. Besides, there are worse things than people talking about you."

"Like what?" I put my foot on the bench, resisting the urge to kick her with it.

"Like when they aren't." She stood up so we were face-to-face. Then she actually *winked*.

I suppose I played right into her trap, and I should have known better. No matter how ugly the rumor is, she doesn't care, as long as people are talking about her.

Maybe you think karma caught up with me. Maybe you think I'm the bitch, or the petty one. I'm not denying I'm a bit of both. But Tabitha is something worse. She's a taker. And something to know about takers is that they never have enough.

12

BRIDGET

TABBY YANKS A BRUSH through my hair. "I didn't do anything wrong. This is so fucking typical. Everyone always believes the guy. I hate living in this world."

As if there was another option.

I'm going to school today—it's the second week back, and the first day of cross-country practice—so Tabby got up early to put my hair in two French braids, the same way she did it last year, when I was a freshman. I'm superstitious like that, especially since last year was my big moment. *She has so much potential*, Coach Taylor told Dad at my first meet—I won a silver medal I barely had to work for. *She could go far*. I wasn't used to the attention, but I liked it.

She liked the attention. Some anonymous classmate said that about my sister. The video ripped through the internet like wildfire. Reporters have been calling our landline—I have no idea how they got the phone number, but they want to talk to Tabby. At least, they say they want to talk to Tabby, but really they just want to talk about her. About her temper, suddenly legendary.

"I'm sorry," I say as her fingers work methodically in my hair. "This isn't fair."

"Life's never fair for us." She yanks just hard enough to hurt. "You'll tell me what they say, right?"

Tabby got a three-day suspension for pushing Lance Peterson in the hall, then my parents decided it would be best if she didn't go back to school until things settle down. Detectives have been poking around, stealing Tabby away to talk, leaving cold half

46

cups of coffee on our granite countertop. Mom and Dad seem sure that things will settle down, that life will go back to normal. I'm not so sure.

I have this feeling it will only get worse.

"I'll tell you what they say, but don't listen. They're losers."

I don't even know why she wants to hear it, why she's desperate for every word, like it's her new sustenance. I guess she's bored, sitting at home. I don't know what she does all day.

Now she loops her arms around my neck and hugs me from behind. In the bathroom mirror, I look at our faces pressed together, similar but so different. Tabby's electric eyes, the freckles summer brought out on her nose. Her hair is naturally reddish like mine, but she has been dyeing it black since we came to Coldcliff. Raven, the color is called. It comes from a box.

"What are you going to do today?" I ask.

She rolls her eyes, her cheek still adhered to mine. "I don't know. Elle's bringing my homework over later. I guess I'll find some way to entertain myself."

For some reason, I don't like the thought of Tabby at home alone.

I'm not denying that she has a temper. I'm her sister—I've probably seen it more than anyone. When we were kids, she once cut the hair off all our Barbies because I had the one she wanted and wouldn't trade. After she and Beck broke up she went into the backyard and screamed at the top of her lungs. Just screamed at the sky, like it made any difference, being loud. Maybe it did. I mean, if you're a girl, too, you know what it's like to basically be told on a daily basis to be quiet.

"Go out there and kill it today," she says. "Show them exactly who you are."

Kill it. Not exactly a great choice of words. But that's something I love about my sister—she doesn't sift her thoughts, trying to find the perfect words for any given situation. She says what's on her mind and thinks about the consequences later. It's an honest quality, and one that most people don't have anymore.

When I get home from practice, French braids still intact—I did kill it, I didn't spend the summer running every day not to— Tabby is at the kitchen table, cross-legged on a chair. She's not alone.

There's a cop with her.

Obviously the cops already questioned Tabby. And like I said—they've been around, the cops and detectives. She told them everything about that night. What else could they possibly have to ask her?

"Hey, Bridge," she says, turning around. "This is Stewart." She sounds almost bored.

I fiddle with the zipper on my shirt. I imagine zipping myself up. Stuffing away all the things I thought about Mark. The things I said to him.

The thing I did.

"It's Detective Stewart," he says. He's pissed off. He doesn't like my sister. She told me that when she got home from being questioned the first time, her eyes red and bleary. *That cop hates me, Bridge.*

"What's he doing here?" As soon as I say it, I realize how wrong it sounds. I'm talking about him like he isn't in the same room. "I just—I thought he already talked to you a bunch of times."

"I did," Stewart—Detective Stewart—says. "I'm here to talk to you, Bridget."

Hiker's girlfriend suspected in murder after backpack found

By Bryce Jules

Nearly four weeks after Princeton student Mark Forrester, 20, was found dead in Coldcliff's Claymore Creek, police divers have retrieved a backpack from the creek, filled with rocks, which they believe Forrester had on his back when he plunged into the water from the Split, nearly forty feet above him.

Records from the Boulder REI store show that Forrester's girlfriend, Tabitha Cousins, 17, purchased the backpack for him as a birthday gift in late July. Cousins has been under scrutiny since Forrester's death, with a video of her assaulting a male classmate going viral last week.

Cousins did not return our request for comments.

13

KEEGAN

"WHAT ARE YOU LOOKING AT?" Kyla asks. She comes up behind me when I'm sitting on my old corduroy couch and wraps her arms around my neck. A *Kyla necklace*, she once called it. Feels more like a noose.

"Nothing." I shut my laptop.

(I was watching the video, again. It keeps popping up on different sites. And yeah, that's the real her. I'm so glad somebody had the balls to post it. I guess it was some chick at Tabby's school. I wonder what Tabby did to piss her off.)

Let me guess. You fell for it. You thought Tabby had nothing to do with what happened to Mark. I guess I can't be that hard on you. I mean, lots of people fell for it. There's this Facebook group, the Tabby Cats, all about how she's getting shit on in the media. I think it's mostly horny guys hoping to have a chance with her. I bet they'll write her letters in prison if she ends up there.

I sure as hell hope she does.

I can tell a very different story about Tabby Cousins, from the day they met to the day Mark died. That day, Mark knew something was up. He fucking knew.

I can show you the last text he ever sent me, before they left on that hike. I already showed the police, even though I knew it wouldn't prove shit. He didn't mention Tabby, but he didn't have to.

> I'll let you know how it goes but I don't think it's gonna go well

How is that not fucking ominous?

Tabby didn't even like doing anything outdoors, unless it was smoking up outside at a party. Then all of a sudden she wanted to go for a hike. Even suggested the Mayflower Trail, which is long and steep and leads up to this lookout point. Mark told me when she first mentioned it, rolling his eyes like he knew it was never going to happen, just like it never happened when Tabby said she would stop drinking or stop being jealous of every girl Mark looked at.

"We should go out or something," Kyla says. She always wants to go out. I mean, I used to like that about her—she's outgoing, and yeah, she's blond and tanned and I'm sure a lot of guys have liked that about her. But she seems to conveniently forget that I work at a grocery store and can't exactly afford to take her on dates. Besides, there's nowhere for us to go in Coldcliff. Just a sketchy eastside bar where bikers hang out and some downtown restaurants that cost way too much.

I should be focusing on my own relationship here, but whatever. Somebody has to tell the truth about Tabby, so I'm your guy.

I never liked her. It's not a secret. She was a bad idea. I figured she was something Mark had to get out of his system. And yeah, I understood the appeal. High school girls, you get to be a man around them. You get to be their college guy fantasy. Don't crucify me for saying that either, because you know you were thinking the same thing. And honestly, we didn't even know she was in high school at first, because that was one of her very first lies. Her and Elle, barely wearing any clothes, but covered in a shit ton of makeup. Who dresses like that for mini golf? Mark

51

and Tabby argued all night. I knew he was turned on. Mark was on the rebound, fresh out of a relationship with this chick Sasha who never had anything to say. Mark wanted a fight.

The end of the night—Mark and Tabby in the back of my shitty Civic, practically clawing each other's skin off. Me and Elle sitting in the front seats like the parental chaperones. I could almost hear Mark in my ear, telling me to put a move on Elle, and normally I would have because she was there, and she probably would have gone for it, but I just had this feeling that if I did, it would end badly. So I kept my hands to myself.

Mark didn't. He was always touching Tabby. His hands on her shoulders, cupping her ass, tilting her head back to kiss her. "Dude, she might actually be the one," he told me when he was drunk.

I've talked to the cops twice. There are at least two of them on the case—Detective Stewart is the one I trust. He's the one who knows Tabby did it. He keeps asking me questions about their relationship, and the more I talk, the more I realize how fucked up it really was.

They were always fighting, constantly on the verge of breaking up. It was their thing. You know that couple you never want to hang out with, because you know they're going to be at each other's throats all night? Well, that was Tabby and Mark. She'd yell at him and he'd make some comment he knew would get her all riled up, usually something about all these big plans he had for when he graduated from college, and they'd get into it, right in front of everyone.

"You're a fucking dumbass," she said once. "You think you know everything. Well, you don't."

Mark stayed silent, which pissed her off even more.

"Just wait," she spat. "Something's going to happen that you didn't see coming."

Looking back, everything she said was a thinly veiled threat.

Mark made it sound like the hike was pretty spontaneous, but I know she had been planning the whole thing, probably for way longer than anyone could have suspected.

You're wondering why I didn't say anything, if I knew Tabby was going to do something like that. But it went the other way, too. When they didn't want to rip out each other's throats, they wanted to rip off each other's clothes. It was like whatever fueled their relationship was dialed up to the max. They didn't know how else to be except extreme.

"Why don't you just end it?" I said to Mark more than once. He always had the same answer.

"I can't just get rid of that girl. You don't understand."

I hated that last part. *You don't understand.* Like Mark felt something deeper than I ever had, or maybe ever would.

Stewart asked me what that text really meant, the last one Mark ever sent. "Was Mark planning on breaking up with Tabitha?" Those were his exact words, like an awkward parent probing for information about your relationship.

"I don't know," I told him. "He said he was a couple weeks ago. Then he changed his mind. It was hard to keep track."

Mark really did say he was going to do it. At a party, the week before he died.

"She's a lot to handle," he told me at the end of the night, when Tabby was crying in the bathroom. "I think I should just break up with her. Start the year without any baggage."

Then he didn't bring it up again. Maybe he thought they could fix it. Mark was big on fixing shit that other people would have just thrown out. When we first got our driver's licenses, he liked to cruise around looking for the shit people put out at the curb on garbage day. Tables missing legs and old dishwashers and stained armchairs that looked like they'd been punched in the overstuffed gut. I'd help him load up the back of his dad's truck, and when we got back to his house, we'd lug everything into the

53

basement, where he'd make magic happen. One day he wanted to turn it into a side business. You know, when he wasn't busy being a hotshot lawyer.

So it's no wonder he thought he could fix Tabby, fix whatever they had that was so deep and so worth saving. He was too blinded by whatever power she had over him that he couldn't see what the rest of us already knew. That the girl is broken.

His cause of death was drowning, and now there's a backpack. The fall didn't kill him, but that stupid creek did. It doesn't make any sense. Mark was a champion swimmer, and he never would have drowned. Something else killed him. Someone.

"I'm bored," Kyla says in the pouty voice she uses that she thinks is cute. "Come play with me."

I don't want to play with her. But I also don't want her getting too far away.

14

BRIDGET

YOU WANT TO KNOW WHAT Stewart and I talked about, and I'm not going to tell you. I'm not supposed to talk about it, and I won't. At least, not yet.

What I will talk about is the backpack, because it's not at all what people think.

Here's what really happened. Tabby asked me to go shopping with her for Mark's birthday gift. She wanted to get him something special.

"I'm not going to be helpful," I told her. "I have no idea what guys his age like." I don't know what guys any age like, except that they don't like me. Or they just don't notice me, not in the ways they notice Tabby. I am fifteen but look closer to twelve. I'm *so cute* and *adorable* and my friend Laurel's mom even called me *precious* once, which made me want to die. I am supposed to be sexy by now. Boys started noticing Tabby when she was still in middle school, her new curves changing the way her clothes fit. Changing the way she fit.

"You always have good ideas. Come on, don't make me beg."

I didn't. I let Tabby grab my hand at the outlet mall, pulling me into the REI in Boulder, a store I didn't think she would ever set foot in. It was for outdoor people, the kind who liked breaking a sweat.

"What are you getting him? A new sleeping bag?" As far as I knew, Mark didn't like the outdoors any more than my sister did. He was a swimmer, so the pool was his second home.

"No," she said. "Something else. I'm gonna surprise him."

Mark's Instagram was public—I'm sure you saw it, before it got taken down. It was basically the chronology of a golden boy. Witness the great swim champion, arms raised in victory. See him at the beach with his shaved chest, hairless and tanned. At a party, a drink in each hand, a girl under each arm.

Then there's my sister's Instagram, the Tabby and Mark show. Kissing on a porch swing. Pressed together on Elle's deck, sweaty from the summer heat, both in jean shorts and tank tops. They say married couples start to look alike—I don't know if it's true, my parents just look bored—but the truth is, Tabby has always started to look like her boyfriends. In little ways, at first. When she was with Beck, she bought a leather jacket.

Then she changes in other ways. Starts to mimic their personalities and mannerisms. When she was Beck's girlfriend, I was "sweetheart" and my parents needed to "chill." Maybe she doesn't even know she's doing it.

Tabby stopped briefly in the women's clothing section, fingering the edge of a sports bra. Then I followed her through a display of yoga mats and running shoes, straight into a wall of backpacks. Some of them were practically as tall as me, the kind people brought on a summer trek through Europe.

"Is Mark planning a trip?" I asked.

"No. I mean, maybe. We talked about going somewhere. But not until I'm finished with school. What I'm looking for is something like this." She pulled a camouflage-print backpack off the rack, holding it up like a trophy.

"It's, uh . . . kind of ugly."

"It's totally ugly. But Mark will love it. He told me he wants to do more hiking and outdoorsy crap. I'm trying to be more supportive of his lifestyle. See, this one has pockets for water bottles and everything."

"Okay," I said. "Whatever you say."

We walked up to the checkout. I stared at the assortment of

freeze-dried foods near the cash register with a mixture of curiosity and disgust.

"He wants me to hike the Mayflower with him," Tabby said. "Before summer ends. Isn't that where you had your cross-country regionals last year? And where we went running once?"

I was surprised she remembered it, but I let the feeling pool in my stomach like warm butter. The memory is less my gold medal and more Tabby screaming at the finish line, arms in the air, shirt raised to show her stomach. There was a sign on the ground in front of her, bristol board with glitter paint. I ♡ YOU BRIDGE!!!!!

"Yeah," I said. "The Mayflower Trail. There are a ton of roots. You basically have to stare at the ground the whole time."

"Duly noted," Tabby said. When we got to the car, she thanked me. The backpack was slung over her shoulder. It looked funny there, the camo against the baby pink of her tank top.

"I didn't do anything," I said.

"Typical Bridge. You always think you didn't do anything. Sometimes just being somewhere with somebody is enough."

It was exactly the kind of thing Tabby said that made me remember how deep she is, how thoughtful. People tend to think girls like Tabby are surface level. That if you like makeup and partying, you can't also like books or care about world issues. Tabby is the wild one. I'm the workhorse. She's the girly one. I'm the sporty one. She's the slut, and I'm the prude. She's the bad one, and I'm the good one. The universe is always trying to split girls in half. Half angel, half demon. No wonder so many of us turn into monsters.

I know every inch of the Mayflower Trail. Every root, every bump in the ground, every twist and turn, like a book with a plot that surprised me the first time around, but not anytime after that, because I'm smart enough to see everything coming.

"It's really easy to get lost in there," I said. Hot air puffed out when I opened my car door.

"Good thing you drew me a map," she said with a wink.

I never told Tabby this, but one of the times I ran the trail over the summer, I smelled something other than dirt and old leaves. Pot smoke. Then I heard the laughter. It was a group of guys, sitting on the fallen tree trunk just over two miles into my route, where the Cider Creek trail ends and the Mayflower begins. Tabby hated when I ran in the woods alone. "It's dangerous," she would say, sounding more like a stern parent than our actual parents.

"I know where I'm going," I always said defiantly, even though I liked that she worried about me. It felt good, somehow, to be doing something dangerous enough for somebody to worry about.

"Yeah, you do," she said. "That's not the problem. The problem is someone else knowing where you're going, too."

She made me promise not to run with earbuds in. *You never know who's watching*, she told me. So I kept the promise. Besides, I like hearing my feet hit the ground, having my breath be the soundtrack to my route. Harder and more labored going up Salt Hill, almost like a hiss going back down. The only people I ever saw that deep in the woods were random hikers or the same two middle-aged women with sweaters tied around their waists, greyhound dogs running ahead of them.

Except that day, I saw boys. Then I saw who was among them. Mark and his friend Keegan, the one Tabby didn't like. Mark had something in his hand. A joint. Don't get me wrong, I have no issue with people smoking pot. But Mark was always Mr. Anti-Drugs, the poster child for Don't Kill Brain Cells. I'd heard him chastise my sister more than once for drinking before they headed out to some party, even though he drank, too. I also remembered him telling Tabby he couldn't believe she had tried pot, because he thought she was better than that.

Mark's gaze flickered over me, then he looked down. He

was going to pretend he didn't know who I was. His eyes, in the moment ours met, held some kind of warning. *Don't tell your sister.* I could feel the other guys leering at my bare legs and the strip of stomach my tank top didn't cover. It was the exact way boys never looked at me before, but their collective gaze didn't empower me like I expected it would. For the first time, I did feel scared in the woods—a girl under the trees, too far away for anyone to hear her scream. For the first time, I turned around instead of completing my full loop.

"Tell her yourself," I shouted over my shoulder, increasing my speed as the guys laughed.

People are saying that Tabby isn't a nice girl. But I grew up with her, and they didn't. She brought me soup in bed when I was sick, and they didn't. She took me to the hairdresser to fix the terrible dye job I tried to do myself, and they didn't. She cried to me when her first boyfriend broke up with her—because she wouldn't put out—and they didn't. She raged to me when that first boyfriend spread rumors about her being terrible in bed, a bed she was never even in. They didn't.

They don't know my sister. I do.

I wondered how fast I could run in the woods that day. Maybe Tabby had to figure out the exact same thing.

15

SLATE FORD,
SALESPERSON, REI BOULDER

YEAH, THAT GIRL? She was in the store, asking a whole bunch of questions. Of course I went over and helped her. You always want to chat up the hot ones.

Told me she was going on a hike. Didn't say where. Said it was with her boyfriend. I thought maybe she was making up a boyfriend so I wouldn't hit on her.

She asked about jackets. Said it was gonna be a long hike. Then boots. Said she didn't want anything too heavy on her feet.

Then she picked up a walking pole and said, *This could be a murder weapon*. Laughed. I laughed, too, because she was kidding. Maybe even flirting. She left without buying anything, and I didn't have the balls to ask her out.

They're gonna say it was normal for her to be in the store if she knew she was going on a hike. But I read the news and she's saying the hike got sprung on her partway through August. That it was his idea.

If that's true, why the hell was she in the store talking about the hike back in May?

Excerpt from Tabby's Diary

September 13, 2018

I haven't written in a while, but I've been busy. It's hard with Mark back at Princeton. I knew it would be hard, but I thought we would still be us. I'm still me, but he's not him anymore. He's someone who doesn't have time for me, or at least not the time he promised. Plus, I can't seem to stop stalking his Instagram and seeing there are other girls in the photos. He told me we'd Skype every night, but he has excuses. Like having to go to bed super early for practice, except then I'll see someone tagged him in a photo from a party. He used to text me back instantly, almost before I was done hitting send. Now it takes hours.

Maybe I'm just being paranoid. I'm trying to be the cool girl, but it's hard. A month until he's back, for the homecoming game. Maybe I just need to make him miss me more.

Map, diary found in home of dead hiker's girlfriend
By Sally Kelly

A search of the Coldcliff, Colorado, home of Tabitha Cousins, 17, has revealed a map to the Split, the lookout point from which her boyfriend, Mark Forrester, 20, fell to his death on August 16. The map appeared to be hand-drawn, although it hasn't been confirmed whether Cousins was the one who drew it.

A diary kept by Cousins was also recovered, but police haven't revealed what, if anything, the diary reveals about Cousins's relationship with Forrester. Evidence is expected to be analyzed in the coming weeks. In the meantime, as previously reported by the *Coldcliff Tribune*, police are continuing to search Cousins's phone records from the weeks leading up to the fateful hike.

16

ELLE

I DON'T KNOW HOW THINGS changed so quickly, how Tabby went from being Mark's widow—it's a morbid expression, but I heard it somewhere and it stuck—to being a suspect. Or a *person of interest*, as she called it. Because Mark's death is no longer considered just a tragedy, or an accident.

Mark's death is now basically a murder.

And as far as everyone knows, there was only one person in the woods with him that night.

I don't know if it was the YouTube video or something the police found that they haven't disclosed, but everything's different now. Tabby has pretty much been quarantined at her house, and they have a warrant to search her cell phone. Yesterday she called me from her parents' landline.

"It'll blow over," she said, followed by a laugh. I had no idea how she could make a joke.

"What if it doesn't?" I said. "What if they actually think you did it?"

"They already think I did it, Elle. But they won't be able to prove a goddamn thing."

She must be scared, under it all. She must be terrified. But Tabby never lays all her cards on the table. She rarely lets people know she's hurting. Even me—I'm her best friend, and it's like she still wants to protect me from something. From herself, maybe.

Lou Chamberlain is in my first-period English class. She's nice enough to me in public and always sends me Facebook invites to her parties, but she's the one who posted the video. She's the reason why everyone's eyes are on Tabby. Something like two hundred thousand sets of eyes—how many people saw that video before it was taken down? The comments still dart in front of me, the things people said. *Violent. Crazy. Psycho bitch.*

I told anyone who would listen that Lance provoked her. Nobody cares. They share a common enemy, and now she has been ousted.

I force myself to march up to Lou's desk, even though I hate confrontation. "Why did you do it? Why did you post that video? Do you realize what you've done to Tabby?"

Lou arches a blond eyebrow. She's pretty, in a generic way. I don't know what Beck sees in her. Civilization, maybe. Or it could be that he just ran out of girls.

"What I've done? Honey, somebody had to do it. Don't hate the messenger."

"What do you have against her? She never did anything to you."

Lou squints, like she's seeing me for the first time. "Maybe you don't know her as well as you think. Maybe she wanted it that way."

I grip my knuckles and picture the mark they would leave on Lou's petal skin. "What the hell are you even talking about?"

"Just—never mind. But honestly, do you think it adds up, her version of the story? Ask yourself that. All I want is justice to be served."

"You didn't even know Mark," I say. She didn't. The closest she and Mark ever got was attending a few of the same parties, with dozens of bodies between them. They'd probably never exchanged a word.

"I'm not saying I did," she says. "But he didn't deserve how he died."

Sometimes—in this dark part of my brain—I think Mark

planned all of this. The hike was his idea. Obviously. I mean, Tabby hated exercise. Bridget inherited all of the athletic ability in that family. Tabby and I used to joke that we were the two laziest people in existence, two overgrown house cats.

"Mark wants to go on a hike," she told me. I think it was the Monday before he died, and we were at the Brody Community Pool. I have a pool in my backyard, but my dad hates taking care of it, so we always end up at Brody instead. I like it better there anyway. More opportunities to see and be seen.

"Does Mark know you? That's hilarious. What did you tell him?"

She spread her towel onto a lounger. "I told him I didn't have hiking shoes."

I sat down beside Tabby and kicked off my flip-flops. "And then what?"

"Then he said don't worry about it. That I could just wear a pair of Bridge's running shoes. I should take an interest in his hobbies, right? He says his coach is on him to do some cross-training outside of the pool. Like, work on his leg strength or whatever."

"Maybe," I said. "But does he take an interest in yours?"

I couldn't see Tabby's eyes behind her sunglasses, but I imagined she was rolling them. "What, he should support all the reality TV we watch? It's not like I'm on a sports team. Or ever will be."

I knew I wasn't going to win this argument. I didn't want to have an argument. Tabby and I barely ever fought, but when we did, we were two opposing storm fronts, both hurtling too fast to turn back first. Besides, we were still in the frosty aftermath of my confession from last week, because Tabby wanted to pretend I never told her the things I'd whispered in the dark. It was easier that way.

I saw him with another girl. It was dark. I couldn't tell if they were kissing but their heads were really close—

"Oh, great," Tabby said, stretching out her legs. "We're being watched."

I sucked in a breath when I saw who was watching us. Lou. She was wearing a high-waisted polka dot bikini, a knockoff of something I remembered seeing Taylor Swift wear in her Kennedy phase. Basically everything about Lou was an imitation of somebody else.

"Just ignore her," I said, grabbing my water bottle, wishing it was filled with something stronger.

"I'm surprised she went anywhere without her *boyfriend*," Tabby said, making the word sound hideous.

"She didn't," I mumbled. Because there was Beck, ridiculously out of place somewhere bright and loud like this. He was in profile and staring through the chain-link fence that surrounded the pool.

Tabby laughed. "I guess he doesn't own swim trunks."

I thought of what was underneath Beck's T-shirt. The tattoos. Somebody who was willing to put so many things on his skin wouldn't be like every other boy. Unwilling to commit to anything more than a blow job at a party.

But I was wrong about Beck. I imagined him being tamed by some mysterious powers I never had. I felt his hand covering mine, his hair falling onto my face as he fused kisses to my forehead. Maybe his silence was my favorite thing about him, his ability to be quiet when everyone else was loud. I filled in that silence with what I wanted to hear. I liked my own fiction more than the reality of who he really is. And I let my own fiction ruin everything.

"So you're actually going on this hike?" I ventured, because anything was better than thinking about Beck.

Tabby stared up at the sky. At first I thought she was ignoring me, then her words landed with a thud. "I'd do anything for him, Elle. Like, anything at all. Sometimes it scares me."

Tabby is a romantic—that's something most people don't

know about her. If you've ever been in a class with her, you probably think she doesn't pay attention, because she never puts her hand up to answer any questions. She makes fun of girls who love romantic comedies, girls who ditch their friends when they get a boyfriend, but she's one of them. She wants the great love story.

I suspected Mark didn't want the same thing. But I never knew what he wanted instead, or what he expected Tabby to do in the woods with him that day. Or what he tried to do when she wouldn't do it.

Now Lou isn't paying attention to me anymore—she's staring at her face in a Sephora makeup mirror. "Maybe he did deserve it," I say as the bell rings, my voice drowned out by the din. "Maybe he deserved worse."

You've only been back at school for a few days but it feels different please message me when you get a chance.

Text message from Tabitha Cousins to Mark Forrester,
September 13, 2018, 6:52 a.m.

17

BECK

Coldcliff Police Station, September 16, 3:05 p.m.

OFFICER OLDMAN: Let's talk about your relationship with Mark Forrester.

BECK: We didn't have one. He was some guy I saw a couple times at parties. That's all.

OFFICER OLDMAN: Some guy whose nose you almost broke. Isn't that right?

BECK: We got into it a bit. Once. It happens when people are drinking at a party. And he came at me. The guy was jealous. I guess he saw Tabby talking to me and was pissed off.

OFFICER OLDMAN: What were you and Tabby talking about at the party?

BECK: (cracks knuckles) I don't even remember. Just small talk. I make small talk with a lot of people. Kinda like you and I are doing now.

OFFICER OLDMAN: Were you trying to get back together with Tabitha?

BECK: No. Just because I talked to a girl doesn't mean I wanted to get back in her pants.

OFFICER OLDMAN: Mark didn't file any assault charges against you.

BECK: Because he knew he was being an asshole and deserved it.

OFFICER OLDMAN: You claim you didn't speak much with

Tabby. But you talk to Tabitha's best friend, Eleanor. Elle Ross. Isn't that right?

BECK: (pauses) Not really. We're not friends either. What does all this have to do with what happened to Mark Forrester?

OFFICER OLDMAN: We're getting to that.

18

LOU

I DON'T REALLY HAVE TIME to talk about this right now. I do have a life, you know? And I'm waiting for Beck to pick me up. But whatever, he's always late. And I do feel like it's my duty to let people know the Tabby I know, not the angelic girl she's suddenly trying to be. (Seriously, she wore *lace* to school the day before she stopped coming. Who does that?)

I remember where I was when I found out about Mark. On my bed, doing a face mask, waiting for Beck to text me back. I had sent the last text, and it had been almost three hours, not that I was counting. And I mean, Beck isn't glued to his phone like everyone else. But when my phone went off, I pretty much expected it to be him. Sometimes he texted to tell me he was standing in my backyard and I'd get this thrill, sneaking down to meet him, careful to wear cute underwear.

But it wasn't Beck. It was my friend Trish. *Did you hear? It's all over Facebook. Mark Forrester is dead. Some kind of hiking accident.*

My first thought, as totally horrible as this is, and I'd never admit this to anyone else—I hoped Tabby was, too.

(Tabby. It sounds like someone's house cat, right? If she's a cat, she's one of those feral ones constantly in heat.)

What you really want to know is what happened at Elle's last party before Mark died. And honestly, I'm not totally sure what went down that night, and I don't know why Beck got in Mark's face, because he wouldn't tell me. But I know it has something to do with Mark's death, like some chain reaction.

If you've been to one of Elle's parties, you know they get pretty wild. She has them only a couple times a year, when her parents go out of town and basically give her their blessing. They're, like, teen-movie party clichés, complete with people doing it in the upstairs bedrooms. Not that I'd ever do it in an upstairs bedroom at a party. Even though Beck is super hot and we're pretty much doing it every day.

Well, sort of. I mean, it's really none of your business, is it?

And this isn't about me and Beck. It's about Tabby and Mark. What I saw. What I think I saw anyway. It was all kind of confusing. I'd had some wine. I don't usually drink. Not like Tabby does. I hate how people like to use alcohol as the reason why they turn into somebody else. It's exactly what my mom did last summer when she cheated on my dad with some random guy she met at the bar. She went away for this girls' weekend with her mom friends, and apparently confessed the whole thing to my dad when she got back. She was all, *I had too much to drink, I wasn't thinking clearly.* It's such a convenient excuse.

Anyway, I was kind of tipsy and looking for Beck. You can't miss him. He has this whole bad boy thing going on. Before him, I only ever dated jocks. Football, basketball, baseball. They were all the same. Boring and predictable, and into their balls—ha— way more than me. I didn't want some guy to pick me up for a date in his polo shirt, driving his dad's Honda. I craved something wilder, something to match the wilderness I know is inside me.

I couldn't find Beck anywhere, which bothered me a bit, because we were supposed to be at this party together, and maybe more so because the fact that I couldn't find him made it really clear that I didn't know him as well as I should after almost six months of being together. (Well, I mean, not that we ever had the conversation about being exclusive, because bringing it up would just make me sound clingy, and I don't want to be the kind of girl who needs a Facebook relationship status to have an actual relationship. Even though, between you and me, the validation would be nice.)

I have no idea why I opened the door to the pool house. Maybe because I had already opened every other door. I've seen people hot box the pool house at one of Elle's other parties, which is so gross. But I cracked the door just a bit, and that's when I saw Tabitha's back. She was straddling someone whose face I couldn't see—like, it was really dark, and I only know it was Tabitha's back because there was a bit of light coming from a lantern in the garden and it lit up the ugly ivy tattoo she has creeping up her spine. Hands were cupping her ass and her hair was falling down, mostly out of the fishtail braid she'd started the night with.

Anyway, I turned to leave—I'm not a pervert who watches other people do it—but I heard what she said. I heard it and I can't unhear it. *This doesn't mean I still love you.*

It's a weird thing to say to your boyfriend, right? I mean, at first I figured they were in a fight and that doing it somewhere they could be caught was their kinky way of making up. But then, like, a few minutes later I saw Mark inside the house, making a drink. It was definitely him—he had this pink shirt on. (Although I heard him say it was *salmon.*) So I went back outside and the pool house door was still closed and there was no Tabitha anywhere.

So maybe my timeline is a bit fuzzy, but I really don't see how Mark could have gone from doing it with Tabitha in the pool house to doing shots in the kitchen in less than five minutes, unless he's actually two people, like Clark Kent and Superman. Which only means one thing. She was cheating on Mark with someone else at the party.

Of course, my mind rounded up the usual suspects. There was Keegan, Mark's friend, who always tagged along to parties, which meant he must have thought he had a good chance of getting laid. (And I mean, he probably did, because he's pretty hot, although he'd look hotter if I didn't know he worked at the Stop & Shop.) I always wondered if he and Tabitha had something going on. Just the way he looked at her sometimes, like he was some kind of animal hunting for prey. A snake, and if he opened his mouth wide enough, he could swallow her alive.

There was Dean Hanson from the football team. Someone apparently saw him and Tabitha sneaking out of the boys' locker room together after the Red Flags game sophomore year. And Reid Carter, who everyone knows Tabitha hooked up with right before she got together with Mark. Or maybe it was during. I wouldn't put it past her. Oh, and Dylan—I forget his last name because he doesn't go to our school, but one time at the Fall Fair, Katie Saunders saw them on the Ferris wheel and his hand was totally in her shorts.

Then it was like, something in my brain shifted and the entire night was ruined, because what if it was Beck?

Don't get me wrong. I trust my boyfriend with all my heart. I trust Beck. I just don't trust Tabitha, and girls like her have a way of making boys do just about anything.

And besides, as much as I totally hate to admit it, Beck has history with Tabitha. He doesn't talk about it. But before Tabitha deleted her Facebook account, when I was friends with her on there, I creeped her old profile pictures and found one of the two of them from sophomore year, before she and Mark were a thing. Her sitting on his lap, them kissing at some party. They were just, like, all over each other all the time, then suddenly they weren't.

I kept looking for Beck at the party because I could feel myself getting frantic, and I needed to know he wasn't with her. I went back outside. There were a bunch of people in the pool, and the door to the pool house was open. I didn't see Beck anywhere but I did see Tabitha, sitting beside the pool with her feet dangling in, staring into the water with her hand covering her mouth.

74

Then there was Beck. Of course I recognized his back. I mean, he has this long blond hair and always wears a leather jacket and it's pretty much the sexiest thing ever. He was on a lawn chair by the fence, staring up at the sky, smoking, which he'd told me he quit doing. Did you know Beck started smoking when he was, like, twelve? And when we got together and I asked him to quit, because I didn't want him to kill himself, he just said *Sure, sweetheart*, and did it, like it was the easiest thing in the world. That was when I knew he loved me. Even though if we're being honest here, the real reason I asked him to quit is because I hate the smell.

So I went over to him and tapped him on the shoulder. He took my hand in his, as if I hadn't surprised him. Beck never lets you know when he's surprised. Or happy, or sad, or anything, really. He's just, like, super good at hiding his emotions.

"Hey, sweetheart," he said. He always calls me *sweetheart*. Which I used to think was really cute, but sometimes I wish he'd say my full name, like guys do on TV. *Louisa Maria Chamberlain, I love you.*

"Where were you?" I blurted out. "I looked for you everywhere."

"I've been here the whole time," he said.

"You're smoking."

He dropped the lit cigarette and snuffed it out with his boot. "Not anymore."

"You told me you quit," I said, trying to stay mad at him, but I could feel my mad becoming something mellow, just like it always did with Beck.

"I did quit. But sometimes I get in a mood and just need one. You don't understand because you've never been addicted to something." He slung his arm around my shoulders, kissed the top of my head.

I'm addicted to you, I wanted to say, but it was the kind of

75

cheesy line that belonged in a rom-com. I kept my mouth shut. You know, boys get scared off when your feelings get too big.

He didn't apologize for smoking after he'd told me he quit. Beck never apologizes for anything. Maybe because he really isn't sorry. I burrowed into him, tucked my hands against the bare strip of skin where his jacket had ridden up. I sucked in his smell, leather and sweat and, kind of gross, the cigarette. But there was something else there, too, I swear. Perfume. And Tabby must be trying to cover up the rotten stench where her soul should be, because she always wears a shit ton of it.

I know what you're thinking. That I'm paranoid, and making things up in my head because of how the media is slamming Tabitha. I'm dogpiling on her, projecting my own insecurities. That's what my mom would say anyway. She's a psychiatrist, one of the many reasons why I never tell her anything.

But here's the thing. Beck couldn't just quit smoking that easily, even though he told me he had. Maybe he never quite gave up Tabitha either. And sometimes when I'm feeling really pissed off about everything, I wonder if he could have had something to do with Mark's death. If Tabitha and Mark weren't the only two people in the woods that day.

I know, it's ridiculous, and it doesn't even make sense. Beck is with me, and I'm sure he wasn't the one in the pool house that night. But somebody was, and I just have this feeling Tabitha wasn't working alone. A girl like that always gets someone else to do the dirty work.

Dead Princeton student's alcohol level high at time of death

By Madison West

Autopsy reports show that Mark Forrester, 20, had alcohol in his system on the day he died. Forrester and his girlfriend, Tabitha Cousins, 17, were hiking to the lookout point of Coldcliff's Mayflower Trail, known as the Split, when Forrester fell from the forty-foot lookout. His cause of death was determined to be drowning, with Cousins as the only current suspect.

It is unknown what District Attorney Anthony Paxton and his team will do with the new evidence. Cousins has maintained that Forrester got too close to the edge and fell. However, a weighted backpack was found in Claymore Creek, which was later confirmed to be the backpack Cousins purchased for Forrester at an REI in Boulder.

Cousins's family has hired powerhouse defense lawyer Marnie Deveraux to defend their daughter. Deveraux told the press yesterday that the truth would be uncovered, and that her client's innocence is indisputable.

19

BRIDGET

BLINK AND YOU'LL MISS US. We're the people who make up Coldcliff, all seven thousand, eight hundred of us. Let me situate you. You're standing in Coldcliff Heights, which is on the north side, and it's the area the high school is in. It's pretty, you're probably thinking. Look at the view of the mountains.

Do you feel safe? You probably do, all nestled in like this, framed by mountains and thickets of trees. The air probably smells better here than where you come from. Fresh and crisp. Maybe you think our girls look wholesome.

There's no reason to come to Coldcliff. Not really. We don't have any of the Fourteeners protruding from our land, so we get passed up by most of the serious climbers. Our shopping leaves something to be desired—most of us buy everything online anyway. The one mall we have, Forest Glen, is pretty tiny, with more shops getting shuttered by the year. Most people get their groceries at the Stop & Shop, which is in the same plaza as my dad's orthodontic office and the optometry place where I get my glasses.

We have nice neighborhoods, suburbia bordered by wilderness. Most people here are solidly upper middle class, living in two-stories just like ours. Most of us have big backyards. Most of us never use them.

What we do have are some good hiking trails. They draw people here in the fall, when the leaves are changing, a smattering of outdoorsy types with waterproof clothing and bear spray for the black bears that they think are the greatest danger around.

If you've read the news lately, you might think there's another danger now.

We have a new tourist attraction. My sister. They're flocking to the trails with maps made by this one website—Outwit the Split, they're calling it, trying to re-create Tabby and Mark's last walk. Isn't that sick and twisted? I have no idea who was morbid enough to come up with it, or who is morbid enough to actually take the time to do it. But I see them in the woods, because I'm there, running.

And today, along with those lemmings and their maps, I see somebody else. Mark's brother. I recognize the hair—blond curls, so different from Mark's meticulous buzz cut. Also, he's wearing flip-flops. Who hikes in flip-flops? Except I guess I know he isn't hiking at all.

He sees me. I freeze, like a deer caught in crosshairs. I'm not scared, though. Like I said, he's in flip-flops, and these woods are my domain.

"What are you doing here?" he says. "Don't tell me you're one of them." He aims his middle finger at a man and woman in matching khaki shorts with walking poles.

"I'm a runner. So I'm running. Do you honestly think I'm one of them?" I jog in place next to him. I hate losing momentum.

"I don't know. Sorry. I didn't mean to be rude, but these idiots get under my skin. I'm Alex. You're Bridget, right?"

I know what he means by *You're Bridget*. You're Tabby's sister.

"I'm Bridget." I gesture to his feet because I don't want to look at his face. He looks too much like Mark, once you get past the hair and the stubble. Same eyes, same mouth. "Not the best choice of hiking footwear."

"I'm not hiking," he says. "I'm—whatever. Never mind. I just feel closer to him when I'm here. And apparently so do all these other people who never knew him at all."

I stop jogging on the spot and glance up, then drop my gaze, because it's hard to look directly at him. Maybe I read Alex all wrong, the hardened boy I saw at the funeral who hates my sister. Right now he just looks sad and lost. I think about Tabby at home, probably stretched out on the couch watching the *Real Housewives*. Maybe this whole thing isn't as shrouded in mystery as everyone wants it to seem. Maybe it's just a dead boy and the people grieving for him.

"I'm sorry," I say, wiping damp hair off my face. Why do I sound so guilty? I didn't push Mark.

But I did something else, and if I hadn't, things might be different now.

"Let me ask you something, and please be honest," Alex says. I look around, aware that we're utterly alone. "You saw them that day, right? Did anything seem off?"

I shake my head and make the mistake of meeting his eyes, and the intensity there makes me hold my breath. He looks especially like Mark now—Mark when he wanted something. "No. They seemed totally normal." I don't mention that their *normal* was anything but.

"I'm just trying to make sense of it," he says. "I mean, I know what I've been hearing. And I saw the video. This has been hell for my family. Mark and I didn't talk often. Last I knew, he had a girlfriend, but I had no idea if they were serious."

They were too serious. I think about Tabby's locker, the words scrawled there. Alex has no idea.

"I didn't know much either," I say. "Tabby had her own life, and I have mine." I stare at my watch, at the timer that has kept going. I don't want to stand here, because I'm afraid of what he'll ask next.

"I'm heading back to Australia next week," he says. "But if you remember anything, let me know. You know where we live, because I see you running by."

I swallow. My throat is dry.

"I should go." I turn and start to jog, willing him not to follow me.

"Mark mentioned his girlfriend's sister didn't like him," he yells, his voice rising. "Why didn't you like him? Everyone liked Mark."

I break into a sprint.

Coldcliff doesn't feel that safe anymore.

Excerpt from Tabby's Diary

October 18, 2018

How do you stop yourself from loving someone? I seriously need to know. Now Mark is upset at me because he knows I talked to Beck about us. Nothing else happened, but Mark doesn't believe that. Yet I'm supposed to believe him that nothing happened with all the Instagram girls. I even called him out on it, just to see what he'd say. He made me think I was the paranoid one. You're the only one, he told me, but keep this up and you won't be. I feel so alone.

New witness comes forward in boyfriend-killer case
By David Moss

A shocking new witness statement from Coldcliff, Colorado, resident Abe Hendricks, 47, alleges that Tabitha Cousins, 17, was seen at Coldcliff's Crest Beach stuffing rocks into a picnic basket the morning before Mark Forrester's August 16 death. Hendricks called in to the local police tip line with his testimony. While he doesn't have photographic proof of Cousins collecting the rocks, he is certain it was her he saw at the beach that morning.

Forrester's body was found in a creek approximately fifty meters from a backpack weighted down with rocks, leading investigators to surmise there was foul play in the competitive swimmer's drowning death.

"Usually I'm the only one there," Hendricks told the *Coldcliff Tribune* yesterday. "It was early, not even seven. The sun was just on its way up. There was this girl. I didn't think of it again until I saw her face on the news."

A source who did not want to be named reached out to the *Charger* exclusively to report that Cousins and Forrester had recently been fighting at a house party thrown by one of Cousins's friends.

"I couldn't make out what they were saying," the source said. "They kept their voices down. Then she stormed off."

Speculation exists that Cousins was cheating on Forrester with her ex-boyfriend, Thomas Becker Rutherford III, and she may have shoved Forrester when he confronted her about it during their hike. However, District Attorney Anthony Paxton has stated that the plot to kill Forrester was carefully crafted by a dangerous girl. Cousins's attorney, powerhouse lawyer Marnie Deveraux, maintains that the accusations against her client are "absolutely invalid."

CoffeeAddict: awfully convenient that this guy comes forward now. I don't know. Something about this case isn't adding up

KatieKat: I have no idea how she's getting out of this one.

PrincessPea: They were fighting at that party because she was screwing another guy.

>   **Swifty01**: Yeah like you would know

>   **PrincessPea**: I would because I was there.

20

KEEGAN

AS MUCH AS I HOPE she ends up in jail, I can't picture Tabby there. I mean, can you see that girl eating prison food? She used to bitch and complain about the restaurants Mark took her to, like she was too good to be seen there. Made him feel like shit for not feeding her steak every night. Do you know how that makes a guy feel, when he's busting his ass and it's still not good enough, and it'll never be good enough?

I'm at the Stop & Shop today, working a double because I need the cash, and because I do happen to know how a guy feels when he busts his ass and isn't enough. Kyla doesn't have expensive taste. She's the chick who's just happy that you're paying any attention to her. (Don't tell her I said that.) Except lately the more attention I give, the more she needs.

If Mark were here, he'd tell me not to waste my time. He'd tell me to find something I could win at. Mark hated being anything other than first. He once came in second at a meet in high school, the fifty fly, which wasn't even his main event. There was this bonfire after, and I watched him take his silver medal out of his hoodie pocket and shove it in the fire, right underneath everyone's roasted marshmallows and hot dogs. I was wasted, but I'll never forget that moment. Mark hated losing.

I smile at the old lady I'm ringing up. You can always judge a person on what they buy. This granny is all about marked-down meat, stuff that's going to spoil tomorrow, red pulp that's leaking bloody juice all over the conveyer belt. I smile anyway because

I need this shitty job, because I don't have enough money to get the hell out of town.

Mark came over to my place only a couple times all summer. He was always busy doing other shit. Tabby, I guess, or swimming. The Coldcliff Heights Aquatic Center has this Olympic-sized swimming pool. He was so pissed about what happened at the NCAAs. Typical Mark, he only blamed himself, but it was her fault, her calling him up the night before and saying all the stuff she did. It was like she did it on purpose to make him lose.

I don't even look up at the next customer, not until I realize he isn't buying anything. Then I see the uniform, and the stern face.

"Keegan Leach," he says. "Do you have a break coming up so we can talk?"

I already talked to the cops. It came up on Mark's phone that I was the last person he talked to before he left with Tabby. I was pretty brutal with them. I mean, I told them how Mark felt about the whole hiking idea. That he was worried about it. I showed them the text he sent me, which I'm sure they had already seen.

Officer Oldman, that's this guy's name. He isn't the one I talked to before. After my shift, I sit in a hard chair at the police station and sweat, because I hate talking to cops. Find me one person who doesn't feel guilty by proximity, even when they have nothing to hide.

"Keegan." He sits down across from me. "Thanks for coming in. We've been made aware of some new information in the Mark Forrester case, and I was hoping you'd be able to shed some light on it."

I sit back in the chair. It's, like, exceptionally hard, and I guess that's probably on purpose, to make you uncomfortable.

"Someone has come forth saying he saw Tabitha Cousins at Crest Beach on the morning before Mark's death, loading rocks into a picnic basket."

"Okay." I've already read the article. I still can't picture Tabby with a picnic basket, all wholesome.

"We believe these were the rocks that were intended to anchor Mark to the bottom of Claymore Creek. I'm sure you know that we found the weighted backpack, the one that was filled up with rocks, in the creek with Mark's body."

With Mark's body. I can't fucking think of him like that, as two different things. Mark and body. It's so messed up. I'd rather not think at all.

"Yeah," I say. "I heard about the backpack."

Oldman leans forward, all bulk. An intimidation tactic. I wonder if he was the one who questioned Tabby. I wonder if she broke down in front of him. Knowing her, she'd be more likely to break him down.

"We believe Mark was wearing the backpack that day. Some hikers verify that they saw a girl with a picnic basket and a boy with a backpack walking up toward the Split." Oldman's face goes a bit softer. I wonder if he works on his expressions in the mirror at home, like they used to tell us to do for school picture day. "Something just doesn't add up. Why would he carry a pack that heavy without knowing what was in it?"

I shrugged. "That's Mark. He's an athlete. I mean, was an athlete. He probably didn't even notice the weight. He used to go for runs every morning over the summer with a backpack full of his mom's soup cans. Thought it helped his back muscles. Plus, he was just one of those guys who carried his girlfriend's shit without asking. Sorry, I mean stuff."

Oldman nods and gives me a look as if to say, *Women and their mysterious shit.*

"That makes sense," he says. "What doesn't is that we found the backpack underwater, almost directly beneath the drop-off point from the Split. Mark was found almost fifty meters away."

Fifty meters. The hundred-meter freestyle was his specialty. I remember us in high school swim club those early mornings, me sometimes hungover, chugging water bottles filled with a water-Gatorade mixture, because Mark read somewhere it was the best thing for your system before getting in the pool. Mark lapping almost everybody else, in his own league. People saying he was the next Michael Phelps.

"So you're saying . . . ," I start, and Oldman watches me put it together, the whole goddamn mess. Everyone knows Tabby pushed Mark off the Split, even though she's saying he fell. But nobody believes her. I mean, she says he lost his balance. What does she expect? Just like she doesn't have the patience for anything else, she didn't think murder through.

"The fall wasn't what killed Mark. We already knew his cause of death was drowning. But presuming he fell with the backpack on, and it was intended to weigh him down, he would have been found that way, with the pack still on. Mark managed to swim away."

I gulp back the acid in my throat. He was alive. He fought for it. Just like he fought for everything he wanted. Most people think stuff came easily to Mark. Grades, sports, girls. But he had to work for it, just like everyone else.

Oldman folds his hands in front of me. He's wearing a wedding band, a gaudy one with diamonds. "This doesn't prove anything. But it does lead to suspicions that somebody could have held Mark under the water."

"You mean Tabby?" I blurt out.

"We're investigating all leads," he says, calm and professional, the opposite of me.

"Maybe he got tired," I say, because it's too sickening to think Tabby dragged someone else in on this with her, that someone else hated Mark enough to want him dead.

"The creek is rocky leading up to the area where Mark was found. Any traces of wet footprints would have vanished on the rocks. We're working to pick out any shoe prints in the surrounding area that would definitively identify a suspect."

I rub my face with my hands. Mark almost didn't go on that hike. I could have talked him out of it—I was with him that day. But I didn't try at all.

"What I'm wondering," Oldman continues, "is what you might know, as Mark's best friend and arguably the closest person to him. Did he have any enemies? Is there anyone you can think of who might want Mark dead?"

"No," I say. "Everybody loved Mark."

Except maybe the one person who was supposed to love him the most.

You said you were going to call me and I've been waiting up for hours. Was supposed to study for this huge bio test and now I'm going to fail and it's your fault. Where are you? *10:34 p.m.*

Did you even open the Snap I sent you? *10:36 p.m.*

Why did you not comment on the pic I tagged you in on Insta? Are you ashamed of me? *11:17 p.m.*

Do you even want to see me this weekend? *11:21 p.m.*

Do people at Princeton even know about me? *2:17 a.m.*

Text messages from Tabitha Cousins to Mark Forrester,
October 18–19, 2018

Text message history reveals jealousy, possible motive

By Julie Kerr

New evidence has been revealed in the death of Mark Forrester, 20, a Princeton championship swimmer whose hiking accident in mid-August is now being treated as a possible murder. Forrester's girlfriend, Tabitha Cousins, 17, who was with him at the time of his death, asserted that Forrester fell. However, text messages retrieved from Forrester's phone, found in the creek, show a tumultuous relationship with a possible motive for murder. Cousins frequently sent messages to Forrester accusing him of cheating, and she sent an ominous text the day of the hike.

Cousins's lawyer declined to comment on the story.

21

BECK

Coldcliff Police Station, September 23, 10:16 a.m.

OFFICER OLDMAN: I'll get right down to it, Thomas. That's your real name, right? Thomas Becker Rutherford III.

BECK: Nobody calls me that.

OFFICER OLDMAN: We had a warrant to search your phone. You weren't exactly forthcoming when we asked you if you'd been in contact with Tabitha. There was a flurry of calls made from her to you right around Christmas. Then again a few months later. And over the summer. She hadn't lost your number.

BECK: So she called me. I don't see what the big deal is.

OFFICER OLDMAN: The big deal is you picked up. You must have talked about something.

BECK: I told her to stop calling. She did that sometimes. Just wanted to talk. Maybe there was nobody else who would listen.

OFFICER OLDMAN: Did she tell you she was upset with Mark?

BECK: No, because we didn't talk about him.

OFFICER OLDMAN: Did she want anything from you? When she called? She must have wanted something, if she kept calling.

BECK: Sometimes she'd want to be picked up from a party. She knew I wouldn't judge.

OFFICER OLDMAN: Judge what?

BECK: Her. For being wasted. Or whatever.

OFFICER OLDMAN: Tabitha drank a lot.

BECK: So do most people at parties.

OFFICER OLDMAN: You picked her up, then. On your motorcycle.

BECK: Yeah.

OFFICER OLDMAN: And what did you talk about, on those rides? Where did you go?

BECK: It was too loud to hear anything. You ever been on a bike before? Can't hear much, besides the road. I'd drop her at home. Well, a block away, then I'd watch to make sure she got inside okay.

OFFICER OLDMAN: Why not walk her to her door?

BECK: Her folks didn't like me much.

OFFICER OLDMAN: Why not?

BECK: Do you have a daughter?

OFFICER OLDMAN: Answer the question, please.

BECK: Maybe it wasn't that they didn't like me. They just didn't know me.

OFFICER OLDMAN: Do you feel like a lot of people don't know you?

BECK: Are you a cop, or a shrink now, too?

OFFICER OLDMAN: (clears throat) Those nights you drove Tabitha home. You never went to Queen Anne's Woods?

BECK: No. Why would we?

OFFICER OLDMAN: If you and Tabitha—(pauses, is interrupted by another officer coming in) One moment, Thomas. I'll be back shortly.

BECK: My name's not Thomas.

TABBY CATS—JUSTICE 4 TABBY!

Welcome to our Facebook page!

This group has grown to almost 20K members, how great is that? Looks like there are LOTS of us out there who know Tabby didn't do it. With all those unfair articles popping up, we need to help our girl and spread the word however we can. How many of us have been accused of lying? Slut-shamed for having sex? How many of us have been swept under the rug by some golden boy? I haven't ever met Tabby, but I don't need to meet her to know she's telling the TRUTH. I can see it in her eyes. I bet if Mark wasn't a star athlete, or a rich white boy, everything would be different. Don't let them keep getting away with it!

We'll be marching in downtown Coldcliff this week-end, wearing cat ears. Come join us! And tell all your friends!

👍 4.1k Likes 💬 252 Comments ➤ 311 Shares

Write a comment... 📷 ☺

94

22

ELLE

IF YOU FEEL LIKE you've spent some time with me and still don't know me very well—that's fair. I keep people at a distance. Even Tabby. She doesn't know everything, and it's better that way.

I see her as often as I can. Today, I show up with powdered doughnuts from Milky's Variety—her favorite. She has makeup on, even though she doesn't leave her house. There's a news van camped out by the curb. I shoot my middle finger at it before cutting through the gate and knocking on the glass patio doors.

"You're the only one who visits," Tabby whines, reaching down and taking a doughnut. "It's like everyone forgot about me."

I wonder if that's true. Not that everyone forgot, because obviously nobody did, but whether I'm really the only one.

"You're too good to me," she says, brushing white powder from her lips. "I owe you big-time. The next time you're a person of interest in a possible murder, I'll bring you doughnuts, too."

I smile, but the truth is, I'm the one who owes her.

I'm not ready to tell my truth. So I'll keep telling Tabby's.

The first time Tabby and Mark had sex was at my house. We were all downstairs playing video games, then she said she was going to get a drink, and he followed her. I was left with Keegan—sometimes I got left with Keegan when we hung out. I didn't have a problem with him or anything, but it was like we were expected to hook up by default, and he really wasn't my type.

So eventually I went upstairs to see where Tabby was. I called into the kitchen, but she wasn't there. Then I heard a noise coming from my bedroom. I walked up and stopped abruptly. They hadn't even bothered to fully close the door. Mark was on top of her, and her hands were wrapped around him, digging into his skin. He said something I couldn't quite make out, but it sounded a lot like "You're mine."

They had known each other for five days.

It wasn't that I was judging Tabby for having sex with a guy she didn't know all that well. But that comment was super creepy and possessive. *You're mine.* I knew Tabby would have seen it as romantic. It was an embrace. A promise. She wanted somebody who wanted her, needed somebody who needed her. She became a mirror for whoever she was with.

I closed the door. I went back downstairs to where Keegan was sitting. He had paused his video game, which was unheard of.

"What's up?" he said.

"Nothing." I sat down on the couch, leaving an entire cushion between us.

"Are they fucking?"

I stared at my jeans, feeling my cheeks turn red. "I don't know."

He laughed, but it wasn't a nice laugh. "Yeah, you do. Get used to it. This is his pattern."

I curled my legs underneath me, wanting to make myself as small as possible. Ever since I became aware of my body, I was always trying to take up less space. "What do you mean, his pattern?"

Keegan picked up the controller without looking at me. "He meets a girl. He gets obsessed with her. She messes up, and it all blows up." Some kind of explosion happened on the TV screen, followed by two red words in the middle. *Game over.*

I wanted to tell Tabby everything he had said. It was something she needed to hear before she got invested and fell too hard for Mark. But later that night, when the boys were gone, I could tell I was too late. She had already fallen.

"He's so amazing, Elle," she said as we walked to Reid's Ice Cream. A blanket of humidity hung in the air, making her hair curl around her ears. "You know when you meet someone, and he's the one? Well, I think Mark might be the one."

I don't think so, I wanted to say. I was sure that Tabby was one in a string of girls that Mark liked to play with. Maybe he only went after her in the first place because he suspected she was in high school. That she didn't know any better.

"Great," I said instead. "I'm happy for you." I reminded myself that Mark was a summer fling. He was going back to Princeton for his second year. He'd be in New Jersey, almost two thousand miles from Coldcliff, Colorado.

"We're going to Skype every night," Tabby told me at the end of the summer. "I even bought some new bras and stuff. You know, to keep it interesting."

I could tell she was panicking inside. Her face did that thing where her eyes told a different story than her mouth. She was worried about the college girls. The ones at Mark's swim meets, the ones sitting in front of him in class, the ones at parties, bra straps slipping down their bare shoulders as they chugged cheap beer. Mark had probably promised her she was the only girl for him. *You're mine.*

Things would get better when Mark went back to school. Tabby would go back to normal. Maybe they would break up, and maybe they wouldn't, but he wouldn't be all she thought about.

"You're my only friend, you know," Tabby says now. "I don't know what I'd do without you."

I return her hug, hoping she doesn't feel the tension coiled in my shoulders. Because I have a feeling that without me, things would be a whole lot easier for her.

Tabitha Cousins: Good girl gone bad?
By Oberon Halton

The internet is buzzing about Tabitha Cousins, the 17-year-old arrested for the murder of her boyfriend after a hiking accident. Now wherever you look, there's someone saying something new about Tabby, as she's known to family and friends. A source close to her revealed exclusively to me that Tabby was having doubts about her relationship, but didn't know how to end it.

"She was scared of what he might do," said the source, who asked not to be identified.

This presents an interesting dichotomy. Tabby's case has proved especially polarizing in the media, gaining recent traction on big news sites. A Facebook group that now has nearly 40,000 members is called the Tabby Cats. But a rival group, Remember Mark Forrester, is full of people who claim Tabby wanted him dead. A lot of commenters are comparing Tabby's case to that of Amanda Knox. On one website, she was given the nickname "Blue-Eyed Boyfriend Killer," which seems to have stuck.

Readers have asked me what I think, and honestly, I'm torn here. I'm new to the scene and it means a lot that you trust my opinion. At first I looked at Tabby and thought: guilty, guilty, guilty. Then I started thinking more about it. Recent speculation that it may have been a suicide pact gone wrong actually holds weight with me. Maybe Mark went through with it, and she backed out. I definitely think she knows more than she's saying, but maybe because she's protecting him.

My DMs are open to discuss, and feel free to leave a comment or reach out to me if you know anything about this case.

PenIsABitch Suicide pact? Hell yes. I said that from the start. It's only a matter of time until they find her backpack.

Ares: She's protecting somebody, but it's not Mark. No way did that girl do it alone.

23

LOU

LATELY HIS *SWEETHEART* sounds more like he's talking to a small child. A small, stupid child. I'm not sure what changed between us, besides his ex popping up in, like, every news article ever, even though she hasn't officially been arrested yet. (I keep waiting for that one!)

It's not easy being Beck Rutherford's girlfriend. Not most of the time. Not when he asks you to do things you sometimes don't want to do. (No, not like that, you perv.) I mean — ride on the back of his bike without a helmet. Go for walks at 2 a.m., which requires sneaking out of the house. My mom caught me once, and now she thinks I need to see someone to talk about all the *feelings* I'm experiencing. My mom's big on feelings, which I guess makes sense, since she listens to other people's for a living.

You've probably seen Beck's name tossed around online. It's super frustrating. I don't even know if he has seen it, since he doesn't have social media (or much in the way of social skills, ha). He deleted his Facebook account after he and Tabby broke up.

He's not great at responding to my messages. I think I already said that, right? Well, today has been even worse. I can't get in touch with him at all, and he never came over last night like he was supposed to. I don't think boys understand sometimes what we go through to get ourselves ready. Like me. Every time I get that text, *you around*, I take a shower. I shave everywhere. I rub on the body lotion I know he likes. I put on my makeup, even though I took it off to go to bed. Then I respond. *I'm here!*

(The exclamation mark is a bit much, right? My friend Tessa says exclamation marks are desperate. But Tessa has also been with the same boring boyfriend for four years and has only ever been in the missionary position.)

I'm stewing about it after school when the doorbell rings, and I know it must be Beck, here in broad daylight for once. Except when I open the door wearing just a tank top and my underwear, I realize it's not Beck. It's a policeman, a young one. His eyes go big, then back to normal as I hide behind the door.

"Sorry," I say. "I thought you were someone else."

"Louisa Chamberlain?"

"Yeah. What's going on?"

Except I already know, don't I? It must be something to do with Tabby. I knew they'd get to me eventually. They've already talked to a bunch of other people. Elle, Bridget, Beck (although good luck getting him to talk about that), even Mr. Mancini.

"Is your mother home, Miss Chamberlain?"

Well. I'm not expecting that. First of all, my mother is always at work, and also, this better not be the Guy. The one from her girls' weekend. He has had so many different faces in my head. Ugly, handsome, bearded, blue-eyed, tall, squat. She never said his name, just refers to him as her mistake, like another possession she owns. I hate picturing it. My mother, drunk at a bar, probably screaming along to some terrible song from a band she saw in concert in the nineties, before I came along and made her practical. My mother, flirting with some guy, any guy who gave her a compliment and bought her a drink. My mother, going home with him.

"She's not home," I say flatly. "Why?"

He doesn't answer. He's way too young for my mom, but maybe that's her type. Maybe any guy who isn't my dad is her type.

"Actually, we wanted to speak with you as well. Regarding Beck Rutherford."

A flush starts at my neck, which I know already looks blotchy, because that's where I wear my emotions, in the space along my collarbone. Stress, embarrassment, lust, anxiety. All red and covered in welts—the world's ugliest necklace.

"What about him?"

He reaches into his pocket, hands me his card. "Give me a call when it's a good time for you. There are just a couple questions I have."

I take the card. I realize he doesn't want to come in, because I'm a teenage girl in my underwear, and also because he doesn't need to come in. I did nothing wrong.

I tell him I'll call him (I won't) and shut the door. From the window, I watch him walk away. He has no swagger at all. His card says his name is Detective Blake Stewart. I forgot to see if he had a wedding band on, or maybe I didn't forget, because it doesn't matter. A little piece of metal does nothing.

I go back upstairs and open my laptop. I used to just check the *Tribune* for updates on Tabby's case, but now her face is everywhere else, too. Perez Hilton made her into a meme. I can't help but think she'd love the attention.

Then I found Sharp Edges Crime. Don't ask me how. But now it's, like, my new obsession. That sounds awful, but isn't everything about this story?

There was a new post yesterday. *Good girl gone bad?* Like she's an overripe avocado. Have you read it? It's actually pretty good journalism.

I refresh the page, read the new comments. Tabby defenders. Gross.

Don't believe what you read. Don't believe what you see. Every time they show her leaving her lawyer's office or whatever, she's all buttoned up and big-eyed. (How do they know where she's going to be all the time? Who are *they*, exactly? She's orchestrating this entire thing, I'm telling you.)

She's their darling. They're determined to prove she didn't do it. Remember what she told the *Tribune*? She was *scared*.

So scared. So scared that she bothered to put on her fake eyelashes. And they all fell for it. Her tears, the way her hands shook. She loves this, becoming infamous. Her Insta, before it got taken down, was public, all super-filtered selfies and those Marilyn Monroe quotes every basic bitch loves to plaster over their lives. *If you can't handle me at my worst, you don't deserve me at my best.*

But now, the truth is coming out. Now, they found a backpack and all those nasty texts, and it's only a matter of time until they find the next bombshell. And all I want to say is *I told you so.*

You haven't even told me which dorm you're at I think it's ridiculous I don't even know where my BOYFRIEND lives. *11:23 p.m.*

Who's the skank in all your photos? I guess she's good enough to be in your life but I'm not? *11:41 p.m.*

You made a really big mistake crossing me. Two can play this game. *2:16 a.m.*

Look, I'm sorry for sending all those texts last night but I'm super upset, do you think we can talk? *6:14 a.m.*

Text messages from Tabitha Cousins to Mark Forrester, October 24–25, 2018

Girl, 17, only suspect in Princeton student's murder

By Talia Sims

The death of a promising young man, which rocked the community of Coldcliff, Colorado, is now shaping into a murder investigation. On August 16, Tabitha Marie Cousins, 17, and her boyfriend, Mark Forrester, 20, were hiking to a lookout point known as the Split. Cousins told police that Forrester lost his footing and fell over the edge, and that she could barely find her own way back out of the woods, as the couple had hiked to see the sunset but ended up out after dark.

However, when a backpack filled with rocks was found in Claymore Creek by police divers, Cousins was questioned by police and is now the only suspect in her former boyfriend's death. She maintains her innocence. A statement by her lawyer said that Cousins had no knowledge of the contents of the backpack, or why Forrester got so close to the edge.

A police search of the text message history between Cousins and Forrester, who had been dating for approximately one year, revealed a tumultuous relationship, with jealousy and accusations coming from Cousins. Sources close to the couple say that in the months leading up to Forrester's death, things seemed better between them, when Forrester was home in Coldcliff for his summer break from Princeton.

"They literally seemed perfect," said a source, who requested to not be identified. "You'd never guess there was anything wrong."

Police are continuing their investigation, with District Attorney Anthony Paxton stating there is sufficient evidence to prove Cousins is guilty.

Forrester was due to enter his third undergraduate year at Princeton. He planned to take the LSAT exam that fall, his brother said. Friends describe Forrester as studious, loyal, and generous.

"He'd give anything to you," said Forrester's best friend, Keegan Leach, 20, also of Coldcliff. "The guy would give you the shirt off his back, even if you'd just met. I can't believe he's gone."

In addition to his academic achievements, Forrester was a gifted swimmer, receiving several scholarship offers before turning them down to attend Princeton, his father's alma mater. He swam competitively for Princeton, earning NCAA championships in his freshman and sophomore years. He was heavily favored to win the 100-meter freestyle in this year's event, but failed to advance to the finals.

"The stress got to him," said a teammate who wished to remain anonymous. "It's true, what everyone is saying. It was her. Always on him. I knew there was something wrong."

Cousins, a high school senior, has been called the "Blue-Eyed Boyfriend Killer" as media scrutiny increases around her. She is expected in court next week to hear the charges against her.

COMMENTS

Kiley_R_Loves_B: omg she totally did it, look at that pic of her. she looks sooo guilty

XmanCometh: Because she's wearing makeup? How can you tell if someone is guilty from a photo?

MsPenn: I tried to look up her Instagram but it's gone, so is his. I'm so curious about what happened. Girls don't just kill their boyfriends. He must have done something to deserve it.

Swifty01: One does not simply go hiking with a backpack full of rocks.

HeadPerson: She goes to my high school!!!! And I know at least 5 people who slept with her

BeeYoTiful: Maybe he killed himself? Just because they had angry text messages doesn't make her a murderer. I mean if the cops found what my hubs and I sent each other they'd probably lock us both up.

Kenn-A-D: I used to know this girl. She definitely did it.

24

LOU

I CAN'T FUCKING BELIEVE IT. She made *People*! Not just, like, if you scroll way down the site either. There's her face, right there, the biggest of the crime stories.

Do you get it now, why I think she planned it this way? No publicity is bad publicity, right? And that girl wants to be famous. She wants people to stare. And she wants them to talk. I've known it ever since *A Streetcar Named Desire*.

I find Beck today during my spare period, under the bleachers. He's smoking again. He doesn't try to hide it.

"I'm not going to kiss you if you taste like ashes," I say.

"I never asked you to." He taps his foot. That's new. He's—I don't know. Nervous?

I linger back. "You know, you're killing me right now. In a secondhand kind of way."

He cocks his head. "Sweetheart, nobody made you stand this close."

"You're an asshole. Are you not going to say anything about the article? I know you saw it. Do you believe it now? She's guilty, Beck. They must have something on her."

"Maybe," he says. "Or maybe they just hope they do."

Beck didn't always talk in riddles like that. When we first met, he and Tabby were way over. We don't exactly run in the same crowd—actually, Beck doesn't have a crowd—and it took some planning (scheming is such a nasty word) to make sure we were at the same party at the same time. It was a costume one, and I dressed as an angel. It was a risk, but I wanted to be the light to her dark. We hooked up that night and just kept hooking up and it turned into more.

When Tabby first saw us together—I knew she was going to be pissed. She was with Mark, but the way she stared at Beck— she still wanted him. It was widely known that Beck dumped her for cheating on him. But you know what? She smiled. At me, or at him, I'm not sure. Almost like she liked the idea of us. Like nothing I did would shock her.

"The Blue-Eyed Boyfriend Killer," I say. "Honestly, how stupid is that? I'm sure she thought of it herself."

Beck just shrugs and crushes what's left of his cigarette under his boot.

Things are different without Tabby around. He looks different. Almost, like, cheaper. Not the authentic bad boy of your dreams but a Halloween costume, pleather instead of leather, cologne where he should be gritty. But that's just how boys look in the absence of competition.

"They questioned me," Beck says just as I turn away. "I'm getting a lawyer."

"I know. She's trying to drag you down with her. Don't let her get away with it."

You know what this means, though, right? The fact that her face is literally everywhere? (Besides the fact that she loves the attention?)

It means they really have something on her. Or they're about to.

25

ELLE

YOU ALREADY KNOW that Tabby lawyered up. What you probably don't know is that I'm not even allowed to talk to her anymore. She's more cut off every day, a princess in a two-story. I want to know what they have on her, besides a whole lot of crap supposedly proving that she's not innocent. As if not being an angel translates into being guilty.

I'm not innocent in all this either. I played a role. I'm still playing one.

When I'm at school today, I lose myself in a swirl of girls, the same ones who come to my parties but don't know me at all. It's not their fault. When Tabby came into my life, I let everyone else slip out of a grasp I hadn't even been aware I possessed. Now when they ask me anything—*What are you doing after school? Are you going to the party in the woods?*—what they're really doing is trying to wedge me open so I let Tabby's secrets sprinkle out.

I don't say a word. I tell them I'm fine and let my smile do the rest. My mouth is my deadliest weapon. I've told lots of lies with it. Two of my lies started out gossamer thin, with barely any substance. But they got so tangled that it stopped mattering.

I know Dallas has algebra second period, and I've aligned my days so I don't have to see him. But today, he's coming out of Mr. Mancini's office as I'm walking to the cafeteria, and I dart into a random classroom so he doesn't see me. Not that it matters. Dallas has been texting me nonstop. *Elle, what's going on? What did I do wrong? Just talk to me. If I did something, don't I deserve to know?*

He did something. But I'm the one who did something wrong. This time, by not talking. See? My mouth really is my deadliest weapon. If it says something, it gets people in trouble. If it doesn't, it gets me in trouble. Sometimes being a girl is a lose-lose situation. Like now—I have to hide not because I'm afraid of what he'll say but because of what everyone else will.

Beck's text, which comes in right after I get home, is one I don't ignore. Seeing his name on my phone still turns my ribs into a vise, gripping my heart. *I got a lawyer. Are they still talking to you?*

It's my fault he's involved at all. Just like it's my fault Tabby and Beck ended, and my fault she met Mark. I'm the catalyst for everything, and I'm the only one who knows it.

She's cheating on you. Those are the words I said to Beck when he and Tabby had been together for four months. I was drunk, barefoot in someone's backyard, and I was irritated at Tabby for ignoring me and worshipping her leather-clad bad boy. She was so fucking starry-eyed. And she kept on flirting with other guys, even though she didn't call it flirting. She called it being friendly. If she had seen Beck like I did—really seen him, his softness and the sensitive parts he swept underneath the hard exterior—she never would have been so *friendly*.

He confronted her, and she didn't deny it, because it was true. She had cheated on him. A kiss with Sawyer Hartman, who she didn't even care about. I saw it, a quick grazing of their lips at the bus stop. I didn't even know Tabby took the bus anywhere. Maybe that's what bothered me most, that she had secret pockets in her life that I wasn't invited into.

Two days later, she and Beck were done. My poison acted fast. Tabby was a mess, of course. I took her for ice cream and dried her tears and listened to her talk, knowing I was the reason she hurt but saying nothing.

But Beck never stopped caring about her. I could tell. They weren't friends, exactly, but something else. Two people who went through something together. One who had been screwed over by the other but still managed to care.

(There's an analogy here for me and Dallas, but I'm choosing to ignore it. Because what I did to him is much worse.)

My phone buzzes when I'm in the middle of composing a message to Beck—something long and emotional that I know I'll never send. The new text is from Dallas. *I know you saw me today—just talk to me, please.*

I delete it instantly and erase everything I was typing to Beck. I send something else instead. *It doesn't matter—they don't hear anything I say anyway.*

What I said to Beck two months ago—what I told him about Mark—I knew it would set something off. I'm not sure why I did it. I guess I wanted to see how far people would go for Tabby.

Maybe I can't handle the answer.

26

KEEGAN

I THINK IT WAS HOMECOMING when it all started to fall apart between Mark and Tabby. Yeah, like, three months in, that's when relationships start to get tough. I'm not being sarcastic. This is why I don't do girlfriends. Although now Kyla keeps asking me what we are, and I know what she wants to hear, but I just want to tell her we're humans, and we're basically another kind of animal.

But at homecoming, Mark had this whole thing planned for Tabby, this romantic dinner the night before the football game. Then a few hours later I got a text saying he wanted to go out, so I figured they had yet another fight. We went to some house party. He drank, but not as much as I did. When I asked him what happened to his big date, he just let out this giant sigh. "She's not returning my texts. I have no idea who she is." He slapped his head. "I mean, where she is."

"Tons of girls here," I said, gesturing around. It was the same old crew, mostly seniors from Coldcliff Heights and some leftovers like me, trapped between high school and the Real World that comes after it, but they'd be new to Mark, at least a body to keep him warm.

"But you don't get it," he said, sitting on the arm of a dingy brown couch. His arms were giant, like they were about to hulk out of his shirt. My body used to look like that, once upon a time, when I swam and worked out with Mark. Not anymore. "I don't want tons of girls. I want her."

But why, I wanted to ask. Sure, Tabby was hot, but so were most of the girls there. She must have been magic in bed or something. Maybe she could unhinge her jaw. Mark was too good a guy to ever talk about shit like that with me, not like the guys at the Stop & Shop. Tabby came in a lot to get random stuff. Diet soda, makeup remover, sometimes girl shit like tampons. She always wore the same tiny pajama shorts and tank top with no bra, almost like she was daring the poor guy cashing her out to picture what she looked like naked.

I tried telling Mark once, and he just laughed. "Typical Tabby. She hates getting dressed if she doesn't have to. Come on, haven't you ever left the house in your pajamas because you were too lazy to change?"

That was when I knew he had picked a side. That was when I knew there were sides to be taken at all.

I'm not gonna say what happened later that night. I mean, I was pretty wasted, and I lost track of Mark. I have no clue how he got home, and apparently I left the party without my shoes, because I woke up the next day with the soles of my feet black, my socks in a wrung-out clump on the carpet, two dirty snakes. There was a strange girl in my bed, and I didn't think about Mark at all until he texted me later to say he was heading back to school early to get more time at the pool.

When I got around to responding, I asked him if he'd ever heard from Tabby, and he answered with one word. *No.*

I figured they were over. I hoped they were. I wanted Mark to go back to Princeton and find a girl his age, maybe one who was also super into sports and understood him. Mark wasn't a guy who complained, but he'd told me a few times that Tabby just didn't get it, all the hours he had to spend in the pool, at the gym.

"She wants to talk every single night," he said. "She doesn't get that I'm in bed by nine and up at four. I woke up today to seventeen missed calls from her, and a nasty text."

I asked him to read me the text, so he did. It was long.

Something along the lines of *I know you're out with another girl and that's why you're ignoring me, well if you're gonna do that to me I can do that to you too, two can play that game, motherfucker. You think you're so smart but I'm onto you.*

"Just dump her," I said. It was like talking to a kid, trying to explain the multiplication tables to somebody who just didn't get it. "She's crazy, dude."

"But she's not," he said. "She's just . . . had a rough past. Guys have lied to her a lot. And I love her. I just wish she trusted me."

I knew—seriously, mark my words—I knew then that the rough past was bullshit. Tabby is the type of girl I know well. Basic upper-middle-class suburban white trash, made up of Starbucks cups and makeup and diet drinks and size-two dresses that are too short. She's the type who likes to claim bad stuff has happened to her, but let's face it, the so-called bad stuff—she's the root of all of it. She's the common denominator. And Mark fell for it. Weird, because usually I'm the one whose type is bad-news girls. He was new to it, didn't know he was trapped, which was maybe why he didn't even want to find a way out.

Now, they're saying Tabby didn't do this alone. That there was another guy, some poor sucker who was in on it with her. And I think I might know who it was.

27

BRIDGET

I'M THE ONLY ONE WHO SEES Tabby now. I mean, me and my parents. She's here, but she's not here. There are news vans camped outside. I wonder about the people inside them, if they have anything better to do. Tabby stands at the window and watches them.

"They're making this my fault," she says tonight, when we're watching Tabby's beloved *Housewives* in our pajamas. "They were always going to make it my fault. I have too many demons."

"Everyone has a past," I say. "They can't hold it against you."

She runs a finger over her eyebrow. "Not only can they hold it against me, but they'll make it into a weapon and impale me with it."

I don't laugh, until she does, and she feels like regular Tabby again, not the girl I see online. Not the Blue-Eyed Boyfriend Killer, the face that launched a thousand comments. She's makeup-free, hair in a neat bun, and she doesn't look capable of hurting anyone.

"It's about time something about this was funny." Tabby gets up and grabs our empty popcorn bowl. "This house is like a tomb. Mom and Dad don't even know how to act human in front of me anymore."

She's right. Mom and Dad are more like apparitions than people lately. Their heads are constantly down and they speak in hushed tones about *everything that happened*. They vacillate between ignoring Tabby and overcompensating by sucking up to her—Mom takes her Starbucks order pretty much daily, and today she came home with a new pair of fleece slippers. *You're stuck in the house, but at least you're properly caffeinated with warm feet!* Sometimes I catch Dad staring at Tabby like he has no idea who she is. I guess he hasn't for a long time.

There were flowers on our porch today. I read the card. *Can we talk??* I don't know who sent them, or who needs to talk to her. I suffocated the bouquet in a big black garbage bag and stuffed it in the garage before anyone could see.

They reminded me of the flowers that showed up for Tabby last fall. They were orchids, blue and purple ones that weren't found in nature, that had to be dyed to look that way. Tabby's favorite. I saw them lined up on her dresser, the orchids, like little soldiers. They were cheap, the kind that came from a grocery store, and they were already wilting, even the newer ones. There was a note on her desk that must have gone with one of the bouquets. *Because u know why.*

I rolled my eyes. Mark was prelaw at Princeton and couldn't even bother to spell out the word *you.*

Then I went back into my own room and started a list that I would continue adding to for months to come: *How to get rid of Mark,* which I tore up when the police first came to our house. In confetti form in my wicker garbage basket, it didn't seem so threatening anymore.

"I meant to ask," Tabby says now, shuffling into the kitchen to open the fridge. "What did he want to talk to you about? Stewart. What did he ask?"

I stare at my feet, my socks dingy against the light hardwood of the living room floor. "I already told you. Just like, the sequence of events. Basic stuff. I didn't tell them anything."

She shuts the door hard, clutching a Saran Wrap–covered

bowl of the macaroni and cheese Mom made for dinner last night. "There's something I have to talk to you about."

She makes me promise it'll stay between us. And I'm good at keeping promises.

Excerpt from Tabby's Diary

October 24, 2018

I'm pretty sure I'm not just paranoid. There are other girls.
Keegan basically admitted it. I'm sure that's why homecoming weekend was so awkward. Part of me is kind of
relieved that it's not just in my head, but the rest of me
is devastated. I guess I was his summer fun. I don't know
why he doesn't just break up with me.

New evidence rocks case of fallen hiker
By Angie Watts

Police have uncovered new evidence in the death of Mark Forrester, 20, who was killed last month when he fell from a lookout point in Coldcliff, Colorado's Queen Anne's Woods. Strands of hair were found on the creek bed of Claymore Creek, where Forrester drowned. DNA testing of the hair is expected to definitively link Forrester's death to his former girlfriend, Tabitha Cousins, 17.

Police are currently investigating footprints near the creek bed and on the surrounding trails, a task that will likely be fraught with challenges given the popularity of the Mayflower Trail circuit. The trails draw hikers to Coldcliff, a town thirty miles south of Boulder, especially in the spring and fall seasons.

28

ELLE

SAINT FUCKING MARK. Death made him a martyr. I guess that's one thing he and Tabby had in common. She never minded being a martyr either. I know that better than anyone.

His Instagram account is gone now—the police must have shut it down as part of the investigation—but there were other girls in the pictures he used to post. He'd be at a party when he told Tabby he was studying in his dorm. He'd say he forgot his phone at home when he didn't respond to her messages, but pictures would magically be posted from his account. And she didn't believe Mark, but she let him get away with it.

I know they had some sort of fight during homecoming, but she didn't want to talk about it, and I didn't press. A few weeks later, when Mark was back at Princeton, we went to the Stop & Shop to get microwave popcorn, me in my ratty pajama bottoms and Tabby in little terrycloth shorts and the red lipstick she suddenly felt the need to wear everywhere. Mark was changing her in myriad ways. Maybe she didn't feel him in all the different places he now took up space, but I did. The invisible weight on her shoulders. The reluctance to drink a whole milkshake. The need to straighten her hair, even though she saw him only through a computer screen.

"We should get some vegetables or something," Tabby said. "Maybe with hummus. Mark says it's a superfood."

Mark says. Mark says. Whatever Mark was doing, I doubted he was saying, *Tabby says. Tabby says I shouldn't drink so much. Tabby says I have a girlfriend.*

"You get hummus," I said. "I'm getting ice cream. And chips." We always got ice cream and chips. She headed into the produce section, and I went into frozen foods with a lump in my throat. I hated the Mark-shaped wedge between us.

When I walked back with my pint of Rocky Road, Tabby was bent over a display of refrigerated goods, her ass practically sticking out of her shorts. Then my eyes flitted over to the checkout lines behind us. Maybe it was instinct, to see who was looking. I like to think it was me being protective of Tabby, but it was probably more me being jealous of her. I always feel as if Tabby is a lot harder to overlook than I am, even though so many people tell us we look like sisters. Maybe it's true, but even with sisters there's always a pretty one.

Someone was watching that day. Keegan. The way he stared at Tabby, it was like—he was taking notes, or something. That was when I knew. He was watching her, keeping an eye on her. And he wouldn't have done that unless somebody asked.

She was his prey, and she had no idea, hinged over reading the label on a container of hummus, probably making sure there weren't too many carbs. He was staring so intently that he had no idea I was there, so intently that I stopped being jealous of Tabby and actually felt scared for her. She was in something with Mark, something bad, and she had no idea. As much as she pretended everything was fine between them, it wasn't fine at all. She didn't trust Mark and it was making her paranoid. Mark didn't trust her and instead of letting it make him paranoid, too, he sent in Keegan to do what he couldn't. Watch her, and make sure she didn't step out of line. I was sure he would report back to Mark later: *She looked like a slut. If that's how she dresses when she's out buying food, can you imagine what she dresses like at school? At parties? Dude, you're in trouble here.*

As I stared, he pulled out his phone. Started typing something.

I held my breath. He wasn't reporting back to Mark later, he was doing it now.

I jogged over to Tabby, my flip-flops smacking the ground. "Did you find what you're looking for? Because my ice cream's melting."

She stood up and tossed her hair over one shoulder, put her phone in her purse. "Yeah. This stuff's premade. Turns out it's a hassle trying to make it yourself. I was just googling it. You need tahini, whatever that is. I'm just gonna take the easy way out. Now I need to get some cucumber to dip in it, because otherwise I'll pig out on chips."

We went through Keegan's checkout line. He acted distant, like he was some guy who barely knew us at all, not someone who had drank and played video games with us. "Hey," he said as he bagged our groceries.

"Hi," Tabby said. When he put the hummus in the bag, she added, "I'm trying to eat healthy." As if he cared. As if eating healthy was going to tell Mark to call off his watchdog. I bored holes into his head with my eyes, not even offering a smile as I gave him my debit card.

"You guys up to anything tonight?" he asked as we waited for the transaction to be approved.

"Girls' night in," Tabby said at the exact same time I said "You never know what we'll get up to."

He didn't flinch. Just gave me my receipt. I didn't look back when we left the store, but I knew he was still watching us. Watching her.

"He's so weird." The words tumbled out when we were safely outside. "He was, like, staring at you. Like he was planning something."

She looked at the ground. There were fossilized wads of gum embedded in the cement like some kind of ugly mosaic. "I just don't think he likes me," she finally said. "He thinks Mark can do better."

Instead of being jealous, I felt sorry for her in that moment. Mark, with his perpetual buzz cut and broad shoulders, the possessive way he grabbed her hand in a crowd, like he wanted everyone to know she belonged to him. She had decided that his affection was the benchmark for her worth.

"You're the one who can do better," I said.

Tabby wrapped her arm around my waist, then started laughing. "I don't think so. Have you seen any other contenders?" I laughed, too, but it wasn't funny at all.

29

LOU

I'M AT THE STOP & SHOP today when I hear a couple people in front of me in line talking about Tabby's case. Two women, probably midthirties, carrying Michael Kors bags. Literally everyone is talking about Tabby, and that's when I see it—her eyes, staring out from one of those tabloids that usually have stories about, like, Meghan Markle's baby or Justin Bieber's married life. But there's Tabby, up there with them, a picture from her Instagram. The headline is what really slays me. *Girl, 17: Guilty or Innocent?*

She's not just Colorado news. She's national news. This is different than seeing her on *People*'s homepage, because I stumbled onto that when I was online stalking her (come on, you do it, too), so I guess I deserved to find it. This feels like a violation, like she's the one seeking me out. Here she is, taking up the spot of a perfectly good celebrity with cellulite. And you know what? She would love it. A bunch of us were talking about Amanda Knox once at lunch, about whether she did it (um, definitely, without a doubt). And there was Tabby, hovering over us, saying something like, "Don't believe everything you read." Like anyone asked her opinion.

That's why she did this. To become infamous. To be the next Amanda Knox, the next pretty girl accused of something. I mean, she's not good enough at anything else, right? She's the kind of girl who has probably been told a hundred times that she needs to *apply herself*. I've seen her in front of Mr. Mancini's office, tugging the waistband of her skirt up. I'm sure she wasn't really in there looking for advice on what colleges to apply to. No, she didn't want to study or *apply herself* like the rest of us, which sounds like we're stick-on decals that just need to find the right surface to cling to.

Tabby may not get the best grades, but I'll give her this. She's resourceful. She knew she wasn't smart enough to get into a good school on her own, and she knew Mark was going to get tired of her drama and dump her eventually, so she had to do something else. And now she's in a tabloid, right next to the Kardashians. She's graduated from the local news and crime blogs to *People* and *TMZ*. Her pretty face, those blue, blue eyes. Now, I'm sure somebody will make a movie about her life. She'll hire some doormat to ghostwrite her memoir. She'll end up rich and men will be terrified of her but they'll want to sleep with her anyway. And nobody will ever know the truth about what happened to Mark in the woods.

I slap down the tabloid, then I realize the checkout guy is Mark's friend Keegan, the one who came to all the parties with Mark, obviously trolling for high school girls to hook up with.

"She did it," I say, because I feel like I have to say something.

"Yeah," he says, practically thrusting the tabloid back at me. "I know."

I pay, like, five bucks for the crappy magazine. I'm sure Tabby would love that.

"Anything else?" he says, because I'm still standing here and there's a guy coughing behind me, all impatient.

"Yeah. We should find a way to prove it."

Second suspect questioned in death of Princeton student

By Mason Livingston

Police in Coldcliff, Colorado, released a statement Tuesday evening that another suspect is being considered regarding the death of Mark Forrester, 20, on August 16.

Thomas Becker Rutherford III, known as Beck, is an ex-boyfriend of Tabitha Cousins, and while police wouldn't elaborate on their lead, they have sufficient evidence to suspect Rutherford's involvement. A source reveals that a call history between Cousins and Rutherford tipped police off to the fact that Cousins may not have acted alone.

The Coldcliff Tribune first broke the story of Forrester's death when it was believed to be a hiking accident. Since then, it is believed that Forrester did not fall from the Split, the lookout point for the Mayflower Trail, as Cousins told police.

Rutherford, 17, has previously been arrested on charges of assault. He has had multiple suspensions from Coldcliff Heights High School, where he is a classmate of Cousins. Sources say the two were previously romantically involved, and that Rutherford would have done anything for Cousins.

"He loved her," the source, who asked to remain unidentified, told the *Vanguard.* "That doesn't just go away."

30

KEEGAN

"YOU'RE ACTING WEIRD," Kyla says. "Is this about Mark?"

We're in my bed. We just—you don't need to know what we were just trying to do. Anyway, it's like Mark is in bed with us because Kyla keeps bringing him up, and yeah sorry, I don't want to think about my dead best friend when I'm supposed to be able to get my dick hard.

"My best friend died. So yeah, there's a lot on my mind. There's a lot going on. I guess, yeah, it's about Mark."

She traces a circle on my chest. It feels like a bull's-eye.

"That's not what I mean." She stands up and slips back into the dress she wore over here. "I know you're upset. But this is more than that. Just be honest. Is there someone else?"

Kyla was supposed to be a party fling. You've seen her type. Hot, but kind of cheap-looking. I'm not saying that to be mean. It's just how she is.

"No, there's nobody else. Just you."

Her eyebrows creep up. "Why don't you stop lying to yourself, Keegan?"

I don't know what else she expects. Last night I took her on a date. She dragged me to this expensive place downtown. Ordered champagne. Made me pay. She doesn't seem to get that Mark is gone and maybe I'm having a hard time dealing. The police keep releasing more statements, like Tabby is one of those wooden dolls my mom used to collect, where you'd open one and there'd be a smaller one inside it. That's what this case is. A whole bunch of layers, encased in something pretty. People are fucking salivating over it.

Now they're deep into Tabby's phone, and there are all these calls to that Beck Rutherford guy, but just calls, no texts. The texts were to Mark, and they show she was pissed off. It makes me happy they found them, actually. Tabby has been trying to make herself out to be this good girl, this sob story, and those messages show who she really is. A head case.

Maybe Beck did help her with it. I saw them together. Plus, I saw him get up in Mark's face at Elle's party. Now his girlfriend, this Lou chick, wants my help trying to figure out the mystery, probably so she can clear his name or whatever. Maybe I should go along with it, though, if I can prove Tabby did it. I told her I wasn't interested, but now I'm kind of wishing I hadn't been such an asshole. Anything to get the two of them the fate they deserve.

"I'm not sure how much longer I can keep doing this," Kyla says.

Doing what? I want to ask. It's not like we're even a couple. I never asked her to be my girlfriend. She just kind of assumed that's what we were. I mean, she goes back to college in January anyway. She told me she was deferring this semester, but I didn't bother listening to the reason why. Come to think of it, I don't even know which college she goes to, or what she's studying.

"Okay," I say. "I don't know what else you want from me."

"I want you to appreciate me," she says. "You might be sorry if you don't." Then she turns and leaves, all dramatic, and there goes any semblance of a boner, and any chance of me being in a good mood today.

I have to see Detective Stewart again this morning. He left a message that he wants to discuss *new evidence*. I see the guy more often than my friends. It's kind of sad, really, because I don't exactly have any friends. Mark was my friend and now he's gone and everyone else was just a party acquaintance, people who weren't there when the hangover wore off.

Today Stewart asks me about Beck. The last person I want to talk about.

"Would you say Mark knew about Beck Rutherford?"

I hate hearing that little prick's name. His grungy leather jacket. The cigarette hanging out of his mouth.

"Yeah. Mark knew. He told me Tabby was fucking around on him. Sorry, screwing around. You know what I mean. He wanted to find proof."

"So that's where you came in." I'm starting to hate Stewart, how he's picking up steam, getting more comfortable the more I sweat in this chair.

"I guess so. I mean, he just asked me to keep an eye on things."

"To spy on Tabitha?"

"Not spy. Just if I saw anything, to let him know."

"So you never spied on Tabitha Cousins. You never followed her home."

It's not like that—I didn't follow her home. It's just that I saw her, on the back of his bike. He dropped her off down the street. I was in my car, inching up, trying to stay hidden. Beck Rutherford with his stupid long hair. He doesn't even wear a helmet, although she did. They didn't kiss, but I'm sure he wanted to, because he stood there and watched her go inside.

I watched, too. I texted Mark and told him she was with Beck. I wanted to confront her myself, to knock on her door and ask her what the hell she was doing with him when she had a guy who loved her so goddamn much that he would do anything for her.

Mark wrote back right away. *Thanks man I'll talk to her.*

I almost chucked my phone. *I'll talk to her?* He was so calm, so together. I wanted to run the guy and his bike right off the road. But I guess that was the difference between me and Mark.

"No," I say, staring Stewart down, picturing him as my prey instead of my predator. "I never spied on that girl."

He switches lanes, pushes his hands out in front of him in a rubbery knot. "According to our records of Mark's whereabouts, you were the last person to see him before he died. Besides Tabitha. What did you and Mark do the morning of the hike?"

"I already told you guys. We went out for breakfast. At this diner we used to go to when we were in high school. It never changed." I don't know why I throw in that last part. It's important, somehow. Rita's never changed, even though we did. Same soggy French toast, same greasy bacon and eggs.

"Did you talk about Tabitha? Did Mark seem nervous, angry, or out of sorts in any way?"

They already asked me all this, way back at the beginning. I said no, just like I do now. He was his regular self. He had the protein plate, ate every last scrap. Mark never wasted food.

I said no, but it wasn't the whole truth then, and it isn't now. There was something he said to me. Something that made all the difference. But I can't tell Stewart. I can't tell anyone.

I can tell he doesn't believe me, and I also know he's turned into the enemy. He's on her side now. Tabby. She got in his head somehow and she's spreading her lies like some kind of disease. The thing you have to remember about Tabby is this: Her poison, or whatever it is, tastes so good you have no idea you're being slowly killed until it's too late.

31

LOU

THE INTERNET HAS such a massive hard-on for her. Did you know they have Tabby makeup tutorials on YouTube? People are, like, copying her *look*. The dark hair and blue eyes. There was even one chick trying to make freckles with an eyeliner pencil. All of it makes me sick. She'll probably end up getting color contacts named after her, and all she had to do was murder a guy to get there.

And now she's taking Beck down with her.

Everyone thinks he's involved because he dated Tabby. (God, it was, like, almost two years ago.) They think the entire thing was this get-rid-of-the-other-guy scheme so they could be together. Maybe I'm spending too much time on Sharp Edges, because murder basically runs through my brain the way song lyrics used to. Or I just eavesdrop on too many of the conversations happening at school. But I know Beck didn't do it.

I'm not expecting him to come over tonight, but he does. Texts me from outside just as I'm falling asleep. *You home?*

I pull a hoodie on, but keep my legs bare. He's standing in front of the tree out front, pacing, which isn't like him. When I come outside, he grabs me by the shoulders.

"You know I didn't do it, right?" he says. "Even my parents think I did it. They're walking around me like I'm some kind of monster living under their roof. My mom leaves me dinner in the fridge, like she can't even look at me."

I slip my arms under his jacket, where I know his skin will

be warm. This is the most I've heard Beck talk about his parents ever. I guess I can thank Tabby for this, in some twisted way.

"I know you didn't do it," I say. And then I say something else, because I can't help myself. "But where were you, the night it happened? You never texted me back."

"I was just out riding," he says. "Sometimes I do that when my head gets complicated. I stopped at Pacers and got a beer, but nobody remembers me being there. It's like this whole thing is coming down on me."

He's never like this with me, never frantic, never loses his cool. I sink into him and he lets me, cupping my head with his hand.

"I knew you weren't with Tabby," I say. "But why did she call you all those times? You never told me about it."

He sighs, rubs his eyes. "I mean, I don't know. She just wanted someone to talk to her."

I pull away. "She has Elle for that. Why does she need you?"

"I guess she thinks I understand her. I can't really explain it."

My voice is shaking like it does when I know I'm about to cry. "But you dumped her. I didn't know you still talked to her."

"I don't tell you everyone I talk to. What does it matter? And who told you I broke up with her anyway?"

I literally don't know if I want to laugh or cry. Sometimes Beck is not worth the effort. He's a puzzle with too many pieces missing.

"Why did you actually hit Mark? At the party?" I'm not even sure why I'm asking, other than that it seems important, suddenly.

He tugs on the ends of his hair. "We got into it. I told him I was watching him. He just looked at me like he had no idea what I was talking about. He's manipulative, Lou. He knows what he's doing."

"Was. Knew. He's dead, Beck. And they don't think Tabby did it alone."

This time when he pulls me in, I resist, but only for a second. I remember what his hands are capable of, the good and bad. That's the essence of Beck. Tough with other people. Knuckles that have been covered in blood, a mouth that smokes and spits out swear words and threats. But gentle with me. A mouth that calls me *sweetheart, sweetheart,* as it presses into my skin, and hands that worship me.

"Just believe me," he says. "I didn't have anything to do with it. And neither did she."

Why didn't you text me back that night? I want to say. *Where were you really?* But I don't ask, because this part of me that won't be quiet is saying I don't actually want to know.

"I believe you," I say. "I'll figure out a way to prove it."

I make him think it's just for him. But I've always been the kind of person who just needs to know. I have an investigative mind, my mom once said. I used to want to write for the school paper, until I realized nobody read it, and nobody cared about cafeteria food exposés. So I did my own thing instead.

This isn't for Beck, and it's not for Tabby. It's for me. And you, really. Because the truth shall set us all free.

32

KEEGAN

SOMETIMES I'M HAUNTED by Mark's final scream. How it might have sounded, the last noise from the guy who thought the world was in his hands. A lot of these nights I wake up disgustingly sweaty, hearing him in my head, all the different versions of him. Happy Mark at parties, the guy everyone talked to. Sad Mark, when he had a sluggish day in the pool. Even drunk Mark, the good-time guy, belting lyrics to old bands I had never heard of. He knew the words to practically every song.

I wonder what he was thinking in those final moments, before he put the backpack on. Before she hugged him, kissed him, and shoved him over the edge.

Maybe he didn't scream at all. Maybe he was too shocked to make a sound. I have no idea how long that fall would take, but the Split is high up. I went there once when I was a kid, the summer my stepdad tried to get us to become active. My legs were rubber and I got queasy looking down and I was too shit-scared to stand that close to the edge. I'm still scared of heights.

I wonder if his head made a sound when it hit the rocks. I wonder a lot of morbid shit. Mostly how Tabby looked staring down at what she had done. Her face when she realized he was still alive.

I should have been a better friend to Mark. I let that girl get in the middle of us, just like she was trying to do. She had a birthday party for him and didn't even tell me about it. Who does something like that? She was doing everything she could to distance him from the people who actually cared, but he didn't see it at all.

It bugged Mark that Tabby and I didn't get along. "I don't expect you to be best friends," he said. "But can you at least try? She'll be around for a while."

He said that over Christmas break, I think, and literally a week later, when he was back at school, Tabby was in the Stop & Shop, wearing leggings and those weird slipper boots girls wear, makeup perfectly done. She didn't bring her regular shit to the counter. No diet soda or candy or tampons. She brought a box of condoms. Magnums, if we're keeping score.

Mark wasn't due back from Princeton until the end of April.

She was totally daring me to say something as I rang her up, but I didn't. She wanted to get a rise out of me, and I wasn't giving it to her. I stuffed the condoms in a plastic bag and made sure to charge her the extra five cents for buying a bag. Sometimes I let the hot chicks get away without paying for one.

"Any plans tonight?" she said. She was baiting me. She didn't give a shit about my plans.

"Yeah, and they're none of your business," I said.

"You don't like me," she said, then laughed. "That sucks, because he's going to pick me every time."

"I don't give a shit one way or another," I said. "Sixteen seventy-five."

She traced her belly button through her shirt, stuck her debit card in the machine. I wondered what she looked like under all the shit she always wore, if that makeup was hiding a hideous monster underneath.

I stuck my middle finger at her back as she walked away. She looked back and winked at me. It was all a game to her. Life. Mark. Even me.

I texted Mark as soon as she left. *Your gf was just here buying a giant box of condoms*

He wrote back a couple hours later, when I was home. He never used to take so long to respond. I know he always wrote back to Tabby right away, always called her exactly when he said he would. If you looked up *boyfriend* in the dictionary, Mark's picture would be right there.

She likes to be prepared, can't complain about that ;)

He had such a gigantic blind spot when it came to that girl. It was less a blind spot and more a goddamn eclipse.

I scrolled through my texts with girls I'd hooked up with recently. Most of them were one-night stands who insisted on swapping numbers because *this was fun*. I never had a reason to text them again. I was done with girlfriends, but I was also bored as hell and needed something to do.

Then there was a knock on my door, and I didn't have to text anyone after all.

THE COLDCLIFF TRIBUNE

October 10, 2019

DNA found near dead hiker a match for girlfriend
By Julie Kerr

DNA found near the body of Mark Forrester, 20, has been positively linked to his former girlfriend, Tabitha Cousins, police indicated in a statement released yesterday. This evidence, along with a half footprint matching Cousins's Nike shoes, near the creek bed where Forrester was found, is enough for police to formally charge Cousins.

A separate set of boot prints near the mouth of the woods has been identified as belonging to Thomas Becker Rutherford III, 17, with whom Cousins had a previous romantic relationship. Rutherford's lawyer could not be reached for comment.

33

KYLA DOVE

SO YOU DON'T KNOW ME, or at least not well, which is fine. I'm not offended. Nobody knows me well. There's really nothing that sets me apart from anyone else. My blond hair comes from a bottle and I wear a lot of makeup to cover up the fact that my skin breaks out on a regular basis. My body, I barely cover up, because the parts boys like distract them from seeing that my face isn't beautiful.

Anyway, this isn't about how I look. For once, it's about what I have to say.

I don't think she did it. Tabby. I'm sure she would be shocked I'm standing up for her, because I know she doesn't like me. Every time we hung out as a foursome—me and Keegan, her and Mark—she barely acknowledged I was there, and I heard her call me *desperate* at one of Elle's parties. And it makes me feel sad, because I think in another time and place we could have been friends. But not this time and place, because they pit girls against each other for all kinds of reasons, don't they?

They say we're born with female intuition, but we're great at ignoring stuff when we don't want to deal with it. Tabby would hate that I'm lumping her with every other girl, but I strongly feel that she had no idea what was happening until it happened. You're wondering how I know she didn't do it.

Because I know who did.

34

BRIDGET

NOBODY KNOWS HOW TO ACT around Tabby anymore. It's not house arrest, exactly—nobody is outside guarding her, unless you count the perimeter of news vans, and she doesn't have an ankle bracelet monitoring her, like I've seen on TV—but our house has become her prison anyway. Last night I heard her arguing with Mom and Dad about being allowed to go back to school.

"Can't I just live a normal life?" she pleaded.

"We think it's best that you stay here until all this blows over." That's Dad—he always sounds like that when he argues. *We* this and *we* that. I'm not sure when he and Mom became this amorphous blob of *we*, but that's how it is now.

"Do you think I did it?"

They don't respond right away. Then Mom says, "Of course not, sweetie."

She's lying. They're afraid. Afraid that Tabby did something. It's like we stop being little girls anymore and they stop knowing who we are. We're under their roof, brushing our hair, letting them kiss us good night, but something is different. We aren't candy sweet. We're opaque where we used to be transparent. Our skin hints at a storm, so they stay away.

My parents liked Mark. He was *such a good guy. So polite.* Of course, he was following Beck's act, and Beck never had an act, so it was easy for Mark to look good. Beck never came for family dinners. He never shook Dad's hand and promised to take care of his daughter.

I find Tabby curled up on the couch watching a movie. I'm stretching against the wall and can see what she's reading on Mom's iPad. A new article. The same one on BuzzFeed that Laurel and Sydney were looking at after practice. It has a click-bait title: *What this girl did after fighting with her boyfriend will shock you.*

Tabby's lips are laced into a smile. She's wearing lipstick— actually, a full face of makeup—even though she isn't leaving the house.

At least, she says she isn't leaving the house. But it's not like Mom and Dad are home to keep an eye on her. Mom is a teacher at the elementary school and Dad is an orthodontist, so they're both gone all day. Dad even did Mark's braces, back when he was a teenager, before he was ever part of our lives. Sometimes I picture how awkward that must have been when Mark first came to the door to pick up Tabby. Dad having all that knowledge of the inside of his mouth. Dad having tortured him by tightening wires and elastics. Dad having an understanding of how that smart mouth of Mark's worked, but still eating up every single word that came out of it.

"How can you possibly read that?" I snap. "Don't even give that stupid website any more traffic. Do you actually want to know what they're saying about you?"

She rolls her head back to stick out her tongue at me. "Bridge, come on. It's better to know what they're saying than to wonder about it. Everyone else knows. Why shouldn't I?"

I guess she has a point. It's her right to know. I'm a runner. I prepare for every race, every practice. She's preparing, too. For the next time she's at school. The so-called facts people will spew in her face. For the next time she's at a party and some mean girl asks who she's going to kill tonight. She wants to have all of the information, even though I'm not sure what she's planning to do with it.

"Maybe I'll just run away," she says suddenly, tossing the iPad aside. "That'll give them something new to talk about. What's here for me anymore?" She laughs, but her eyes well up.

"You have me," I say.

"For how much longer?" she almost whispers. "You'll turn on me, too." Then she grabs the iPad and stalks upstairs, slamming her bedroom door loud enough to shake the house. I have this thought, *I bet the reporters outside heard that.* I bet they're spinning it into whatever web of bullshit they've made, with my sister stuck in the middle. Their black widow.

I text Elle when I can't sleep because my brain keeps treading over all the things Tabby could do in her spiral. To other people. To herself.

She broke down earlier. She threatened to run away. I think she might actually do it.

Elle's reply is almost immediate. *She won't. She has a court date. She has police to talk to. She knows it would just be trouble.* Her words hold a certainty I lack, like she knows her version of Tabby better than I know mine.

I have a feeling, I type, then pause before sending the rest. *I think she's going to do something bad.*

Bad how? Elle responds, but I put my phone down without answering, either because I don't know what to say or just wish I didn't.

The next day, Mom confiscates the iPad. Tabby's antsy without it, walking the loop through the kitchen and living room and down the front hall a thousand times, slippered feet shuffling. "They're not going to find anything," she tells me. "They think I have all these secrets."

"Do you?"

She stops walking and grips my hand almost hard enough to hurt. She painted my nails earlier in a fit of boredom and they're still slightly tacky. She insisted on black.

141

"They know everything about me," she hisses. "If they all put their dumb heads together, they'd have a whole person."

It's the last thing she says to me before we both go to sleep. I wake up to noise and lights and the cold certainty that as bad as things have been, they're about to get a lot worse.

PART II

Jack fell down and broke his crown

Girlfriend in dead hiker case arrested, deemed a flight risk

By Julie Kerr

Tabitha Cousins, 17, was arrested last night and taken into police custody at a juvenile detention center in Colorado Springs. Cousins will be held in custody until her trial, which has been tentatively scheduled for late November.

A Coldcliff resident who wishes to remain unidentified told the *Tribune* that Cousins had a packed bag at the time of her arrest and had been planning an escape for several days, maybe even weeks. "She knows they'll find out what really happened, and she'll spend her life behind bars," the source said. "Being on the run would be a lot easier. And I don't think she was planning on going alone."

Anyone with additional information has been asked to contact the police department's tip line.

1

ELLE

HERE'S WHAT HAPPENS when a girl gets arrested.

The police come to her house. Maybe they look smug about it, because they never believed her story in the first place. Maybe they're rougher than they need to be when they put her in handcuffs, right in front of her parents and sister. They tell her she has the right to remain silent. As if they would hear her even if she screamed.

They let her know the crime she's being charged with: the murder of Mark Forrester. They notice she's wearing tight jeans, that she has makeup on, even though it's eleven o'clock at night. They see the packed bag and wonder where she planned to go. She thought she got away with it, the little brat. She thought she had everybody fooled with those big eyes and the story she came up with, the story that made her out to be totally innocent. *We went for a hike. We wanted to see the view. He leaned over too far. We. We. He.* Never me. She didn't do anything wrong.

This is what happens when a girl gets arrested. She gets questioned again, and again, and again, because they think they can wring the real story out of her. They know Mark didn't fall. Mark was not the kind of guy who fell for anything.

"You did it," they say. "We know you did it. If you admit it, this will go a lot easier. We can make a deal. Do you want to spend the rest of your life in prison?"

They wonder why she hasn't cried. She must be a monster, devoid of emotion, running purely on instincts. It's a good thing they arrested her, because who knows what she's really capable of. They don't know that she has cried, but only when nobody is around to see her do it. They don't know that when she finally falls asleep at night, she has to flip over her pillow, because it is wet with tears.

She's seventeen, so she's held at a juvenile detention center. She sleeps in a ward with other scared girls. She wonders why they're here, if they have been accused of the same thing. She didn't do it. She couldn't do it.

What she doesn't tell the police: yes, she was angry at Mark on the hike. Yes, she walked behind him and for a second, maybe longer, she allowed herself to fantasize about what his sweaty back would feel like with her palms pressed against it, how she would feel being the one with the power. But she didn't do it. She's not capable of murder.

"I'm scared," she says, practically a whisper. "I'm scared I had something to do with it."

I know all of this because she's allowed to have visitors.

"Just tell me what happened," I plead. "We'll get through it together."

I'm not allowed to touch her, but I mentally touch her hand and hope she feels it.

"I can't," she says. "It's just, I didn't want him to die, okay? I never thought he would."

I wanted to ask her what that meant, but our time was up.

2

BECK

OFFICER OLDMAN: I'm sure you heard that Tabitha attempted to leave town last week, and now she's being held in custody. If you have something to tell us, we need to know it. Was she on her way to meet you?

BOBBY GOOD, BECK'S LAWYER: Go ahead and answer that.

BECK: Why would she be?

OFFICER OLDMAN: Seems to me that if someone tries to run, it means they have something to hide.

BECK: Seems to me that if someone thinks everyone hates them, what else are they gonna goddamn do?

BOBBY GOOD: My client was unaware of Miss Cousins's whereabouts, as he has already asserted.

OFFICER SCHULTZ: A resident on Shady Lane claims she saw a bike drive past around seven p.m. Says the sound of it made her look up from her game of cards. Did you drive your bike down Shady Lane the night Mark Forrester was killed?

BECK: I have no reason to be on Shady Lane. I don't ride my bike around rich people's neighborhoods.

OFFICER SCHULTZ: The entrance to the woods where your boot print was found is close to Shady Lane.

BECK: Ever think Durango might have made more than one pair of boots? Maybe in a weird attempt to make money?

Half the guys who hang out at Pacers wear these boots. Check into them.

OFFICER SCHULTZ: I assure you we're following all leads.

OFFICER OLDMAN: Your girlfriend, Louisa, lives on Shady Crescent. But she said she didn't see you that night.

BECK: Yeah, because we didn't see each other.

OFFICER SCHULTZ: But you were supposed to make plans, isn't that right? And you didn't reply to her messages?

BOBBY GOOD: This is irrelevant to the case at hand. You have no evidence tying my client to the scene.

OFFICER OLDMAN: What about the text message Mark sent you?

BECK: Yeah, I don't even know how he got my phone number. Must have found it in Tabby's phone. He seems like the kind of guy who'd look through his girlfriend's shit.

OFFICER OLDMAN: He told you to stay away from Tabitha. Is there a reason why he would have felt the need to say that?

BECK: I don't know. He was a possessive guy.

OFFICER SCHULTZ: Did Tabitha tell you that?

BECK: She didn't have to. You could tell. Went to a few parties, and his arm was always around her.

OFFICER OLDMAN: It seems like you paid a lot of attention to Tabitha.

BECK: Well, she's the kind of girl people pay attention to. The whole country is doing it now, right?

BOBBY GOOD: What my client is trying to say is that he wasn't the only person who noticed things.

OFFICER OLDMAN: Tell us about what happened last homecoming weekend.

BECK: That was so long ago, how am I supposed to remember?

OFFICER SCHULTZ: So you didn't meet up with Tabitha at a party that weekend?

BECK: No, I didn't even see her that weekend.

OFFICER OLDMAN: We've heard from various sources that she left a party with a boy in a black leather jacket.

BECK: Well, it wasn't me.

OFFICER SCHULTZ: It sounds like we hit a nerve. Are you still in love with Tabitha Cousins?

BOBBY GOOD: That's irrelevant. You're investigating a boy who died. My client's love life didn't kill Mark Forrester.

OFFICER OLDMAN: We'll be the judge of that.

BECK: Kind of hard to love a girl who only loves herself.

3

LOU

IT'S LIKE A BLESSING in disguise, or whatever you want to call it. Tabby finally gets arrested, which is what she deserves. Obviously she wasn't as clever as she thought. I should be happy about all this, but I'm not, because they're dragging Beck into it even deeper, and now he's all grumpy and quiet and doesn't want to talk about any of it. He doesn't even want to touch me, to be honest.

"A lot of people own those boots," I say when I see him at school today.

"I know, sweetheart," he says, brushing my hair off my face—I love it when he does that, especially in public. "But nobody wants to believe me."

The boots—they're clunky black ones. Durangos. I've never seen him wear anything else.

"You don't even go into the woods," I say. He's super quiet, his hand balled up on my shoulder. So quiet that I'm not even sure he's breathing.

"You don't even go into the woods," I repeat. Then, "Do you?"

"No," he says. "I'm not much for hiking and shit."

I have no idea why it takes him so long to answer, and why his answer just sounds like what I want to hear. Maybe I've been spending too much time online.

4

BRIDGET

TABBY COMPLAINED ABOUT Louisa a few times. Basically stuff like, *Why does she hate me so much? I've never done anything to her.* And I'm not sure, but I think it was less about what Lou had against her and more about what stood between them. Who stood between them. Beck. From what I've heard, Lou thinks my sister hooked up with Beck after they started dating, or something like that.

(Don't ask me about what's happening with Beck, as if I'm supposed to know. He's just a guy my sister used to sneak out to meet. I don't have any inside knowledge of him. I know as much about him as you do, which is probably very little. When Tabby and Beck were "together"—whatever that even means—he didn't feel the need to even acknowledge I existed. At least there was some honesty to that, unlike Mark, who tried on that "cool older brother" act at first. It didn't work.)

Anyway, Lou started all of this about my sister. If she hadn't posted that video of Tabby shoving Lance, would any of this be happening? Maybe it would have happened anyway. Maybe there was no way a girl like Tabby could sneak through unscathed. But the video didn't help. The video was what made people feel entitled, its comments section the first battlefield. If the situation were reversed and I was the one who had gotten taken away by the police, I know my sister wouldn't be skulking through the halls like a shadow.

So today I find Louisa Chamberlain.

I have to wait to get her alone, because she's always

surrounded by these same girls—I think their names are all variations of Kaylie or Kacie or Kylie, all of them in pastels, like sidewalk chalk lined up in a row. They must be really vapid to have Louisa as their leader. I have to wait until the end of the day, when Louisa is walking to her car in the parking lot—an Audi, which makes me smile, because Tabby once said only assholes drive Audis.

I'm supposed to be at practice. We're going into the woods, doing repeats of Salt Hill, short and steep, but I don't want to be in the woods right now. Not because Mark died there. Maybe I'm morbid, but that part doesn't bother me. It's Tabby's death that bothers me more, the way she gets murdered a little more every single day. Every comment on every article a new knife wound, a fresh stab.

And I need to blame somebody, so today I blame Louisa.

I trail her until she's almost at her car door. I'm good at that—coming up from behind. It's a skill I've honed through all my years spent running. I don't have a flashy style. I rarely lead from the start, choosing to tuck myself behind the leaders, staring at their backs until I notice the signs of them getting tired. Hunched shoulders, shorter strides, shallow breaths. Then I make my move. That's why freshman year, my teammates started calling me the Silent Knife.

"You're unassuming, until you're not," Laurel told me.

Now, I'm not.

"Why did you do it?" I call to Louisa's back. I hate her hair—it's always so precise, these precious ringlets that obviously didn't come from nature.

She whips around. "Excuse me?"

I stand my ground. "Why did you take the video? And why did you post it? Are you so jealous of my sister that you have to try to ruin her life? You realize this isn't just some feud over a guy, right? She's in juvie. She might actually go to prison."

I'm no good at confrontation. My voice has already started to become thin, like the tread of shoes that have run too many paths. I think about the Nikes Tabby wore in the woods that day—my brain keeps coming back to them, like they're supposed to mean something.

"I wasn't the only one who took a video." Louisa drums her nails on her arm. "It's not like she tried to keep it a secret. If she didn't want people to see, she shouldn't have acted psycho in front of everyone."

"She's not psycho. She was angry. Do you even know what Lance said to her?"

"The question is, do you?" Lou says. "Look, maybe you don't know her as well as you think. I saw what I saw. And that wasn't the first time I've seen Tabby mad. I don't know. If she gets that mad when she knows people are watching, imagine what she's like with nobody around."

I know what she's getting at. Tabby has a temper, and now everybody remembers every outburst she has ever had. If Tabby were a quiet girl, this might be a different situation. Because somewhere along the line, we decided to equate quiet with good, which means loud became bad by default. In the world we live in—our girl world, bordered by our bodies, trespassers violated accordingly—everything is an extreme.

"Lance didn't say anything. He was just making a comment about the swim team missing Mark. He didn't mean anything by it."

I clench my jaw. *I'm* supposed to be the quiet one. The innocent one. But just because there are things I haven't done doesn't mean I haven't thought about them. Right now, I'm thinking about my fist making contact with Louisa's skin. The satisfying crack my knuckles would make on her cheekbone.

But I'm not going to do it. Because it won't be me Louisa comes after. It'll be Tabby. My violence will be her fault. I must

153

have seen that rage somewhere. I was always *such a nice girl*. Something must have happened for me to shed that skin and pull a heavier, angrier one around me. I'm not myself anymore as much as I am an extension of Tabby, another limb. When I bruise, she does. If I break, she does, too. So I have to stay intact, for both of us.

"Just stop spreading rumors about my sister." I turn away. I hope she hears the venom in my voice and knows it isn't just for show. Because quiet girls might be the most dangerous type.

5

ELLE

MAYBE YOU'RE WONDERING who Dallas is, and how he fits into this. He shouldn't fit into this at all, but I listened to Tabby, so now the three of us are part of it.

Dallas is a year younger than us—a junior—but you wouldn't know it by looking at him. He's tall and rangy, long-legged. Actually, everything about him is long.

(Wait, I didn't mean that in a dirty way. If Tabby were here, she would have laughed. A sexual innuendo never goes over her head. I wish she was here.)

Anyway, the other thing about him is he's nice. There was a bird with a broken wing in our backyard, and I took it in a shoe-box to the animal sanctuary over on Waverly. Dallas volunteers there. He somehow fixed the bird, then found me at school and asked if I wanted to be there when he set it free.

I'm sure there's some kind of metaphor here. A boy and a girl and a broken bird that had to relearn how to fly. But if there's a meaning, I can't find it. Because of the three of us, the bird was the only one who came out healed.

"Elle. Elle, hey. Can you please talk to me?" He catches up with me in the parking lot as I'm walking to Mom's car.

"I have nothing to say. You made it clear exactly what you think of me."

"I was pissed off, okay? But you didn't even give me a chance to explain."

I spin around to face him. "Why should I give you the chance to explain anything? You weren't there."

"Yeah, because you wouldn't let me be. Elle, you know I like you, right? I still like you. But you shut me out."

It's always the people you don't care about hearing from who have all the right words. The ones you need. It's like life designed them to come from the wrong mouths. Life designed everything wrong to come from my mouth.

"Just leave me alone," I say, turning away, my eyes blurry. He's wearing his Nirvana T-shirt, the one I teased him about, because I don't think he can name a single Nirvana song.

"I know you're going through a lot," he says. "With Tabby in juvie and everything—"

And everything.

Mark died. Tabby got arrested.

If I had stayed closed, none of it would have happened.

Was there another woman in the Blue-Eyed Boyfriend Killer case?

By Talia Sims

Multiple sources allege that Tabitha Cousins, 17, had a bitter vendetta against her boyfriend, former Princeton student and champion swimmer Mark Forrester, who died on August 16 under suspicious circumstances. Cousins is currently being held in police custody at a juvenile detention center.

Several sources state that while Forrester was at Princeton and Tabby was attending Coldcliff Heights High School, she suspected that he was cheating on her. One student, who wishes to remain nameless, said that Cousins even made a special trip to Princeton to catch Forrester in the act.

"She crashed this party he was at and pulled him away. It was super awkward," the student states. "And Mark was just friends with that girl."

That girl, according to Forrester's now-deleted Instagram, was Madeleine Swanson, 20, a junior at Princeton. Swanson could not be reached for comment. One of Forrester's friends, who reached out to us anonymously, said Cousins was jealous of every girl Mark ever talked to.

"He didn't cheat," the friend said. "He treated her like gold. But she never believed that. She hated all those other girls. She used to talk about things happening to them. Bad things."

Since this speculation started up, Swanson's roommate, Gloria Wheaton, said Swanson has received death threats from Cousins's legion of fans, known on social media as the Tabby Cats.

"They need to leave Maddie alone," Wheaton said when reached by phone. "She didn't do anything wrong. If Mark did cheat with someone, it wasn't Maddie."

The story continues to develop as Cousins's trial has been slated for early December. If tried as an adult, she faces life in prison.

Excerpt from Tabby's Diary

November 5, 2018

I thought my boyfriend would be happy that I surprised
him, but he was just fuming. He didn't even want to
touch me. All I want him to do is love me the way I love
him. He accused me of keeping tabs on him. The truth is,
sometimes I feel like I'm being watched. Like Mark has
eyes here somehow.

6

ELLE

THE PRINCETON TRIP. I knew it was going to come up. So here's how it went down.

We took Tabby's mom's car. We left on Friday afternoon, right from school. Tabby had told her mom she was sleeping over at my place that weekend, and I pulled the same lie with my parents. Mom told me to have fun, but I could tell she was disappointed we were going to Tabby's house instead of staying at ours. She loves having both me and Tabby under our roof, bringing us snacks and asking Tabby about her homework and her boyfriends and her life. Tabby indulges her in a way I never do. The way Mom interacts with her—Tabby is the daughter she really wanted, the beautiful and charismatic one. In Mom's eyes, Tabby can do no wrong.

Tabby told me Mark invited her. That he knew we were coming. "I can't believe we haven't done this already," she said. She was driving too fast, and it was cold out, but her window was open, the air coming in and slashing our skin.

It was absolutely insane, driving halfway across the country—it would take us an entire day just to get there. I struggled to stay awake when it was my turn to drive, chugging coffee that settled in my stomach like acid. I didn't want to go to a party. But Tabby and I stopped at a shitty rest stop and did our makeup in the bathroom. I watched her apply her signature black eyeliner, even though she was already wearing a ton of it. I let her put bronzer on my cheeks after she said I looked pale.

"Where exactly is the party?" I asked when we were finally off the highway, ensconced in city traffic.

"Some guy's apartment," Tabby said. We were at an intersection and she pulled out her phone, where Mark's Instagram was already up on the screen. That was when I first doubted that we had been invited anywhere. "It should be right around here."

To this day, I have no idea how she found out where "some guy's apartment" actually was. Later, I searched Mark's Instagram for the same clues she had to work with. There was a picture of him and some other guys who must have been his college friends, plus one girl with dark hair. The photo was posted the day before we arrived. Someone had commented on the photo: *Can't wait to see you assholes tomorrow!*

Someone else had posted *Igor's parties are the best parties.*

That was all she had to go on. The name Igor. If you pull up his Instagram, you'll see a picture from September of an apartment building, and a guy standing in front of it who must be Igor. *First grownup digs*, it was captioned, with the hashtag *#adulting*.

I didn't know this at the time, when we pulled up in front of the building. You needed a buzzer to get in. Tabby searched the directory, probably for Igor's name, but it was the kind of directory without names. She looked at me, shrugged.

"Why don't you call Mark?" I said.

"I want to surprise him." She touched her lips.

"So he doesn't know we're coming."

She broke into a big smile, as if I'd be happy about being lied to. "Well, not exactly. I knew you'd think it was crazy. But I need to do something to get his attention."

His attention. I hated that attention was all we ever wanted, and it was the hardest thing to get. If people just gave it to us from the start, maybe we wouldn't do such wild things to get noticed.

I bit the inside of my cheeks. I was nauseous—the inside of the building smelled sour, like body odor and stale perfume.

"What's your plan, exactly?" I asked, just as her plan strolled through the lobby. A guy, probably midtwenties, who was leaving and held the door open for us. Tabby flashed him a smile.

"We just follow the noise," she said.

Except there wasn't any noise. This wasn't a high school party, one that ricocheted through the neighborhood, the kind I had somehow become synonymous with because Mom wanted to be cool and let me get away with it. The only reason we found Igor's apartment at all, after taking the elevator from floor to floor, was because a girl got in the elevator with us and Tabby asked her.

"Do you mind letting me know Igor's apartment number? I'm such a space cadet."

The girl laughed. "Yeah, no worries. It's four-eleven." She went down, and we went up.

What happened next was embarrassing. We opened the door to Igor's apartment and let ourselves in, me following behind Tabby like a shadow. People were standing in clumps, talking, some of them dancing, and they stopped to stare at us. Mostly everyone was in jeans and sweaters. Tabby and I stood out, in our short skirts and ripped tights, cleavage everywhere. I wished I had never come.

"Can I help you?" a guy in a thick wool turtleneck asked. Later, I would recognize him on Instagram as Igor.

"We're looking for Mark Forrester," Tabby said. "Is he here?"

Something like confusion passed over Igor's face, then he rebounded with a nod. "Yeah. He's here. Not sure where, though. Who are you guys?"

"I'm Elle," I started to say, but Tabby cut me off. "I'm his girlfriend."

It was obvious from Igor's face that Mark had never mentioned a girlfriend. In that moment I hurt for Tabby. She must have been mortified.

Igor started to say something else, but Tabby pushed past him, into the apartment. She didn't bother taking her boots off, even though everyone else was in socks, shoes piled by the door. I took mine off. I just wanted to sit down, or lie down and go to sleep.

"Elle," someone said, and it was Keegan, a beer in his hand. "What are you guys doing here?"

"I don't know," I said, because I couldn't think of something better to say. "Tabby's looking for Mark."

Tabby stomped back a few minutes later, brushing tears from her cheek. "Let's go," she said.

"Go where?" I said. When she looked at me, I noticed how red her eyes were. Then she saw Keegan sitting behind me.

"What are you doing here?" she spat.

"I was invited," he said. "I've been here since Thursday. I have the weekend off."

Mark showed up maybe a minute later, followed by a girl. The dark-haired girl in his Instagram photo. He tried to put his hand on Tabby's shoulder, but she shook it off and sat down, practically on Keegan's lap. She took his beer out of his hand and held it to her lips.

We didn't go. Tabby got increasingly drunk, flirted with Keegan to piss Mark off, to make him pay for whatever he was doing with that girl when she arrived. I let somebody hand me a cup of something, but I didn't drink it. I watched it all unspool, whatever was happening between Tabby and Mark, the flickering of eyes, Tabby's narrowed and Mark's pleading. By the end of the night, they disappeared together, and the dark-haired girl was nowhere to be seen.

Keegan seemed as annoyed as I was. "She shouldn't have showed up. Things were fine without her."

"Who was the girl?" I asked.

Keegan shrugged, but he liked the question. I could tell.

Maybe it felt good for him to see that Mark wasn't perfect. "I don't know that one's name."

I ended up crashing on a couch in Igor's apartment, the one adjacent to Keegan. When I woke up the next morning, it was still dark out, and I had no idea where I was. I stumbled to the bathroom, where I hovered by the toilet, thinking I needed to throw up, even though nothing came out.

Tabby and Mark must have been in the hall outside, because their voices came into focus. Mark saying *We were just talking. She's having a hard time with her boyfriend right now.*

Tabby. *I don't care. You're* my *boyfriend. Don't forget it.*

On the drive home, I told her what Keegan told me. *I don't know that one's name.* Tabby needed to know what that meant. That there were others.

"We talked about it," Tabby said. "We're good now. I believe him that nothing happened."

Except she didn't, and I didn't believe it either.

7

MADELEINE SWANSON

MARK FORRESTER WAS A GOOD GUY. I have no idea how I got drawn into this. I saw some stuff online—my roommate reads all the celebrity gossip—she showed me some post about "the other woman" in the Blue-Eyed Boyfriend Killer case. She said, "Maddie, isn't that the back of your head?"

It's a picture of me and Mark at a party. I think the party was last November. That's when Jason and I were fighting a lot. I met Mark in my Stats class freshman year, and we stayed friends. Sometimes we'd grab a drink on a random weeknight and catch up. Jason went to Brown and things were hard, but I never considered cheating on him with Mark. It wasn't like that with us. But I did talk to Mark about Jason. I asked his opinion. For Mark, it always came down to being honest, even though it's damn hard to do.

I do remember that party now, because it's the night Tabby showed up. Mark never mentioned a girlfriend to me—probably because it was always me talking about my drama, and that's really embarrassing to admit. I didn't go to Princeton to become a girl who cries over boys. I came here because I'm smart. But Jason made me doubt myself. Right before that party, he told me he wanted to take a break.

"What do you mean?" I'd asked.

"Exactly what you think," he said. "This isn't working for me." Then I heard someone laugh in the background, and realized he wasn't alone, that he was dumping me over the phone in front of people. It's still the most humiliating moment of my life.

Of course, I didn't want to go to the party after that. I wanted to stay in my room and put my pajamas on and cry over sappy movies. But my roommate dragged me out. "It'll be fun," she said. "Don't let that asshole ruin one night, let alone your year."

So I went. It was at a guy named Igor's apartment. My roommate had been flirting with him for weeks. She liked that he lived off-campus, even though the apartment itself wasn't anything special. I was feeling okay when we got there. I was doing fine, thinking I could rock the single life without Jason's deadweight. Then that fucking song came on. The one Jason and I danced to at our senior prom. "This is our song," he had whispered in my ear, his hand low on my back. "I'll love you forever."

I had believed it.

I knew I was going to cry, so I tried to get into the bathroom and do it in private, but the door was locked. Mark saw me standing there, rubbing my eyes, and it was like I couldn't hold the tears in anymore. He just folded me into a big hug and asked if I wanted to go somewhere quiet to talk. We ended up in what must have been Igor's bedroom. I poured it all out to him. The breakup over the phone. The song. I'm sure he thought I was a mess, but he just listened. He told me some things I needed to hear, things that I knew were true but somehow meant more coming from another guy. That I was a catch. That I had a lot going for me. That I didn't need to waste my time with somebody who wasn't totally sure about me.

"He's going to regret this," Mark said. "But you never will."

Those words stuck. As embarrassed as I was that I had cried in front of him, I let his advice buoy me up, inflate my ego. I let myself believe him.

I was about to hug him when the door burst open. It was a girl in a super-short skirt. I had never seen her before in my life.

"What the fuck?" she said.

"Tabby—" Mark said.

"Just what I fucking expected," she said, storming off. Mark got up, scrubbed a hand through his hair.

"Who's that?" I asked.

"She's—it's complicated."

Like I said already, I didn't know Mark had a girlfriend. I thought his life was swimming and school, but of course he had the same needs as the rest of us. I figured maybe he was supposed to have a date with this girl and lost track of time consoling me. I had no idea she had come all the way from Colorado to surprise her boyfriend.

She didn't look like Mark's type. I guess that sounds ridiculous, because how did I know Mark had a type? I guess if somebody asked, I would have pictured him with a more natural-looking girl. Someone who wore jeans with chunky knits, hair in a messy bun, Chapstick instead of the red slash over that girl's mouth. I was even more surprised when I found out she was in high school.

Maybe I didn't know Mark quite as well as I thought. But I do know that girl—Tabby—looked wild when she opened the bedroom door. She didn't even look surprised, really. It's like she knew she would find Mark with someone. Maybe even with me.

I can't lie. There were a couple times I thought about me and Mark, how we would be together, after Jason. I never did go back to Jason. Every time I got one of his drunk text messages, trying to apologize, I remembered Mark's words. *He's going to regret this. But you never will.*

Mark and I never hooked up, though. That's the truth. That's the story I'm most definitely not selling to some trashy online tabloid. The whole country is obsessed with this story. All I want is to know what happened to Mark, the nicest guy, who didn't deserve any of this.

You can believe me or not, but I'm the girl in those photos.

I'm "the other woman." And I don't think it was an accident, what happened to Mark in the woods. I think revenge is a long game, and Tabby started planning hers the moment she found me and Mark in that bedroom.

Tabby & Beck: The New Bonnie & Clyde?
By Brad Hargrove

At this point, it seems inevitable that Tabby Cousins didn't act alone, but police remain tight-lipped on how exactly they know that. A couple weeks ago, they questioned one of Tabby's ex-boyfriends, Thomas Becker Rutherford III, known to friends as "Beck." Don't be fooled by the roman numerals after his name. This guy is basically a career criminal in the making. He and Tabby had a passionate relationship in their sophomore year of high school, with many of my sources even saying she lost her virginity to him.

This leaves us all with so many questions. If Tabby and Beck loved each other, why couldn't they just be together without killing Mark?

I think you guys know where I stand. I don't think she killed him. I'm not sure Beck Rutherford did either, but after being in this job as long as I have, I can tell you the media portrays boys in two ways. Golden boy or bad boy. Guess who's who in this case. Princeton student/star swimmer versus the guy who brawls at parties when he has too much to drink? Mark's gone and can do no wrong.

Somehow *People* got a photo of Tabby and Beck earlier this week, supposedly from when they were a couple. (You can see it here if you haven't already, although I hate to give that site more traffic.) See where her hands are on him? One on his face and the other on his back, and he has a cigarette dangling from his fingers, and the other hand is on her ass. They're basically eating each other's faces. What struck me about the photo, besides two people who were obviously very into each other, was that hand placement. She calls the shots. This girl was in control. Now, if you look at photos of her and Mark (here and here in my previous posts), see his hand covering hers as they walk, or how far apart their bodies were, even when his arm was around her shoulders? It's not like I'm a body-language expert, but I can't help but wonder if this guy got controlling when he didn't get what he wanted.

More information is coming soon—thank you, my readers, for being willing to talk to me. Now, let's solve this thing before the cops do, and get famous. (Kidding.)

COMMENTS

SkullGirl: Another trash article from a trash site, don't call this a job, ur a hack in ur parents basement

Marley: It's always the angry ex-boyfriend! What a shame, he's super hot. I'll be his prison wife when he goes away for life for this.

LittleWreck: What do you want to bet he gets life and she walks?

DogLover101: Is it wrong that I find that kind of romantic? My bf can't even kiss me in public . . .

WhenDovesCry: There is so much wrong here. Everyone has it all wrong.

8

ELLE

THIS IS SOMETHING I HAVE TO DO.

Just like what I did *That Day* was something I had to do.

He hasn't been in school much. Maybe because he's getting questioned by the police—I'm sure he's not talking to anyone about that. He never went to class much before anyway. Why did I like him so much? Was it because of him, or because of Tabby?

I can name the things I like about Dallas. His smile and the way my name turns into a precious dollop when he says it. The certainty of his hands on my back. Beck was just a boy—someone I had gone to school with for most of our lives. Just a boy, always the one getting into trouble, dirty hands from playing outside and a mouth that liked to shock. Beck was just a boy, until there was a girl who decided he was something more, and then I saw him differently, too.

Maybe he's like Tabby in a lot of ways. Smart. Calculating. Easily bored. She could have been sleeping with him the whole time she was with Mark. Today, I need to know, so I'm going to ask.

I take Mom's car and drive to the woods after school. He's sitting on the trunk of a fallen tree right near the south entrance. The leaves crunching under my feet are loud, and Beck turns around. He's not wearing his leather jacket but an oversized hoodie. "You following me?"

"Hello to you, too. I'm not following you. This is a public place. Anyone can walk here."

"Doesn't look like you're dressed for walking." He hunches

forward and his eyes skirt up my body. My shorts and crop top, his snail-slow gaze a warm trail. Tabby isn't here and I'm dressing like her, in little ways. A slice of skin. More makeup. I'm not even sure why I'm doing it. Maybe so Beck would look at me the way he is now. We're alone—no Tabby. I could touch him, or even kiss him, and see how he reacts.

I'm not sure if it's the fear of rejection or the fear of betraying Tabby that stops me.

"What are the police asking you?" I blurt out. "Do they think you're involved?" *Were you involved?*

"It's just stupid shit." He takes out a cigarette. "Same stuff they're asking everyone. I'm not sure what they think, but I don't really care. Besides, we're all kind of involved, aren't we?"

He knows. He knows what I did, and that he's this involved because of me. My mouth goes dry.

"I guess we are. But they found your footprint. You were here that night."

He swivels the heel of his boot into the ground. "I wasn't here. Lots of people have these boots. They just want it to be me because it's easy. They don't want to think she was capable of doing it on her own."

"You think she did it?" It's something I haven't even allowed myself to consider, because confronting that pitch-black place in Tabby would mean recognizing it in myself.

"No," he says. "I don't. But if she did, she wouldn't need anyone's help. We both know Tabby. That girl isn't in the habit of letting people in."

We're both quiet, maybe both considering how far we were let into her orbit, and how much of us lingers there. Tabby and I used to crave the same things, and maybe it was only when she had something that it became worth wanting.

"Do you still love her?" I ask. "Was she cheating on Mark with you?"

He lights the cigarette and takes a long drag. "Maybe I never loved her at all. Maybe we just used each other, same as everyone else."

He doesn't answer the second question. I know he isn't going to. And now I'm thinking about who I used, and who paid the ultimate price.

Tell me about the girls
By Oberon Halton

Everyone seems to think Tabby's ex, Beck Rutherford, had something to do with Mark Forrester's murder. Yes, they have a boot print, and yes, the guy seems a little bit dark. But what I'm wondering is, what about the girls closest to Tabby?

Sources at Coldcliff Heights High School reveal that Tabby didn't have many friends—she mostly spent time with Elle Ross, whose summer party was the setting for the mysterious Beck-Mark altercation before Mark's death. Where does Elle fit in all of this? Because you're naive if you don't think she fits somewhere. Best friends tell each other everything—what has Tabby told Elle?

Then there's Tabby's sister, Bridget. I've heard sibling loyalty runs deep. And Bridget runs, too. She broke out in her freshman year to get a silver medal in the Colorado State cross-country championship, and is predicted to win the event this year. Rumor has it she knows Queen Anne's Woods better than anyone. So why is everyone focused on Beck Rutherford when there are two totally more plausible suspects right in front of their faces?

9

LOU

I'M GLAD SHARP EDGES posted that. I'm glad somebody pointed it out. Oh look, here are two girls who know Tabby better than anyone, and if she didn't work alone, she probably worked with one of them. Right?

I see both of them at school, and I watch them. Elle kind of slinks around like a shadow, like she's guilty of something. Not how she was last year, her and Tabitha always loud and over the top, like they were trying to one-up each other. Maybe they were, and Tabitha won, because *Hey bitches, I killed my boyfriend, what did you do last weekend?*

And Bridget—well, she has always been a wallpaper girl. You know, the kind you don't really notice until somebody points her out, and you realize she has been there the whole time. I don't have any siblings—pretty sure my parents didn't even want me and I'm here because of some divine condom mishap that I seriously don't want to think about. I never would have thought Bridget was capable of anything, but when she came up to me that day at my car, I saw another side of her. A side that looked a lot like Tabby.

Anyway, whatever. Beck is on his way over here, and my mom isn't home, so we can be alone together. I'm dying to talk to him about all this, but I also want to not talk, you know? I can hear his motorcycle, which means he's actually on time, which almost never happens. He must want to see me as badly as I want to see him.

I swing the door open before he can even knock on it.

"Hey, sweetheart," he says, but it's short and clipped, not his usual long drawl. I throw my arms around his neck—he's wearing this sweatshirt that smells like cigarettes, gross—but he kind of stiffens and pulls back.

"What's wrong?" I ask.

"You're not gonna like this," he says, crossing his arms. "But I think we should cool down for a while."

He's still on the porch. I'm in the foyer, leaning against the door, dragging my sock across the tile floor. I'm not actually hearing what he's saying because, seriously, he didn't even make it to the welcome mat before trying to break up with me.

"Cool down," I repeat. "We've barely seen each other lately. You never respond to my texts."

"I know," he says, his boot tapping on the ground—I can't tell if he's nervous or just wants to get this over with. "Look, I'm sorry. But there's a lot of shit going on in my head right now. I don't think we should hang out until I figure it all out."

Hang out. Like we aren't anything more than that.

"Seriously? You're being such an asshole. Is this because of Tabby?"

He stares at the ground, and his hair swings over his cheek, and I want to cut it off and cut him off and stop always caring about the wrong people.

"I just wanted to tell you to your face," he says. "I'm sorry, okay? You deserve to be with someone who can be all in."

"Wow. Fuck you," I say. I wish I had a better comeback. I'll think of one later, when my head is on my pillow and all my thoughts are swirling above, a mishmash of everything I said and didn't say.

"I know," he says. "I'm an asshole. But there's so much going on right now." I shit you not—for a hot second, it looks like he's about to cry. Like, something scared Beck Rutherford. "I might actually go to jail."

And as much as I want to punch him in the face, I also want to hug him and tell him everything will be okay. Even though it might not.

"You're not going to jail," I say. "You had nothing to do with it."

"I didn't kill Mark," he says. "But it's like they're trying to prove I did."

Now, I'm severely annoyed. Beck doesn't believe in himself at all, and he needs somebody who does. He needs somebody to believe him. To prove Tabby did it alone and that he wasn't involved.

And maybe I'm the only one who knows them both well enough to figure it out.

"This isn't her first time": Former classmates speak up about Blue-Eyed Boyfriend Killer

By Darla Burns

Several former students of Chester Prep School in Rochester, New York, have come forward to reveal exclusively to the *Ring* that Tabitha Cousins, the Blue-Eyed Boyfriend Killer, had a history of getting what she wanted—at any cost.

"Everyone knows what she did to Jordan Bosch," said a source, who used to date Jordan in high school. "She ruined his life, then her family mysteriously moves away and she starts at a new school. It's really not a surprise that a few years later, she ruins some other guy's life, too."

According to two other former classmates, Cousins was at a party with Bosch and had previously told a friend that she wanted to lose her virginity to him.

"She was really serious about it," said Kennedy Baker, Cousins's former best friend. "She was willing to do whatever it took to make it happen."

Baker lost track of Cousins at the party, but Cousins left with Bosch,

who consequently crashed his car, ending his promising football career. Reports showed Bosch's blood alcohol level was over the legal limit. Cousins was uninjured in the crash, but faced vicious rumors at school, which sources speculate was a reason why her parents uprooted the family to Coldcliff.

"She said it was because of her dad's job," Baker said. "But we all knew the truth. She was done in Rochester. It was time to move on to somewhere else. And someone else."

Attempts to reach Bosch for an interview were not returned, but his father, who separated from his mother last year, says his son has moved on and made something of his life.

"Whatever happened with that girl, he moved past it," said Jack Bosch. "He doesn't want to be dragged back into it."

Cousins is being held at a juvenile detention center until her upcoming trial.

AlleyCat: Okay she looks like a baby prostitute in that pic. I wouldn't let my kid out of the house wearing that.

SkullNBonesXX: I heard about that story way back when. Jordan went to my HS. What do you wanna bet he wasn't even driving the car?

TakeMeAway: The friend just wants her 15 min of fame. All these people do. This trash website just eats it right up.

BethWanderer: WTF is with this reporter painting the boys as golden all the time? I knew Jordan in college. Guess what, he's totally capable of being a drunk driver and crashing his car, and I bet he led the girl on. What was she, 13? Just saying.

10

KENNEDY BAKER

I'M THE ONE WHO TOLD the *Ring* about Tabby's secret past. Some of my friends have told me it's low, that I went to a tabloid because I want fame and a payoff, but really I just want the truth to be out. I guess it didn't follow her to Coldcliff, but here I am to tell you the story of the first boy Tabby ruined.

We were in seventh grade, but dressed like we were high school seniors. Tabby already had boobs and a butt and she knew exactly how to work them, even though she complained to me about how she wasn't sexy, wasn't pretty. She just wanted a compliment. So I dished them out, because she gave them right back.

Here's the thing to know about Tabby Cousins. She'd hitch a ride with anything promising. She had a pattern. Star athletes were her thing. I had a feeling that in twenty years she'd be one of those wives on *Real Housewives*, which my mom watched religiously. On husband number two or three and boob job number ten, spending twenty grand on a kid's birthday party.

The star athlete at our school was Jordan Bosch. He was four years older but this really talented football player. People were always talking about him being scouted for the NFL before he finished high school. Tabby had close proximity to him because we were on the dance squad.

So Tabby, she got really cozy with Jordan. Always waiting for him with a water bottle after his games, offering to rub his shoulders. It was bad because Jordan had a girlfriend, this girl Bella, who was the valedictorian.

The day after the regional game—which we won, of course, thanks to Jordan—Tabby comes over to me with this huge smile. "Kennedy, we're going to a party. I got us in. Just tell your mom you're sleeping over, and I'll tell mine the same thing."

She had the lie all planned out. We met at the bus stop and did our makeup in a McDonald's bathroom, Tabby plastering her face with bronzer and dark eyeliner, pouting at her reflection. "I'm going to hook up with Jordan," she said, pulling a little bottle of vodka, the kind you get on airplanes, out of her purse. "Just wait and see."

"He's with Bella," I said. "He's not going to cheat on her."

She shrugged and took a swig, then passed the bottle to me. I didn't have any. It didn't bother me that she liked Jordan—whatever. It bothered me that she was conceited enough to think he'd leave his girlfriend for her. And it really bothered me that she didn't care about Bella at all, that she was willing to do that to another girl.

I lost track of Tabby at the party. I have no idea why she bothered bringing me, because obviously her plan was to ditch me the entire time. I ended up calling my mom to pick me up and going home, and I got grounded for a month.

The next day, I heard what had happened. How somehow Jordan and Tabby left the party together. How he was driving the car that crashed into a tree. How his blood alcohol level was super high, even though he claimed to have had only one drink at the party. How his knee was mangled, and his football career probably finished.

Tabby claimed he had pushed her head down. That she got in the car because she wanted to leave. She had no idea there would be drinking at the party, and she felt uncomfortable, so when Jordan said he could give her a ride, she got in the car.

Of course, Jordan thought the ride meant something else, and Tabby learned that when he pulled over and started undoing his pants. She refused and tried to get out, and apparently that's when Jordan locked the doors and started driving away, faster and faster, freaking her out, until the car hit a tree and Jordan was slumped over the steering wheel and she got out and called for help.

People at school were divided on Tabby, but most of us were firmly in the camp of *she lied*. Jordan wasn't like that. Although thanks to what happened, Bella broke up with him. Tabby got the typical slut-shaming at school, until the principal intervened and her parents got called in and suddenly, boom, just like that, they were moving, the entire family. The SOLD sign hit their lawn before anyone even knew the house was listed.

She never said goodbye — she was done with me. I had been used, whatever purpose I had served completed, even though I still don't know exactly what the purpose was. But I just so happened to be out walking our dog on the day Tabby's family pulled away from the house in their baby-blue Ford Escape. And I swear, I'm not making it up when I say that she turned around, pressed her face to the back window, and put a finger to her lips, as if to say *shh*. Then she gave a little wave and a wink.

It was hot outside, but I got a chill. I still have one when I think about it. I didn't know where Tabby was going, where she would end up, but I knew she'd land on her feet, just like a cat. I knew there would be a new Jordan eventually, the latest guy with a promising future whose life she would ruin. I knew, but what could I do? I was a teenage girl. Nobody would have believed me anyway.

11

ELLE

TABBY IS A MESS. Her face is puffy and her eyes are red, and she looks smaller, somehow, sitting across from me at the detention center, her shoulders hunched under lank hair. Maybe it's the absence of me that makes her smaller. Her shadow doesn't take up as much space without me by her side.

"Has anyone else come to see you?" I ask. I know the answer before finishing the question. I had to get approved to come for a visit, and driving up to the complex of buildings, squat like trolls, made me want to turn around and head home. Getting past security and marching down a narrow corridor, shoes squeaking, made me feel like a criminal, as if the walls themselves were breathing in my secrets. People would rather hide behind their computers than make that walk.

She laughs dryly. "My parents. Bridge. Who else would come? I don't have anyone."

That's the irony. She doesn't have anyone, but she has the whole world on her back, bending her in half under the weight of its collective suspicion.

"Are you okay? Like, actually okay? I think about you—" I cut myself off before I make it worse. Of course she's not okay. And it's partly my fault.

"I'm fine," she says. "I like to pretend I'm just living in a shithole apartment with a bunch of bitchy wannabe actresses." She sucks in a breath of stale air. "Home sweet home."

She wants me to laugh—she needs me to laugh, to know she's okay, and I do, even though it's not funny. This room is gray and windowless and the girls in it, dotted at other tables across from their own visitors, are all wary eyes and drawn faces, blending into the somberness. Maybe after enough time, this place will soak Tabby in like another one of its stains. I can't let that happen.

"What are they saying about me?" She pulls her hair over her shoulder. "I need to know. Tell me everything."

"Nothing," I say. "I mean, everyone has their own stuff to worry about. They're not talking as much as they used to."

"You're lying," she says, bringing her hands together in a knot. "I could always tell."

Not always.

"They think Beck had something to do with it. I don't know. This is all going to blow over, you know, right? Obviously Beck won't say anything."

She arches an eyebrow. "Say anything about what? I thought there was nothing to talk about."

I hold her eye contact for two seconds, three. Those eyes, always bright, always unnatural. I'm the one who looks away first.

"You'll be out soon, Tabby. Fuck everyone. They just have nothing better to talk about."

Suddenly she leans across the table and grabs my wrists, almost hard enough to hurt. We're not supposed to touch—one of the guards is coming over now. They see everything.

"Make it stop," she says. "Do something to make it stop."

I can't, I want to say. It's only when I'm watching her retreating, as she's dragged back to wherever she came from, that I realize maybe there is something I can do.

12

BRIDGET

YOU'RE STILL WONDERING what that detective asked me before. You'll find out, eventually. But today, on a Saturday morning, when I should be in the woods doing hill intervals, they're questioning me again. Stewart, his hands in a meaty clump across our kitchen table. Tabby isn't here, but they don't think they've wrung enough out of me.

Mom brings over two coffees, like it's normal having Stewart in our house. Maybe it is by now. She knows he takes his coffee with cream and sugar. We never even kept creamer in the fridge until Stewart started making these appearances.

"What did Tabby say to you in the days leading up to the hike?" I hate his voice, slow and measured, like I'm a baby who doesn't understand.

"Nothing unusual," I say. "She was just going because Mark wanted to."

"You know those woods well, from what I've heard," he says. *From who*, I want to ask.

"I'm a runner. That's where I go."

"You drew her a map," he says, either a statement or an accusation.

"Yeah. I told you that already. It was in case she wanted to go running again. I guess she held on to it."

"Running again?"

Shit. I shouldn't have said anything. Now they're going to take that and twist it around, another weapon to use against my sister.

"I took her running with me once. She had no idea where she was going."

"You say she held on to the map. But she never took it with her that day." He leans back, like it's some kind of big revelation.

"She must have forgotten it. And look what happened. She did get lost."

"Look what happened," he echoes. "Did you run in the woods that day?"

My mouth, bone-dry. "Yes. I run there almost every day."

"Did you happen to time your run to see your sister with Mark?"

I shake my head. It doesn't matter anyway. I only got a glimpse of them, walking together. I stayed hidden in the trees. They were laughing, not fighting, Tabby trailing just a few steps behind. Mark was singing a song. I left, because they looked okay.

"You didn't like Mark, did you?"

My head snaps up. "Why do you think that?"

"Because of what you said to him at Crest Beach. Some may have taken it as a threat."

Keegan. That asshole Keegan. No wonder my sister hates him so much.

"It was a joke," I say. "He just didn't take jokes very well."

Stewart nods, his chin bobbing. "Thanks for answering my questions. If you can think of anything else—anything at all— you have my card."

When he gets up to leave—another unfinished coffee in his wake, how many of those has Mom made him?—he turns around. "One more thing, Bridget. What size shoe do you wear?"

I open my mouth, but no sound comes out. "Seven," I finally manage. "Sometimes seven and a half."

I'm not sure why I tack on that last part, but it feels important somehow.

Let's get something straight. I'm guilty of nothing except trying to protect my sister, because she's the one who needs me. I see what the media does to girls like Tabby. Everyone says *boys will be boys*, but girls? Girls will be monsters.

Let's talk about sex (and what it leads to), baby
By Oberon Halton

Got your attention with that headline? Well, keep paying attention. I have the inside scoop on some photos that shed some light on when things started going downhill between Mark and Tabby, and it's not just because somebody got bored or someone had a wandering eye. No, it's because someone got knocked up.

Photos sent in by one of our readers show Tabby heading into an abortion clinic. As you can see, she's wearing a Princeton sweatshirt, which is pretty cruel since Mark knew nothing about the baby at all. The photos were published on an Instagram account belonging to someone who obviously created the account just to post them, and post them they did.

The question is, when did Mark find out about the abortion? Some speculate it was when he crashed and burned at the NCAAs, failing to even make the finals after being favored to win a gold medal. Others claim he didn't know until they went into the woods, and when Tabby tried to tell him, he freaked out, and something happened up there on the Split.

I don't know about you all, but this bombshell has made me rethink everything. If you know anything else about the situation, help a friend out! Let's shed some light on this mystery.

COMMENTS

LookCloser: Those pictures don't even show her face. It could be any girl in a sweatshirt. Also, the Princeton could be photoshopped on, if someone hated her enough to do it. And sounds like they did.

WhenDovesCry: There are other guys who could have been the father.

Excerpt from Tabby's Diary

March 29, 2019

Great, now he doesn't believe me about this abortion
thing. It wasn't me—truthfully, I swear to God, and I told
him that, but he doesn't believe me. He said we'd talk
about it later, but now it's later and we haven't talked
about it. I watched his heats online and he wasn't himself
at all. He didn't even make the semis. He's going to be so
livid, and it's all because of me. I'm scared that he'll break
up with me, and I'm scared he won't.

13

BECK

Coldcliff Police Station, October 24, 10:43 a.m.

BECK: I just don't have anything else to say. (pauses) Am I gonna be here much longer? Because I have a test tomorrow. I don't want to fail.

OFFICER OLDMAN: You don't want to fail this test either. Just a few more questions today, Beck. Do you recognize these images?

BECK: (shuffles through photos, closes file folder) Nope. Never seen them before in my life.

OFFICER OLDMAN: I find that hard to believe. I was under the impression that almost everyone in your class had seen them. They went live on a new Instagram account in March.

BECK: It's a girl in a sweatshirt. So?

OFFICER OLDMAN: A Princeton sweatshirt. Look where she is.

BECK: Some building. Don't recognize it.

OFFICER OLDMAN: It's right near your house, though. You ride past it on the way to school. It's a clinic that performs abortions.

BECK: Okay. Guess I never noticed it before.

OFFICER OLDMAN: Did Tabitha ever confide in you about getting an abortion? Did she tell you she was going there?

BECK: No. Why would she? And how do you know that's even Tabby? It could be anyone in a Princeton sweatshirt.

OFFICER OLDMAN: That's the sweatshirt sources say Mark gave her. Who else would be wearing it?

14

ELLE

YOU WANT TO KNOW about her abortion. Namely, if she got one or not. And honestly, I'm not the right person to ask, because I don't want to talk about it. Some things, girls have to go through on their own. Tell one other person and suddenly you're too big to fit through it.

All I remember is Lou making a comment at school. "Tabitha put on weight," she said to me when we both happened to be in the bathroom at the same time, washing our hands practically in tandem.

"Oh," I said. "I don't think so." I felt like I should defend her, because Lou barely ever even talked to me, and my allegiance was with Tabby, no matter how weird she had been acting lately.

"Maybe because you see her, like, every day. But in gym class she had a doctor's note to avoid jumping on the trampoline. And I wasn't looking or anything, but I saw her when she was changing after class. Her stomach looked super bloated."

I thought about Tabby. The girl I saw eat less and less every day. Maybe I hadn't noticed her putting on weight, but she hadn't been losing it, no matter how many Cheetos she ditched in favor of celery sticks.

"I thought you might know something," Lou said. I shook my head. She was gone before I could ask her about the trampoline, about what that had to do with Tabby's stomach. But it only took a few seconds for me to figure it out. The same thing every teenage girl is taught to be terrified of.

But Tabby couldn't be pregnant. I hadn't seen her drink in a while, but that was only because she was trying to cut out alcohol. She didn't like how she got when she drank it, didn't like how it made her forget. Mark didn't like who she became.

Had she told Mark? Would he be happy? In my head, there were two versions of him. One who wanted to go to every doctor's appointment and put together a crib and time contractions. Another who accused her of lying to keep him around, who spat out lines like *How do you know it's even mine?*

"Are you okay?" I asked her when we were out for a walk at night, something we used to do when we needed to get away from the boxes that were our homes, the ceilings that trapped us under the stars. "Are things okay with you and Mark?"

"What's up with you?" she said, kicking a pebble with her pink Converse. "Things are fine. You know, we have our moments. But we're making it work."

Making what work? A baby? A relationship? Suddenly I felt like a little kid tagging along, trying to get my big sister to notice me.

"Here's the thing about Mark," she said, and tilted her head back to the sky. "I love him more than he loves me. But I think I'm okay with it. I mean, every relationship is a bit off-balance. One person always cares more."

I thought about me and Dallas. There was so much to say.

"You know you can tell me anything," I said. The words came out of me so loud that they were practically a shout. They were a demand. *Tell me anything and everything because there is so much I need to tell you.*

She rubbed her arms and pulled the sleeves of her shirt over her hands, making her fingertips disappear. "Sometimes," she said, dragging out the word for so long that I wondered if she even had the rest of the sentence planned. "Sometimes I wish I could stop apologizing. Like, not everything is my fault."

"What do you mean?" I asked. She just laughed, but it wasn't her normal laugh. It was hollow, like she had been emptied out.

"You know what I mean. Every girl knows. We all apologize for everything. It's like, genetic. In our DNA."

She was right. I lost track of the number of times I said sorry on a regular basis. Sorry to the lady in the cafeteria for not carrying cash. Sorry to teachers for not knowing the answers. Sorry to girls for hogging the mirror in the bathroom. Sorry to boys for being too much and never enough.

Sorry for my body, for all the ways I fought with it. Even sorrier for the hot clash of emotions in my chest, the way they all churned there nonstop.

"You can tell me anything, too," she said.

So I did. I told her everything about Dallas and nothing about how I wished it was Beck instead. Beck was the one whose thumbs I felt tracing my jawline, his arms pinning me beneath him. *You're beautiful, Elle* was supposed to spill from his lips. But of course, I left all that out. Tabby listened to my ugly truth, her hand finding mine, fingers tangling together, and she made it less ugly somehow.

"I can't believe you kept all this from me," she said. "I can't believe you wouldn't tell me. I thought we told each other everything."

As much as I love Tabby, there was a tiny part of me that was annoyed. She managed to take something wholly and utterly mine and make it all about her. But I wasn't pissed off for long. There was too much going on inside my head.

Weeks later, I heard the rumors, same as everyone else. Somebody saw a girl about Tabby's height wearing an orange Princeton hoodie in front of the clinic. The hoodie—remember that, because it was an important detail. That was Mark's college. Mark's sweatshirt.

And when Mark found out—that was when Tabby fell apart.

15

BRIDGET

I HAVE NO IDEA how he got my email address, but the message that appears today proves that he has his ways.

The truth is coming out—you may not know your sister as well as you think. I'm not trying to be creepy—I can just tell you're not like her.

It's from Alexander. Alex. He's back in Australia by now, but still finds a way to send a chill down my spine. Especially since his message comes around the same time that article goes up on Sharp Edges about the abortion.

Honestly, I don't have much to say about that. I heard the rumors the same time as everybody else. I was at school before fifth period, getting my math textbook from my locker, and there was Elle, wanting to talk. Which was weird, because Elle never wants to talk to me. She's Tabby's friend, someone I've always been jealous of by association. People think Tabby and Elle are sisters. I used to see the comments on Tabby's Instagram. *OMG you two are twins!* Yet when Tabby and I go out in public together, nobody ever comments on the resemblance.

"Tabby didn't meet me at lunch," she said. I could tell by her pinched face that she was upset about a lot more than lunch. "And she missed a big bio test. I texted her a bunch of times." She leaned against the locker next to mine. "Bridge, I have to ask. Has Tabby been acting strange lately?"

There was Tabby, pushing food around, cradling her laptop in her arms like it was her baby, staring at Mark's Instagram. There was my sister, shiny as a gold band, dulled down to something that didn't even catch the light. I considered lying to Elle, but part of me thought I could save Tabby with the truth.

"Yes," I said. "Ever since Mark went back to Princeton."

The bell chose the seconds following to split the silence.

"We need to talk more about this," Elle said. "I think something's going on."

Later that day, I saw what they had done to Tabby's locker. Someone had spray-painted two words over it. BABY KILLER. I couldn't move when I saw them, but somehow I kept walking. The longer I stared, the less I would be able to convince myself it wasn't true. Somebody else, though—somebody else apparently couldn't keep walking, because he was staring at the words like they were going to move. Beck Rutherford. I wondered why Beck cared now after he made it very clear to Tabby that he didn't want her. A whole month of not returning her texts or calls. A month of Tabby's tears, where she didn't want to go outside or to the mall or anywhere. She always let boys become her earth, while she orbited them like an obedient little moon.

The next day, my parents got a phone call at home. They got called into a meeting with Tabby and Principal Stanton. I heard them talking about it, my ear up against their bedroom door, like an eavesdropping kid. It was exactly what I had been reduced to.

"She's in trouble," Mom was saying. "Ryan, we need to help her."

Then Dad said something I would never be able to forget I heard. "Paula, you remember what happened last time. Sometimes I think she is the trouble."

He was a traitor, our father, another boy who didn't believe a girl when she was screaming the truth right in front of his face.

I'll never know what happened at that meeting. I saw them all getting out of the car—Dad driving, Mom in the passenger side, Tabby climbing out of the back seat in a dress I had never seen her wear, knee-length and all buttoned up, hair pushed back with a headband. I saw her for what she was. Young and scared.

When we got to school on Monday, Tabby's locker was back to normal. I never asked her about the words there, if they were true. I never asked her what Mark made her do. I never asked, but I should have. The truth was, nobody helped Tabby. So whatever happened next was on all of us.

You don't believe me, do you? I don't know how many times I have to say that I didn't get an abortion. I don't even know where your sweatshirt is. Somebody stole it. *9:21 p.m.*

Why are you being such an asshole? I don't give a shit about your race, I care about US and I think we're falling apart. *10:11 p.m.*

FYI I would never get rid of our baby *1:57 a.m.*

Text messages from Tabitha Cousins to Mark Forrester, March 27–28, 2019

16

LOU

OKAY, THE ABORTION. You all think I took the photo outside the clinic, but trust me, I didn't. I knew Tabby had hooked up with guys, so I figured she had her business taken care of, if you know what I mean. I mean, I went on the Pill last year, when I was dating Braden Hall, even though we never ended up doing it. Anyway, I was wrong about Tabby. Maybe she's like the rest of us. Too afraid to ask a guy to find a condom because that ruins the moment, and ruining the moment can sometimes seem worse than ruining your entire life.

I heard about the abortion from Leslie Sears. Leslie knows I hate Tabitha, and one day she's at my locker, telling me her older sister saw it. Tabitha Cousins at the abortion clinic. Wading through the Jesus freaks and their signs, YOUR BABY IS THE SIZE OF A CLENCHED FIST or whatever.

"Is there proof?" I asked, and there was. A picture. You can't really see Tabby's face, but you don't need to. She had the sweatshirt on, that one of Mark's that she used to fold herself into like it was some kind of security blanket. It was her way of broadcasting to everyone at our school: *I'm dating a Princeton guy.*

Okay, so I'm not totally proud of what happened next. Or what I did. I started a new Instagram account just to post the photo. Then I sent the link to Mark. I took a chance on what I thought his school email address would be. I also took a chance that he didn't already know, because he wasn't in that photo, holding her hand.

He didn't already know. He replied to the email, *who's this?*

Of course, it wasn't my real email addy, so he had no way of knowing who I was. I wasn't going to write back at all, but then I felt bad, or maybe I was just bored, if we're being totally honest. So I wrote *sorry you had to find out this way, but it's better than not finding out at all.* And I added, just before hitting SEND, *you should know who she is.*

I never heard from him again.

And you know, I carry some guilt over it. I mean, obviously I didn't shove him off the Split. But we learned in school about this thing, the butterfly effect. Which is also a terrible movie with Ashton Kutcher. It's all about how everything you do can lead to something bigger, even something far away. Maybe Mark never wanted to talk about the abortion until they were out hiking in the woods, with nobody to overhear them, and she got riled up and pushed him.

But some people believe her. Just like I believed her, once upon a time. At one of Elle's parties early this year, when she and Mark were long-distance and Beck had called me *sweetheart* for the first time. She watched us together, and later, she cornered me in the bathroom, which felt super aggressive. But she just sat on the counter while I put more eyeliner on.

"You have great lips," she said. Random, right? "You should play them up more. Here, have this." And she gave me a tube of lipstick from her purse, this berry color I knew I'd never wear. I can't even find it now. Maybe I threw it out, because I was sick of having Tabby's leftovers. But I shit you not, the name of the lipstick was Boy Slayer.

"Thanks," I mumbled, hoping she would leave. There were rips in her nylons, but, like, on-purpose rips, which just looked super trashy. At the next party, I'm ashamed to say I wore mine that way, too. Not because I wanted to be like her, but because I wanted Beck to look at me the way he looked at her.

"You have nothing to worry about," she said. "It's totally over between us. And I think you're good for him. He needs to be with a nice girl." She hopped off the counter and ran her hand through my hair, just like my mom used to do before she got busy hooking up with strange men at bars.

I let her leave without saying anything, because what the hell was I supposed to say to that? Later, when I was trying to fall asleep, I thought of a bunch of good comebacks. *I wasn't looking for your approval. I'll go for whatever I want. If it's a competition you want, then bring it.* And one alternate reality where our eyes met in the mirror and I said *What makes you so sure I'm a nice girl?*

It was like Tabby cursed me that day in the bathroom, and I spent every day after trying to prove her wrong, that I wasn't nice. And you've gotten to know me a bit, right? I'm not exactly a peach.

I'm surprised it took the rest of the world this long to find out about her abortion. But I'm glad they know now, because it's part of her story. And let's get something straight. I'm not judging her for deciding to get an abortion. We should all have the right to choose what happens with our own bodies. I'm judging her because I doubt she knows who the father even was.

17

ELLIOTT WRAY,
PRINCETON TIGERS SWIM TEAM

I STILL CAN'T BELIEVE IT. That he's gone. Practices aren't the same without him. He was always the leader—I can still hear his voice, yelling from beside the pool as I worked on my turns. *You can do better than that, man,* he'd say. I guess some people would say he was intense, but he just wanted the best for everyone. He pushed people, you know? Oh man, that was a terrible choice of words.

Anyway, you asked about the NCAAs, where Mark bombed. I know a lot of people were happy to see that. The guys from Boston College practically cheered. It was a really big shock for us. After he lost the hundred free, he didn't want to anchor the relay, so Mike Mathers swam instead. He isn't half the swimmer Mark was, so we didn't advance in that either.

I saw Mark in the locker room after it all happened. He was hunched over the sink, gripping his goggles in his fist. He looked so pissed off. There was this energy crackling around him and I didn't even want to talk to him, because I knew anything I said would just blow up. He had to cool down first.

I didn't think he saw me anyway, but I heard him as I tried to open my locker.

"She ruined everything," he said. "She has no idea how hard I worked, and it's all for nothing."

I didn't know who *she* was. Mark never mentioned a girl. From what I saw, he was work hard, party hard. He didn't have time for a girlfriend. But then again, he was a private person. I mean, he wasn't a guy who went around bragging about who he screwed or whatever.

Mark the Shark, man. I still can't believe he's gone. And the crap he was dealing with all that time. With that weighing him down, I'm surprised he didn't drown sooner.

18

ELLE

MARK WAS SUPPOSED TO WIN, because Mark always won. He had been training forever. I knew he was serious because I creeped his Instagram every day. There were no party pictures lately, no beer bottles in sweaty hands, no blurry faces. There was also no Tabby. It was like she didn't exist.

Anyway, Mark didn't win, and he didn't get a medal, and not only that, he didn't advance to the finals. He came in fourth in his heat and didn't advance from there. All that training, and he had absolutely nothing to show for it.

The night of the meet, Tabby came over crying. Mom let her in. Mom was used to seeing Tabby like that, in tears. Sometimes I got the feeling she preferred it that way, having a broken girl to put back together. I never let her see me like that. Tabby was the daughter she always wanted but never had. She let Mom hold her and rub her back and bring her tea.

But that day, Tabby only wanted me.

She flopped onto my bed, landing with her head between my pillows. "I fucked up so badly. It's all my fault. Mark hates me."

"How could he possibly hate you?"

"I ruined his life," she said. "He told me that."

"He said that to you?" Guilt twisted in my gut.

"He texted it. Same thing. Actually, worse, because now I have a reminder of it."

"Where is it? I'll delete it for you."

But she wouldn't give me her phone. "It's my fault he lost his race. He was distracted. Like, by all those stupid rumors.

Somehow he heard about them. I have no idea who would have told him. He's in college. Who would bother bugging him with that shit?"

Those stupid rumors. The clinic on Swanson Road. The baseball cap, the flick of a ponytail over the hump of a Princeton sweatshirt. The roar of traffic on the street. Sunglasses not big enough to cover her face. The sun a hot hand on her lower back, pressing her toward it but away, playing tug-of-war with her body.

"I know who could have told," I said, because I didn't want to think about that anymore. "Keegan. He's here, and Mark's not. He's keeping tabs on you for Mark."

Tabby snorted. "That's ridiculous. Keegan—he must have his own life. I don't think he cares what Mark and I do." She sat up, hugging the pillow to her chest. "I just have this feeling I'm about to lose everything."

"I told you not to—you know," I said. "I told you I could handle it. Then you wouldn't be in this mess." I hated how everything was her idea, that she stepped so easily into martyrdom. I hated that lately, I went along with it.

"It was something I had to do," she said. I wanted to argue—*No, it wasn't, until you made it that way*—but suddenly I had no energy to fight with Tabby. Especially over this.

"I'm sure Mark is just pissed off at himself for losing his race and needs some time to cool off. He'll probably apologize tomorrow."

"He never says sorry." She wiped her eyes, and I knew the crying was over, the tears hardened into something else. "He has a temper, Elle."

"What do you mean?" I asked. But she never got a chance to answer, because Mom chose that moment to knock on the door, brandishing hot chocolate with Irish cream, forever the *cool mom*.

I wish I would have asked again.

I love you, I really do, that's why this distance thing is so hard for me. It'll be better when we have the whole summer together with no distractions. We need that, or else I'm afraid something really bad will happen.

Text message from Tabitha Cousins to Mark Forrester,
April 25, 2019, 10:19 a.m.

19

KEEGAN

I MEAN, I HEARD about the abortion from Mark. He asked me about it, like I knew anything. I really don't have anything to say, except that she should have told him, because he would have been there for her, because he loved her. He would have respected whatever she decided to do and understood that it was her body, her choice.

That's pretty much all I have to say about it.

20

ELLE

TABBY CALLS ME FROM JUVIE. They get phone privileges. I picture her lining up to use a shitty pay phone, like in *Orange Is the New Black*. She must be going crazy in there without her iPhone. I know I'd be losing it without mine. Mom loves to get on my case about being addicted to my phone, but she's just as bad with hers, with her mommy blogger websites and rounds of Candy Crush.

"Tell me what they're saying," she says. "I don't get the internet in here, obviously. So tell me."

"Nothing much new," I say. Her silence, just a few seconds too long, makes me think she knows I'm lying. "How are you doing anyway?"

"I shower with forty other girls. Just tell me what they're saying. I need to know."

"The guys on the swim team started this campaign to raise money for a scholarship in Mark's name. It's some GoFundMe thing. And there's this Remember Mark hashtag on Instagram, where people are posting pictures of him and stories about nice stuff he supposedly did." I leave out the post about the abortion and the comments that festered underneath it.

That gets a laugh. "I bet they are. What else, Elle?"

"It's not all bad," I say. "That Facebook group that started up to defend you. The Tabby Cats. They're doing all kinds of marches and stuff."

"That's cute." I can hear the smile in her voice, the relief.

Not everyone worships Mark's memory. Not everyone let death make him blameless.

"Don't you want to talk about something else?" *Because I do.* I need to talk about something else, and I need my best friend.

"Did something happen?" There's the Tabby I know, the fierce one who would defend me even if it was my fault. And it is my fault.

"He knows it was me and not you," I say. "He keeps trying to talk to me. It was—I feel like a monster."

"You're not a monster, Elle," Tabby snaps. "Do you hear me? I'm so sick of people making us think like this. Like our choices either make us good or evil. Picture it the other way. There was literally no way out where you weren't going to get judged."

I don't think we're just talking about me anymore. We're talking about her. Whether she did it or not—whatever *it* even was—people are going to hate her. They already do.

"I heard they found Beck's boot print," Tabby says. His name is a stab wound, short and swift.

"Yeah. I saw that on Lou's Facebook. She wrote some cryptic message about the truth coming out."

"Can you do something for me? Talk to him, okay? Tell him this will all blow over."

"I—" I don't want to talk to Beck. I have good reasons to keep my distance.

"Just tell him, Elle. This is totally my fault. He was only trying to protect me."

I hold my breath. I'm the reason why Beck's fist made contact with Mark's face. Because of what I said. *He isn't a good guy, and I saw him shove her.*

I did see him shove her—that much is true. I'd been drinking, but I know what I saw. But I didn't say it to defend Tabby. I did it to test Beck. I needed to know how much he cared. If he still loved her.

I got my answer.

"I'll talk to him," I say.

"I have to go, Elle," Tabby says. "Love you, okay? Whatever happens, remember that."

She hangs up before I get a chance to say it back.

21

BRIDGET

I'M NOT SURE WHY the detectives care about the map at all, as if a girl knowing her way around is the most dangerous thing of all. Yes, I made the map. No, I didn't make it as part of some grand scheme to lure Mark deep into the woods. Tabby only became familiar with those trails at all because of me. Because I asked her to go running with me.

At first, she had laughed, sitting there at the kitchen table, cradling the coffee she only ever drank black anymore. "The only way I'll manage to be fast is if I'm running away from someone."

"Well, you can pretend you're running away from me," I said. "Come on. Just give it a try. They say running gives you endorphins and makes you happy."

"What makes you think I'm not already happy?" she said. "Besides, they also make pills for that. Those require a lot less effort."

I knew I had hit a sore spot. Ever since my parents got called in to school that day to talk about what was written on Tabby's locker, they had been making her see a therapist. Some woman at an office downtown for an hour a week, where Tabby was supposed to spill her soul. I wondered if she lied about Mark, or if he even came up. I had no idea what she talked about in those sessions, or if her therapist had a diagnosis. *Depressed. Withdrawn.* I had my own diagnosis. *In a toxic relationship.*

I was ready to give up on the idea of Tabby running with me, but she stood up and drained the rest of her coffee mug. "Okay, fine. But I don't have running shoes."

I let her borrow a pair of my Nikes. She wanted to wear her Princeton hoodie, even though I told her it was way too hot for that in the woods. But it didn't matter, because she couldn't find it anyway.

"Probably Mom doing the laundry," she said. "I told her I can do my own, but she never listens."

Surprisingly, Tabby was fast. She didn't need to stop and take a break. She didn't double over, head between her knees. Tabby was a natural.

To give you a mental picture, the woods are a circuit of different trails, crisscrossing each other like a spider's web. There's a baby trail, the Boardwalk, for people who only have time for a mile. Then the three- and four-mile trails, Humpback Ridge and the Bottleneck. I know what supposedly happens on those trails. Humpback is for humping and Bottleneck is for drinking, littered with beer cans and bottle caps to honor its namesake. Then there's Cider Creek, six miles, which wraps around everything else like a tight hug. Last of all is the Mayflower, a long and winding eight miles, a too-big belt. Getting to the end means making it up to the Split, a steep rock face, the highest point in Coldcliff, where you get rewarded with an epic view.

I've never been all the way up to the Split. I've heard stories about what has happened there. That people disappeared over the edge, never to be seen again. I know they're cautionary tales meant to keep drunk kids away from the brink, but they're enough to scare me away. Besides, I'm a runner, not a climber.

Tabby and I were on our way around the Boardwalk. If she wasn't tired, I figured we could do another lap. But instead, she stopped and stared at the signs for the other trails. "The Split," she said. "That's a weird name for something."

"It's apparently named that because the rocks split, like, years ago, and there's a rumor that one day it will all cave in."

"One day," she said. She rubbed her bare arms. "Should we head back?"

And even though I was the one who knew the woods, it felt for a minute like she was leading me.

Excerpt from Tabby's Diary

June 1, 2019

I'm so glad to have Mark home for the summer. Things
are better now. I know we have a lot to talk about, but
I'm happy. This is going to be the best summer ever. When
it's over, we'll look back on everything we've done. All the
plans we made. And we'll know we did them all.
I really do love him. I just hope he loves me back.

22

ELLE

WE STILL HAD A MONTH of school left when Mark came home at the end of May. Tabby and I were at my house and he just showed up there on the porch with a bunch of flowers, scooped her into a hug. Keegan was skulking behind him, hanging back like a pet that wasn't allowed indoors. I didn't want either of them in the house, but there was Mom, asking if they wanted to stay for dinner.

"I wish we could," Mark said. "But I want to take my girl on a proper date." I swear, he winked at Mom, and even more embarrassing, she blushed. Mom, forty-two years old, blushing because of a boy half her age. I hated her in that moment, for the baby-pink blotches on her cheekbones, shiny and high like hard candies.

I hated her. I hated Mark. I hated *my girl*, like she was his property. I hated Mark's hand on Tabby's lower back, his other hand clamped firmly around hers, a fleshy seashell. The only thing I didn't hate in that moment was Tabby's face. She was smiling, but it was pinched at the corners, her smile generally reserved for school pictures and the lunch lady in the cafeteria.

"Do you have a vase, Maggie? These should go in water," Tabby said, handing her the flowers. I didn't know what kind they were, just that they were a riot of purple and pink. Somehow I knew the act of passing the bouquet to Mom was a rebellion Mark wouldn't like, something Tabby did anyway.

Suddenly I didn't want to let her go anywhere with him.

"I could eat, too," I said, peeling the skin back from my thumb cuticle. "Maybe Keegan and I can tag along."

That took Mark by surprise. His face clouded over, but only for a second, because he was calculating like that. He wasn't about to show his opponent that she had struck him somewhere it hurt.

"I am kind of hungry," Keegan said. I tried not to show my shock that he was playing along. Maybe he was bored. Maybe he was horny and wanted in my pants. Maybe I didn't even care. Dallas wasn't talking to me anymore.

"I don't see why not." Tabby tugged on Mark's arm as he stood there like a department store mannequin. "We have the whole summer to ourselves, right?"

Mark grunted, reduced to a caveman. There were things he wanted to talk to Tabby about that he didn't want anyone else to hear. If we were there, he wouldn't be able to say them, wouldn't be able to squeeze his words into her. He would be alone with her eventually, but at the time, I really thought putting it off one more day would make a difference.

So we went to this fancy restaurant downtown where my parents sometimes go on dates. Umbrage, the place with the lights strung up around the awning. The four of us got squished into a table at the back. Keegan ordered a beer without getting carded, and when it arrived, I took a big sip. Then his hand moved from the table to my bare leg, and I let it stay there, even though it was heavy and hot.

Mark had recovered by then. His arm slung around Tabby's shoulders like a scarf. I noticed the dark brush of stubble where his hair was growing back. He had to shave his entire body for swimming, Tabby had told me.

"All of it?" I had asked.

"Everything except his head. And, well, he might have left a little behind in other places."

Mark the Shark. His swimming nickname. Once I heard it, I couldn't think of him any other way. Cutting through the water, hunting for prey. He even started to look less human to me. Eyes too far apart, like they were set on his face that way specifically for him to know what was happening on either side of him.

But Mark the Shark was a gentleman at dinner. He even ordered for Tabby, a gesture I thought was chauvinistic and gross, but one she didn't balk at. She eased into his arm, let Mark talk about everything he wanted to do that summer. He said "I" a lot more than "we."

"I'm going to take this girl camping," he said, matter-of-factly, like it wasn't up for debate. "Did you know she has never been?"

I never noticed before how often he called Tabby "this girl" and "my girl" instead of her real name. I wondered how many girls at Princeton got the same treatment. The shiny faces in the background of his Instagram, hair flying, arms in the air, always trying to get somebody's attention, and probably ending up with attention from someone they never wanted, because that was how life worked.

That was how my life worked. Keegan's hand wasn't just on my legs but sandwiched between them, inching upward under the tablecloth.

"Tabby has been camping," I said flatly. "She hates it. Her parents made her go last summer and it was a disaster."

"That's because my dad had no idea how to pitch a tent, and it was pouring rain." Tabby glared at me from across the table. "Just because I tried something once and didn't like it doesn't mean I hate camping."

It stung. She was siding with him in a battle she might not have even known was going on. Keegan's hand slid up slowly, the meaty weight of it a relief somehow.

"And a picnic," Mark said. "We need to go on a picnic, right, babe?"

He was gaining steam because he knew he had pulled out in front. He folded Tabby closer to him, his arm not a limp scarf but now some kind of dangerous snake, a boa constrictor, like the one that zoologist brought to school last year as part of the career fair. We were allowed to touch it, and I only did because Tabby did, because her boldness meant it was okay, that neither of us would get hurt.

"A picnic would be fun," Tabby said. "But only if we can get one of those old-fashioned wicker baskets. I'll make sandwiches and we can bring champagne."

In that moment, I had no idea who she was. Tabby had never mentioned wanting to go on a picnic with an old-fashioned wicker basket. She didn't even own a lunch bag. When she brought her lunch to school, it was in a plastic grocery bag, a hasty afterthought when she was sick of eating cafeteria fries.

"Anything for you, babe." Mark kissed her cheek. I fixated on his fingers, how tightly they gripped her arm. When he pulled away, they would leave white indents.

"I don't know why anyone would want to eat outside," I snapped. "Especially during the summer. It's too hot and there are bugs everywhere." I knew I had lost the battle and that I was verging on pathetic, but I didn't care. I needed her to know I was still armed, that just because her fight had been sucked out didn't mean I didn't have enough to spare.

Keegan had remained almost totally silent, periodically sipping beer with his free hand. I unclenched my legs, an invitation for him to creep in.

"What are your plans for the summer, Keegan?" Tabby asked, choosing that moment to rope him into the conversation, sounding formal and forced. His hand stopped moving, like he couldn't do what he was doing to me and answer a question at the same time. I couldn't tell if I was relieved or disappointed.

"Same old," he said. "The store isn't going to manage itself."

"You got promoted?" she asked. "Congratulations."

"It's a pretty big honor," he said. "The last manager passed the torch to me because he's going to Stanford this fall. He knew a lifer when he saw one."

I felt sorry for Keegan, affection spreading through my chest like fire. In that moment, I forgot that he was more than likely spying for Mark while Mark had been away at school. I managed to clear my head of that. We all did shady things for our friends. I dropped my hand under the table to meet his, to let him know I wanted it there. But his hand, formerly its own animal, was still.

"You could apply for college, too," Tabby said. "Even community college. It's not too late."

Keegan laughed. "It's too late for a lot of things."

Mark cut in. "I keep bugging him about college, but it's no use. People need to do their own thing." Then he launched back into his summer itinerary, one he had apparently put a lot of thought into. The Calloway Carnival in July. The beach. A road trip to Cape Cod to see the turtles. Keegan's hand woke up, his fingers breaching the sides of my underwear. I picked up my water and downed half the glass because I wasn't sure what to do with my own hands.

His thumb, rubbing slowly at first, then faster.

After, I felt like I had done something wrong. Maybe I just felt cheap. I let a boy inside my body at a restaurant and we weren't even on a date. It was the first time anything had been inside since—*since*. When the food came, I barely touched mine. When the bill came, Mark paid for his and Tabby's, and Keegan and I paid separately. Maybe he felt like he had already given me enough.

I never told Tabby what happened. I never told her that as we were leaving, Mark bent down to pick up his wallet and looked up our waitress's skirt. I never told her a lot of things, and maybe if I had, she would have paid me the same courtesy.

23

BRIDGET

MY PARENTS VISIT TABBY every weekend. The first time, Mom brought cookies. As if they were going to let those cookies find their way to my sister. I'm sure the guards ate them and had a laugh at our expense.

I visit when I can, but I prefer not going with my parents. They change things—Tabby is different when they're around, more censored. It's not like she's a liar or anything, but we all act different around our parents. Like the best versions of ourselves, because we want them to be proud.

Mom and Dad don't talk about Tabby. At least, they don't talk about her when I'm within earshot. They must have something to say. The night Tabby got arrested, they both just kind of stood there, frozen, like pieces of machinery that forgot they needed to be recharged. I was the emotional one, the one matching Tabby's tears.

Yes, she cried. People are commenting on how she doesn't look sad in any of the pictures online. *Emotionless*, someone wrote. *She's basically a robot. Of course she killed him. Total sociopath.* But what do you want from her? Do you really need to see her tears? Do you feel entitled to them? If so, ask yourself why. Do you think you're owed water coming from her eyes as some kind of apology?

What did she do to you? Do you even know her, or do you just think you know her because you've read so much about her, because her face has been everywhere? It's a legitimate question. But I know my sister is capable of emotion because I've seen her wearing every single one. I've even borrowed some from her, same as I used to swipe clothes from the hangers in her closet without asking. Funny, now that she's not around to tell me to quit touching her stuff, I haven't gone into her closet once.

The police went in there, though, the night they arrested her. I'm not sure what they were looking for. Some hidden box of secrets, maybe. If you're thinking I should go and search her room myself—because I'm her sister and can unravel the knot of her mysteries better than anyone—I'm not doing that. My sister may have things to hide, but they're inside her head, stamped into her skin. And she's allowed to have secrets. Nobody gets the right to extract and unwrap them just because they don't know exactly what happened that day in the woods.

Today, Tabby is happy to see me. Her spirits are high, considering. She's wearing makeup and her hair has been straightened and she's Tabby again, not a muddy-eyed girl in a prison jumpsuit.

I mean—I guess that's one secret I can tell. Tabby's famously (infamously?) blue eyes aren't blue at all. She has worn color contacts for as long as I can remember, even back when we lived in Rochester. Mom's eyes are blue and Dad's are brown. I took after Mom and Tabby didn't, so she claimed she wanted to match. I used to like it, matching my sister, except the eyes weren't enough for people to think we looked related, and hers were brighter than mine anyway, more electric. Just like she's brighter than me, more electric.

Sometimes I want to tell the media about my sister's brown eyes, just so they'll stop calling her the Blue-Eyed Boyfriend Killer. I hate whoever came up with that. I hate that they reduced her to her appearance. I hate that it's a facet of her appearance that came from a box. I hate that we get judged for changing our looks with things that come from boxes. I hate everything about this.

"The food in here sucks," Tabby says. "But the good news is, I think I'm down a few pounds." She leans back in her chair.

"You don't need to lose weight" is my stock response. Although I'm sure Mark made her feel otherwise. *You could use the exercise.*

"I'm working on my beach body," she says. "For next summer." There's that smirk, the one everyone reads so deeply into. It's just her face. It's just her attempt to find the humor in a situation that is completely not funny. What's so wrong with that? Everyone just wants her to be miserable, a grieving widow. But Tabby was never much for mourning anything. I remember once when she was driving—shortly after she got her license—a bird flew into the windshield and broke its neck. I cried. She didn't.

"What was I supposed to do?" she had said. "Swerve into traffic? That bird had a death wish."

(Don't repeat that story. It'll only make people read into everything more. The way things have been going, that bird will come back from the dead to tell its sob story to a reporter and make Tabby look even worse. *Here's evidence she's a murderer. She didn't hesitate before killing me!*)

"How's school?" she asks now. "I never thought I'd miss it. But being in here is kinda like being there, honestly. The people in here aren't very nice either."

"It's fine." I don't tell her what they're all saying. That some of them are looking at me differently. That sometimes I don't mind, because at least they're looking.

"And cross-country? I know I missed your first meet. I'm sorry." She looks down at her hands. She is sorry. And that's the Tabby nobody else gets to see. My Tabby. The one who remembers every single detail of my life that I deem important, along with details I don't think matter but she somehow knows do.

"Don't be sorry. I won." It's a lie. I didn't win. I didn't even run. But Tabby is here, the one place the truth can't travel. She has no way of knowing—Mom and Dad can't even tell her, because they don't know either.

"Of course you did." Her hands drum on the table in front of us, pale fingers and perfect cuticles, the opposite of my jagged mess. Her nails are painted black. "You know, I'm jealous of you. I always have been. You have all this talent. Your body just knows what to do. It runs. Mine never got the memo."

My mouth is too dry for any words to form. It's a hostile environment, always saying either too much or too little. I just know that there's no way Tabby could ever be jealous of me. She always had more of everything.

"It's not talent," I mumble. "I just work harder than anyone else." It's the truth. They go out and party, drink, smoke, pass out without worrying about the consequences. My life is a routine, structured and disciplined. Lately it feels like a cage.

"You own it, though," Tabby says. "Maybe my problem is I never really worked for anything. If I had, things would have been different. I wouldn't be in here."

But she's lying. I have a feeling Tabby worked at a lot of things. It was making them seem effortless that took so much energy.

"Promise me something," Tabby says. "Just make sure you have your own life outside of them. Outside of boys. Girls. Other people. Because if you let them in too much, you won't be able to see where they end and you begin. You'll lose yourself in the mess."

Our time's up, and I can't ask her what she means by that. Maybe I don't need to, because I already know.

24

BECK

Coldcliff Police Station, October 24, 12:16 p.m.

OFFICER SCHULTZ: You realize what the boot print means.
We have reason to believe you were there that night.
That you and Ms. Cousins had been planning something
together. If we obtain a warrant to search your computer,
what would we find?

BECK: Probably a lot of porn.

OFFICER OLDMAN: Do you have anything else to say,
Thomas?

BECK: Yeah. I need a cigarette.

OFFICER OLDMAN: Now isn't the time for jokes. If you
know something about Tabitha Cousins that the rest of us
don't, this is your opportunity to say it.

BECK: Yeah, I do have something to say. (long pause) She
didn't do anything wrong.

"Blue-Eyed Boyfriend Killer" pleads innocent to murder charge

By Talia Sims

Tabitha Cousins, 17, branded the "Blue-Eyed Boyfriend Killer" after the hiking death of her boyfriend, Mark Forrester, appeared in court yesterday to enter her plea. Cousins tearfully proclaimed her innocence and stated that she loved Forrester deeply. With a makeup-free face and her now-infamous blue eyes filled with tears, Cousins made an emotional statement that she had nothing to do with her boyfriend's death, which shook the town of Coldcliff, Colorado, and has sent the nation into a tailspin.

"Ms. Cousins is determined that the truth will come out," her lawyer, Marnie Deveraux, said in a statement to the press. "My client won't respond to any other questions at this time."

A GoFundMe page has been established by Forrester's family to raise money for aspiring swimmers without financial means to receive coaching. Forrester, a NCAA titleholder for Princeton, was passionate about everyone having the opportunities he did.

While Forrester's immediate family could not be reached for comment, Margot Reed, Forrester's aunt, told *People* that his parents were not doing well in the aftermath of their son's death.

"They're struggling," Reed said. "All because of that girl. And they never even met her. This girl they never knew ruined their lives."

Cousins's family declined our request for an interview.

COMMENTS: (101 previous)

Sparkles: Wow, could this article be more biased toward the poor privileged white boy? How many times do you have to mention he was a swimmer? WE GET IT.

MinutesUP: LOL I was thinking the same thing

Pop_Canzz: Yup. I think Talia Sims has a hard-on for the dead PRINCETON STUDENT (did you guys know he went to Princeton?)

PaintItBlack: You should have seen some of the stuff she posted on Insta what a slut, not surprised the ex BF is involved, sure she opened her legs for that guy and got what she wanted too

Swifty01: Everyone needs to stop pretending like they're detectives and FFS stop slut shaming a girl you don't even know.

Do you realize you've been back for almost a month and we've barely seen each other? Why do I still feel like your long-distance girl-friend? *3:31 p.m.*

Actually I don't even feel like your girlfriend anymore. More like some girl you screw from time to time. *5:57 p.m.*

WHY AREN'T YOU ANSWERING ME? *5:58 p.m.*

You fucked that bitch didn't you? That girl from the party. I know you fucked her. I'd respect you more if you just admitted it. *9:21 p.m.*

Sometimes I think I hate you and I wish we'd never met. *9:22 p.m.*

Text messages from Tabitha Cousins to Mark Forrester, June 28, 2019

When push comes to shove
By Oberon Halton

Here's a plot twist for you! In a video posted to *The Button* yesterday, two people—supposedly Tabitha Cousins and Mark Forrester—were recorded at a party arguing, and at one point, the girl appears to be shoved into the railing of a deck. It's hard to tell if the girl is actually Tabby and the guy Mark. If you read the comments on *The Button*—and we all live for the comments, right?—you'll see that most people do believe it's Tabby, but they think the guy is someone other than Mark. You can really see him only from behind, and let's face it, Mark Forrester was a tall white guy with brown hair, and how common are those?

"I was there that night," a source revealed. "She was flirting with every guy. She and Mark were arguing all night and she kept blowing him off to talk to Beck Rutherford."

Beck Rutherford, who seems to have spawned his own collection of followers around the world (it's the hair, I think), is most certainly not the guy in the video. However, I received an interesting tip claiming that Beck and Mark had an altercation at the same party, although it's unclear whether this was related to whatever takes place in the video.

A perceptive reader also pointed out that the girl in the video—presumably Tabby—goes back to kissing the guy shortly after she hits the railing. Perhaps a lover's spat with Mark? Or with somebody else?

25

LOU

OKAY, THAT VIDEO. Everyone is talking about it, and I'm not sure who took it, but yeah. I'd be the first person to argue that it wasn't Tabby and Mark. Except I was there that night, and I recognize her slutty pleather skirt. And that shirt Mark was wearing, because it's, like, bright pink, except he called it *salmon*.

It has way more views than the one I posted, way back then. When Tabby shoved Lance. I guess I'm starting to think that people only push back when they've already been pushed around.

I don't know. The whole thing has left a bad taste in my mouth. I don't know what to say. Sharp Edges was the first to post about it, of course.

Bridget Cousins is easy to find lately. I don't know if you've noticed, but she's starting to dress more like Tabby. Like, probably stealing stuff from her closet. I guess Tabby isn't around to tell her not to. It's kind of sad, actually. I always wanted a sister, but since my parents didn't even want me, there was a fat chance of that happening.

"Hey," I say when I corner her at her locker. She's actually quite pretty, up close. Not as plain as I always thought. She could probably be beautiful, if she wanted to be. But maybe she wants to be something more. Good for her. I'm sick of the world telling us we have to be pretty in addition to everything else we already are. I'm sick of playing into it.

"What do you want?" she snaps. Her voice—it's *so* similar to Tabby's.

"I saw that video. I mean, did she talk to you about it? About him?"

Bridget leans into her locker. "As if you actually care? You're the one who did everything you could to make her look violent. If it wasn't for you, maybe people would have forgotten about her. You just kept feeding the fire. Now look what happened."

"I'm sorry," I say. I'm not sure if I am, but whatever.

"Mark wasn't a good guy," she says. "Now the rest of the world can see it, too. What's your excuse for him now? You have one, right? Somehow this was her fault, too? Or are you one of the people saying it wasn't him, and that it was one of the many other guys she was fucking around with?"

She turns and storms away. She's wearing heels—they must be Tabby's, I'm sure they wear the same shoe size—and can't quite walk in them properly.

And I'm left wondering if I'm one of those people after all.

26

ELLE

I TOOK IT ON MY PHONE. I don't even know why. It was too dark that night to see much anyway, and you can barely make out that it's Tabby and Mark. But maybe the only way to fight their fire is to come back with our own. Besides, I'm the reason this happened. I'm the one who started the tidal wave and sucked Tabby into every current.

I'm the source. I'm the one who sent that video to the *Button*. People can think what they want. I guess I should have known they'd jump to defend the blurry shadow they're trying to say isn't even Mark and could be any guy.

But I was there. I saw it. He pushed her on purpose. Yes, she was yelling, but so was he.

Maybe when they were on the Split, he tried to do the same thing. He pushed. And she pushed back.

If she did, can you really blame her? What would you have done?

No, honestly. Think about it. Think about being that high up. You're probably already scared of heights, so there's that. And the person you're with takes up more space than you do. And he's raging, and his arms are outstretched, and they make contact with you, just for a second. Do your arms go up to protect yourself? Is it fight, or literal flight?

Because the more I think about it, the more I believe somebody had to go over the edge that day. And if it hadn't been Mark, it would have been Tabby.

The video is from the last party I had over the summer. I

made a Facebook event and left it open so anyone could come. Everyone did, even Keegan. I thought maybe he wouldn't, after what happened at Umbrage. Girls always have to carry the awkward aftermath. Girls carry everything. Boys are unburdened, uncomplicated, mouths slack-jawed and empty, all the promises and lies already dried up and used on someone else.

Almost eleven—I know because I checked my phone—I went upstairs, and I heard them in the backyard. My window was open and I looked down and there they were, skulking around each other, pacing like two lions. Tabby and Mark.

"You're always controlling me," Tabby yelled. "I'm not your puppet."

"I wouldn't have to control you if you would just tell me the truth," Mark said, his voice calm and measured.

"I told you the truth already. He's just a friend."

I cupped my hand over my mouth. Mark knew. He knew about Beck. I remembered Tabby and I, drunk, when she and Mark first got together. *He doesn't need to know anything about my past, so don't tell him, okay?*

"You ruined my life," Mark said, still eerily calm. Then he bent over her, hands on her shoulders, and shoved her backward, into the railing on the deck, the same one that wobbled whenever anyone touched it. I got out my phone and started recording—my body did it instinctively. He shoved her again, then kissed her, his hands quickening up to her face. She pulled away, then he had the back of her head in the palm of one hand—such a huge, meaty thing, capable of so little and so much. In that moment I pictured Tabby's skull like something fragile, a robin's egg, and Mark cracking it in his clenched fist.

That was the first time I considered that Mark could kill Tabby.

She would fight back, of course, just like she was fighting now, scrappy and emotional, words sputtering out between tears.

I couldn't make out what she was saying, and maybe neither could he. Then they were interrupted by someone Mark knew and suddenly both of their faces changed, and it was like they were never arguing at all. Mark's arm went back to its regular post on Tabby's shoulders and her smile formed, like her face knew exactly what to do.

They were both so good at pretending. Then again, it's a survival skill, when you're a girl, seventeen.

27

KEEGAN

I DON'T KNOW WHAT you expect me to say about the video, except I know Mark had a lot to drink that night. Not that I'm making excuses for the guy. I don't know what happened between them because I wasn't part of their relationship.

Here's the thing. Even if he did that—if it was him in the video—did he deserve to die?

Everything starts to feel the same. Maybe Mark was sick of it. Maybe I get it. I'm at a party with Kyla right now and it's like Groundhog Day, because it's like every other party. Kyla wears too much perfume. She dances with a couple of her friends, then comes back to me and presses herself against me.

"Maybe we should go back to your place," she says. I stiffen against her.

"Maybe we should get out of town," I say. "Go somewhere else. Just get the hell out of here, you know."

She pulls back. "What are you talking about, Keegan? Why would we get out of town?"

I focus on the pinch of her eyebrows, then laugh. "Just fucking around. There's nowhere else I'd rather be."

Now she's staring at me like she doesn't know me, and that much is true. She doesn't. The only person who really did is gone now.

233

28

BECK

Coldcliff Police Station, November 2, 5:28 p.m.

OFFICER OLDMAN: Let's talk about the party at Eleanor Ross's house, where you assaulted Mark Forrester. A video has surfaced from that night. Did the altercation in the video have anything to do with your assault?

BOBBY GOOD: Go ahead.

BECK: (laughs) That wasn't assault. That was two guys having a conversation. I have no idea what the video is all about.

OFFICER OLDMAN: Several sources say they saw you go up to Mark and assault him. He had a bruise on his cheek after.

BECK: Yeah, the guy bruised like a peach. That's not my fault. I barely touched him.

OFFICER OLDMAN: What would compel you to walk up to someone you claim you barely knew, and had no vendetta against, and lay hands on him? Did you think you were defending Tabby?

BECK: We just had some business to clear up. That's between him and me.

OFFICER OLDMAN: Business about Tabby. She's the only thing you had in common, right?

BECK: Just business. He got in my face. Kind of pushed me backward. So I got back in his face. I don't just stand there and take someone's shit like that.

OFFICER OLDMAN: Afterward, you left the party, is that right? Where did you go?

BECK: I don't remember. There are lots of parties. I probably got on my bike and just rode.

OFFICER OLDMAN: Maybe you rode to Queen Anne's Woods.

BECK: No. I'm not really much of an outdoor guy.

OFFICER OLDMAN: We have hikers who said a boy fitting your description and a girl fitting Tabitha's were seen together in the woods after dark on more than one occasion.

BOBBY GOOD: That's pure speculation.

BECK: Must have been someone who looked like me.

OFFICER OLDMAN: This would go a lot smoother if you just let me know the real reason why you assaulted Mark at that party. Was it because of what happened in the video?

BECK: The only person who could have answered that is Mark. And from what I hear, he's not doing much talking.

Alleged boyfriend killer to reportedly tell all in upcoming interview
By Beth Caan

Rumors are swirling that Tabitha Cousins, who goes on trial later this month for the murder of her boyfriend, former Princeton swimming star Mark Forrester, may have agreed to a jailhouse interview from Springs Juvenile Detention Center, where she's currently being held. Sources allege that Cousins wants to tell her side of the story and clear up the rumors. News networks would likely enter a bidding war for the chance to speak with Cousins, 17.

A source close to Cousins tells the *Alloyed News* exclusively that "Tabitha is the only one who really knows what happened that day, and she wants to tell the truth. She has nothing to hide."

You make me feel like less than nothing and that is not okay.

Text message from Tabitha Cousins to Mark Forrester,
July 29, 2019, 1:17am

Interview request denied for alleged boyfriend killer
By Mason Livingston

An interview granted by Tabitha Cousins and her lawyer, Marnie Deveraux, reportedly to *Hello America*, was denied by the Colorado Springs Bureau of Prisons on Friday and will not go forward. Anne Leon, who was in talks to interview Cousins, previously stated that Cousins would bare all about her high-profile case and leave no doubt that what happened to her boyfriend, Mark Forrester, was an accident. The world will now have to wait until Cousins's trial, later this month, to hear what really happened that day in the woods.

29

LOU

WE WERE GOING TO HAVE a viewing party for the interview, just like we do for *The Bachelor* when it's on, just me and a few girlfriends and some of my mom's rosé. But now it's not happening, and I'm kind of relieved. I mean, what kind of girl wants to give an interview, which millions of people will watch, just to say she didn't do it? The kind who wants attention. The Tabitha Cousins kind.

I almost, *almost* started to feel sorry for her. But stunts like this remind me that even if she's innocent of Mark's death, she's guilty in other ways. She's a taker. She takes what she wants, no matter who wanted it first. She took Blanche and she wanted to take Beck and now here she is with the world in her lap like a new toy, and I'm sure she'll want more than it can give her, too.

When my mom came home last night, I asked her who she'd been with. I do that, sometimes, just to see if she looks guilty. I mean, if there's one thing I have in common with my mom, it's that we're both good at reading people.

"I saw a patient" was all she said. But I didn't believe her.

So today, when she's in the shower, I sneak into her home office. Well, I don't even have to sneak, because she leaves the door open and her laptop is on, and she has these documents up on the screen. It takes me a couple minutes to figure out that I'm reading a patient's file, a real-life person. Somebody seriously fucked up, I might add. Someone's life in sections: HISTORY, MENTAL STATUS, DIAGNOSES, RECOMMENDATIONS. *History of trou-*

239

ble with boys. Quick to anger. Quick to defend herself. Resistant to therapy. Likes to talk to me about my life, as if we're friends. Has not wavered in recollection of events on August 16. Known history of manipulation.

When I don't hear the shower anymore, I click the screen back to where it was and get out of the room. There's a picture of us on her desk, me and her and my dad, from Before. Maybe everyone's life is split into Before and After. Before one person goes and ruins everything. Before my mom cheated, she told me things, and I told her things. After, she's this big mess of secrets.

The name on that file. *T. Cousins.* How long has my mom been seeing Tabitha? And what are her recommendations for a girl like that?

I pull on my coat and leave the house before I have to talk to her or hear any more of her bullshit. I'm never going to figure out anything by asking my mom. She'll say something about *patient confidentiality*, but maybe it's just in her genetic code to protect another fuckup, another girl who will probably grow into somebody just like her.

Maybe I'm wrong, and Tabby isn't the problem. Maybe everyone else around her is. Maybe Beck is. (Okay, he definitely is, because he broke up with me. Ugh.) And as much as he's an asshole, I can't forget how scared he looked that day on my porch. He genuinely thinks he could go to jail, and I might be the only person who can figure out the truth in time to stop that from happening. Except I can't do it alone.

Keegan's at the Stop & Shop, just like I knew he would be. I'm hoping he's not one of those lifer types, then I realize I don't actually care. He's not my problem. None of this is. But I'm making it my problem anyway, because I need to know.

"Keegan Leach," I say. He kind of eyes me up and down,

totally slimy. I wonder if he thinks I'm hot. I'm definitely not his usual party type.

"What do you want?" he says.

"Same thing as you," I say. "I want her to get what she deserves."

30

ELLE

WE STOPPED BEING A FOURSOME pretty shortly after Mark's birthday party, which Tabby convinced me to host at my house so everyone could use the pool. Keegan—who wasn't even at the party—suddenly had this blond girl hanging all over him on Instagram, and they started hanging out with Tabby and Mark, and I got boxed out. Four's company, five's a crowd. Which meant instead of seeing Tabby almost every day, I barely saw her at all.

Keegan gave me a parting gift, though. I went to the Stop & Shop and ended up in his checkout lane since it was the only one open. I was content to act like strangers, but he had another idea.

"They need to break up," he said. "They're toxic. I've tried. Tell her you saw him kissing another girl at your last party. Just tell her, and she'll believe you."

My last party. Mark's birthday. I wondered if Keegan was absent for a different reason than just avoiding me.

"I'm not going to lie to her." I crossed my arms. "It's a lie, right?"

He didn't answer, just told me I owed eleven seventy-six and asked how I'd be paying.

I don't know what went on between the four of them, if they went on double dates, or stayed home and watched movies, or retreated to different rooms to make out. I didn't know if I cared. I saw the monogrammed wedding napkins in my head. *Keegan and Kyla.* I wondered how long they knew each other before his hand went to her bare leg, drawn to all that flesh like some kind of magnet.

It's pathetic to admit, but I wanted school to start again. I wanted Mark to go back to Princeton and Keegan to disappear from our lives, because they came as a package deal. I wanted it to be me and Tabby again. I'd have the real Tabby, not the phony version who took her place. The last few times I saw her, she was acting totally weird, like she was being programmed to say certain things. *We did this* and *we did that*. She never had time for me.

Mark was leaving for Princeton on August twenty-sixth. I marked—no pun intended—it in my calendar, a countdown, like I used to do for Christmas as a kid. It wasn't him leaving that I needed so much as Tabby returning.

There were three weeks to go in the countdown when my phone started vibrating in the middle of the night. I always kept it adjacent to my pillow when I slept, like it was my pet or something. I guess I didn't want to miss anything important.

With sleep-blurred eyes, I swiped the screen. I figured it was a text. Nobody ever called me. Even Tabby barely texted anymore, preferring to Snap, preferring that all of our conversations vanish. But it was a call, and it was from her, and when I picked up, her voice was desperate and panicked.

"Hey," she said. "I really need to see you, okay? Everything's just so messed up and I don't know what to do."

"Slow down," I said. "Where are you? What happened?"

"I'm in your front yard. Can you come down and let me in?"

I crept down the stairs and into the foyer. As soon as I unlocked the door she was inside, breathing heavy, eyes and hair wild. She had been crying.

"What happened?" I whispered. "What did he do?"

She shook her head, clung to me, buried her face in the shoulder of my T-shirt. "What didn't he do?"

I led her upstairs, as if she hadn't been here before, and the two of us got into my bed, just like we did when we were younger and had sleepovers, even though Tabby used to bring a sleeping bag and roll it onto the floor. She always got cold. She always needed to be close.

"What happened tonight?" I said again when we were tucked under the duvet, her cigarette-and-alcohol smell sharp. "Tell me everything."

She stared at the ceiling with glassy eyes. "We talked about this summer," she said, and it was as if those words dried up her tears, because her voice stopped being broken. "We talked about being together. Everything's just so messed up, and I don't know what to do."

"Break up with him," I said. The words I had been dying to say for weeks, months, shooting off my tongue like darts. "He doesn't deserve you."

She laughed, a crescendo sound that I was afraid would wake up my parents. "Break up with him. We're not even together."

Mark's social media. How her face was barely on it. How it was like she ceased to exist in his public life. Tabby, his dirty little secret, the place his dick camped out for the summer. He was going back to parties and nameless girls in college classrooms who cheered at his swim meets and followed him to bars with their fake IDs. He didn't need Tabby anymore.

"I need to tell you something," I blurted out, not even sure exactly how I was going to say it. "I saw Mark. Kissing a girl at his birthday party. I don't even know who she was. I wanted to tell you, but I didn't know how."

"It's not true," she said. "He wouldn't do that to me."

"I'm sorry," I whispered. "But you can find someone who really loves you."

She rolled away from me, curled into a ball, and I thought she was asleep, but I know what I heard next. *I already have.* I stared at her back, at the white curve of her neck, and she didn't look breakable anymore, not like porcelain but something that wouldn't shatter. And the next morning when I woke up, she was gone, and I wondered if I made the whole night up.

Excerpt from Tabby's Diary

August 6, 2019

It's like all of my worst nightmares are coming true. I trust Elle, and she told me she saw Mark kissing another girl. He couldn't even wait to leave the party to do it. She thinks I should break up with him, but it's not that easy. It never is.

Cheaters never prosper . . .
By Oberon Halton

. . . but they don't deserve to die either.

So apparently there's proof out there that Mark was a cheater. It's in some Instagram photos that have since been deleted (although somebody was wise enough to take some screenshots before the account was taken down—thank you, friend)! I've seen the photos, and I must say, he does look awfully cozy, not just with the Madeleine girl everyone is pouncing on, but some other girls, too. And this was posted out there for everybody to see. Almost like he was daring Tabby to notice and do something about it. Now Tabby is being made out to be a girl with a serious jealous streak, on top of everything else.

One of our readers wrote in privately in response to my last article. He or she asked to remain nameless, but suggested that Tabby might have been so aggressively on Mark about cheating because she was doing the same thing to him, and it was an attempt to save face.

Readers, weigh in—how far have you gone to avenge a cheating boyfriend or girlfriend? What's the punishment they really deserve?

COMMENTS

DarkRoastCoffee: Tabby was definitely cheating on Mark. The question isn't whether or not she was. The question is with how many guys, because I don't think it was just with Beck.

31

BRIDGET

I GUESS I SHOULD MENTION what I said to Mark the last time I saw him, because that's what Stewart wanted to talk to me about. Let me clarify: I don't feel bad about what I said. But I think it's important, what he said back to me.

It was the day we all went to the beach. I don't even know why I was invited, or why I went along. I was supposed to do ten miles, then head to the playground near the woods for chin-ups on the bars there and triceps dips. I was convinced it was my arms holding me back. If I could make them stronger, I would dominate cross-country season. Everyone thinks running is in your legs, but it's even more in your arms, because they dictate what the rest of your body does. They make the decisions.

But there was Tabby, smelling like sunscreen, floppy hat on, dark circles under her eyes. I heard her sneak in again last night. It seemed like she didn't need any sleep at all that summer, like she was running on something else entirely. Driving to the beach, things felt normal. We sang along to Taylor Swift and ate Swedish Fish and I stuck my feet up on the dashboard, which Mom never let us do. *If you get in an accident, your leg will end up going through your body*, she used to say, except she didn't know that Tabby and I were untouchable.

We were the first ones there, spreading out our towels, burying our feet in the sand.

"There are the boys," Tabby said, waving them over. Mark and Keegan, shiny chests, matching navy swim trunks, almost like they had planned it. Mark looked better in his, more chiseled, as if he had spent his whole summer at the pool.

They sat down next to us, Tabby and Mark exchanging a kiss that lasted too long to be in public. I suddenly felt out of place, juvenile and babyish, a kid sitting with a bunch of adults. Tabby's body filled out her bikini, and there was the tail of her ivy tattoo, the one she got freshman year that our parents still somehow didn't know about, creeping up her back. I was flat-chested and skinny, hard like leather, hair limp and face plain.

"There's Kyla," Keegan said, and he jumped up, shielding his face against the sun as a blond girl headed our way. She broke into a run as she got closer, leaped into his arms, her legs hooked around him as he held her. *Why am I here?* I wanted to ask Tabby. *Why am I on your double date?*

"We should go in the water," Mark said. "Come on, Tabby."

"I'm not hot yet," she said. "I need to get hot first." She stretched out, fanning her hands over her stomach.

I looked around us. You hear *beach* and think of this glamorous place, tight bodies and Frisbees flying around and waves coming in, but Crest Beach is a joke. A tiny strip of sand, a rocky shoreline, crushed beer cans left behind. I hated that I gave up my workout to be here, that I let myself get derailed for a day. Maybe that was how Mark felt about my sister, and for just a second, I felt sorry for him for meeting her.

"Come on," Mark said, hovering over my sister's face. "You could use the exercise, babe."

Then I didn't feel sorry for him anymore.

"Give her a break," Keegan said. "Look at the waves, dude. They're too big for swimming today."

It had stormed last night, hard rain beating against the roof. The water was the color of mud and the waves were churning against the shoreline, pulling rocks back out with them.

"They're not big," Mark said, cocky, so sure of himself. "They're baby waves. I'm gonna go on my own." He stood up, kicked off his flip-flops.

"If you start drowning, don't expect anyone to save you," I said.

They all heard it. My eyes were locked on Mark, but I felt their heads turn. Tabby laughed, a weak sound, and then so did everyone else, because that's what it was, a joke. Except it wasn't a joke, and I didn't mean it to be funny at all.

Mark knew it wasn't a joke. He didn't laugh, but he smiled, and standing there in the sun, his perfect white teeth suddenly looked like fangs. He could rip her apart, I realized. In a thousand ways, and hide all the pieces, so that we'd never find her again. I was already having trouble finding her, even though she was sitting right next to me, one of her sandy feet touching my elbow.

"You know I had four scholarship offers for swimming, right? You know I've spent more of my summer in the pool than out of it? That's the last way I would go." He looked at all of us, then honed in on me. "Be careful of the undertow. It can really pull you out." Then he was gone, jogging toward the water line, all pumping muscles.

"Bridge," Tabby said when he was gone. "What the hell was that?"

"He threatened me. Did you not hear that? Be careful of the undertow. It can really pull you out. Is that not menacing?"

Keegan and Kyla weren't listening anymore. She was rubbing sunscreen into his back like a mother does to a little kid. Tabby turned toward me, so close that our faces were almost touching under her floppy hat. "He was just telling you to be careful. He used to work as a lifeguard in high school, so he just doesn't want to see you get hurt."

"You're always defending him. Don't you get sick of it?"

It was like a hush fell over the whole beach. Everyone could hear us. But I needed to know the answer, even if I should have asked a long time ago.

Tabby's fingers were twitching. She needed a cigarette. I didn't know where that bad habit came from, because I at least knew it didn't come from Mark, Mr. Wholesome, Mr. Lean Protein and Vegetables. She was hunting around in her head for a lie, not just any lie, but one that could shut me up. I searched around my own brain for a rebuttal, but it turned out, I didn't need one.

"Yeah," she said softly, for my ears alone. "I guess sometimes I do."

Whatever I was about to say next died on my tongue. I watched Mark power through the water, his arms moving like he was part of a machine, legs a blur of churned brown water. I wished an undertow would find him, like a self-fulfilling prophecy. The swimming champion, drowned in a muddy lake. It had a kind of poetic justice to it. People would call it a waste, like they always did when a boy died. But when a girl does it, there's always blame spliced in with the mourning, reasons why it was her fault. *She drank too much. She was trying to show off.* I willed the lake to swallow Mark, the same lake where we learned to water ski when we were kids.

The lake didn't listen. It brought Mark back safely to shore. But that was one of the last times I would ever see him alive.

32

ELLE

I GUESS IT WAS ONLY a matter of time until Dallas showed up at my house. And here he is, sitting on the porch, holding flowers. It's not the flowers that make me want to curl into a ball and cry. It's his face, open and earnest, more than I deserve after I've been anything but.

"Sorry to be a stalker," he says. "But you wouldn't talk to me. I'm not mad about—you know, Elle. I'm just—I wish you would have let me be there for you." He stands up.

He wasn't there, because he didn't know about it. But Tabby knew, and she was there. The morning of, she met me at my house after Mom left for work. She noticed me shivering and took off her own sweatshirt—Mark's Princeton one—and slipped it over my tank top, pulling my arms through the sleeves like I was a small child. I felt as lost and helpless as one.

When we got to the clinic, I pulled up the hood.

It's me in the photo, the dark-haired girl in the Princeton sweatshirt. Tabby let me out and went to park the car, since traffic made us late, and it was an appointment I didn't want to miss. I have no idea who took that photo, but everyone assumed it was Tabby, hair spilling out of the orange hood. And when the photo appeared online—it was her idea to let everyone believe that.

"Let them judge me," she said. "Let them think whatever they want about me. You deserve better."

So it became Tabby's baby. Tabby's abortion. Tabby's judgment. She was a martyr, all in the name of our friendship. I should have been grateful. I should still be grateful. But a tiny splinter of me resents her, because it's always all about Tabby. She has this way of making everything about herself, even a problem that wasn't hers to solve.

But Dallas—he knew it was me the whole time. That first text he sent—*I'd recognize you anywhere, why didn't you let me be there?* I was angry. He made it all about him, just like Tabby made it about her. And it was about me. My body, which suddenly felt foreign to me.

I shouldn't have let Tabby step into my life and lie for me. She was upset that I didn't tell her about Dallas—she thought we made out sometimes, but that I was still a virgin. *Why didn't you tell me?* That was the first thing she said, all hurt—do you see, how she makes things all about her?

I'm sick of people and their constant *why didn't you.* I'm sick of not having an answer. Maybe I wanted a slice of my life to be private from Tabby. Then she stepped in and shouldered my pain and look what happened. I made the choice not to have a baby. I made Tabby swear not to tell anyone, and she didn't. Not even Mark, when he asked, *If it wasn't you, who was it?* She let the secret fester, the infection sear the skin of their relationship. If I had just told everyone it was me, maybe a lot of things would have been different.

I've spent so much time thinking I don't deserve anything good. I've wanted what I couldn't have. I wanted my best friend's boyfriend, and when I couldn't have him, I made sure she couldn't either. But here, closing the gap between me and Dallas, I just want to be hugged. I just want someone to love me anyway.

His mouth finds my hair. "I'm not going anywhere, unless you want me to."

And in this moment, I don't.

33

LOU

I'M AN INDOOR KITTEN—you probably already got that vibe from me? Well, it's true. I hate being outside. It's always windy, which messes up my hair, and the bugs are gross, and yet here I am, walking in the woods with some guy I don't know at all, looking for everything and nothing. And let me tell you, it's creepy in here. The trees pretty much close in above you, so there's almost no light, and all I have is the flashlight on my iPhone. It's totally disconcerting, because I have no clue what time of day it actually is right now.

I'm not sure if I'm surprised or not that Keegan agreed to come with me. It actually seemed like he was expecting me to come back to the store, like it was a relief I asked. Maybe it's because I told him I needed his help. When you want something from a boy and you bring the word "need" into it, they're, like, a hundred percent more likely to help you. It's engrained in their DNA to be heroes.

He is kind of a hero right now, though, because he has a map. I didn't think of printing one out, but obviously it's a good idea, because I have no idea how anyone gets around in here, and right now it's daytime. If I didn't hate Tabitha so much, I'd almost feel bad for her for being stuck in here after dark.

There's a group of people who look a bit older than me, probably in college, who pass us coming back the other way. They're all holding maps, too, and I catch a snippet of their conversation. *This is where she must have run after.* I heard about this online—the woods are becoming, like, infamous by association.

People are running tour groups up to the Split to see the scene of the crime. *Outwit the Split*. Someone pointed out that it's good for downtown business, people wanting to see Tabby's "haunts." When I was on Insta the other day, I actually saw a Tabby and Beck Halloween costume. I wish I was kidding. And this is why I need to clear his name.

"What exactly are we looking for?" Keegan asks. "Because you know if there was something here, the cops would have found it, right?"

"Maybe not," I say. "I just think we need to look for ourselves. I mean, you knew Mark better than anyone." *And I know Beck better than anyone.*

I'm not sure why I didn't think of coming here sooner. I mean, it's so obvious. I know this case has become huge and all, but cops and detectives miss things all the time. Imagine if I could be the one to *Outwit the Split*, so to speak. Imagine how surprised Beck would be.

Although honestly, this isn't really about him.

It's about me, and that need to know. I hate a story without a good ending.

Keegan kind of grunts, and we keep walking. All the other hikers and wannabe case crackers seem to have disappeared, and the deeper in we get, the more I miss the sounds of voices. Every sound—branches clattering, acorns falling—makes me jump.

Seriously, I don't believe in ghosts. But this is super creepy. And it's getting more closed in. My legs are getting all scraped through my pants. I saw the photos of Tabby online, when she was first called a "survivor" and "lucky." Shorts, dirty legs, cross-hatched by cuts. They even showed her shoes, which I remember because I have the same pink Nikes. She said they belonged to her sister. I remember they didn't even look pink, more like a dark red.

Dark red, because they were wet.

Yes, they found a footprint. But did anyone ask why her shoes were wet? Because she said she ran back down from the Split the same way they came up. She had a huge gash running up one arm, which was apparently from trying to climb down the rocks fast. How did I not notice that sooner?

"Her shoes," I say suddenly to Keegan. "Did you see them? They were wet. This sounds weird, but I have the same ones, and hers looked different in all the photos. Because they were wet."

"Okay," Keegan says. "So what?"

"So it wasn't raining that day, and she said herself that she didn't go down to the creek, because she couldn't see in the dark. But they found a footprint, and her shoes were wet."

She never went down to the creek to see if Mark was okay. She claimed she didn't know how to get down there and it was getting dark and she was scared. Then later on, she changed her story a bit. She felt like somebody was behind her, chasing her out of the woods. She swore she heard breathing.

"I don't know," Keegan says. "Maybe she stepped in a puddle or something."

But the woods are, like, bone-dry. There are just crunchy leaves under our feet. I think it rained a couple days ago, but there's no evidence of it here.

"We're not actually going all the way up, are we?" Keegan asks. "I wore the wrong shoes for that." He stares at his Converse.

"We're retracing their steps," I say. "So yeah, duh. If other people can do it, we can, too." But seriously, I wonder how long it will be until somebody has an accident around here. One of those khaki-clad tourists with a map who wants to know where the Blue-Eyed Boyfriend Killer did it. Then Tabby will be responsible for even more people dying.

Here's where it gets steep, and we have to climb more than hike. I can't believe people do this for fun. My fingernails are, like, destroyed already. Keegan is actually really good at this and keeps reaching for my hand so he can pull me up, which is kind of nice. I'm sure Beck would have been more preoccupied with his cigarettes.

I have no idea how long it takes us to clamber up to the top, but I'm glad Keegan is here, because I don't know if I could have made it up alone. And now I'm wondering how much Mark helped Tabby. If he pulled her up, like Keegan is pulling me up, and if she knew the whole time that she was going to push him over the edge, or if she did it in the heat of the moment. I guess no matter what Keegan and I find today, we'll never know. Only two people will ever know, and one of them is dead.

When we're at the top, it doesn't seem like there's enough room for two people. I'm out of breath—apparently I'm not in very good shape—but Keegan is just standing there, looking over the edge.

"Don't get too close," I say.

"Why?" he says. "Are you planning on pushing me?"

It dawns on me that he could push *me*. I mean, we barely know each other, and now we're at the last place his best friend was ever alive, so he could snap any second, really. Also, it's terrifying because I feel like this whole slab could give out from under us. It's just this giant rock jutting out, like it doesn't belong. I read somewhere that it used to be called the Giant's Thumb, which somehow morphed into the Split.

It didn't look this high from the ground, but it sure does from up here. Down below, there are the rocks that must have practically cracked Mark's head apart. I have no idea how that didn't kill him. They're like this row of jagged teeth, biting through the water. And he had that backpack on, so he probably hit the rocks before he even knew what was happening.

The water down there is pretty stagnant. Maybe Tabby hoped Mark would conveniently wash out into a bigger lake and his body would disappear, but it's not like the current moves very fast. From up here, it kind of looks like a giant slug, right down to the brownish-green color. Mark must have tried to get out of the water, fought his way out of the backpack. I pretend I'm Tabby, seeing him get up, rushing back down.

Then I take a deep breath like I'm in yoga class, and that's when I feel Keegan's hand on my back.

"What the hell?" I snap, backing up so fast I'm afraid I'm going to fall the other way—back down the rocky slope we came up. He puts both hands up, like he's being arrested.

"Whoa, chill. I just said you shouldn't get so close to the edge. Did you not hear me? I don't need another dead body on my conscience."

I cross my arms, rub them where goose bumps have erupted. "Why is Mark's body on your conscience? You're not the one who shoved him."

He scratches his head. He's better looking up close, I decide. He has some freckles on his nose that I bet he hated when he was younger. "No, but it's complicated. I knew Tabby was bad for him, and I had a feeling something was going to happen on that hike, and I didn't say anything."

"Well, would it have mattered if you did? People in relationships only hear what they want to hear." I don't know why I'm trying to console him, but he's kind of pathetic, and I guess I know what that feels like, being kind of pathetic.

"Maybe," he says, but he has this faraway look, like he isn't really listening.

I stare at the view again. That's why people come up here—for the view. You can see some mountains in the distance, which I guess is nice, but honestly, I don't understand the hype. Why put your body through all this just to see everything from high up? I'd much rather spend my life at eye level.

"There's nothing here," I say. I seriously have no idea what I expected. A note scrawled into the rock, or some sort of lipstick kiss from Tabby's victory? But it's all flat and stark and there's absolutely nothing here except the ghost of Mark Forrester. I'm not spiritual or anything, but there's this creepy vibe up here, and I want to get away from it.

"Yeah," Keegan says. "We should go."

I can't decide if he sounds disappointed or relieved.

Getting down is terrifying. I'm sure I'm going to die, and what a huge waste that would be. Tabby would definitely get the last laugh. I manage to scrape up my legs a bunch more times, which I'm sure will look lovely the next time I'm wearing a skirt.

To get to the creek from the trail, you have to cut through this patch of really tall grass, which is slimy and feels like it's licking my legs. Keegan hangs behind. "I don't want to get my shoes wet," he says, but I suspect the real reason, and it's not like I can blame him. He doesn't want to have the mental picture of Mark, dead in the creek, become any more vivid than I'm sure it already is in his head.

A snapping sound makes me jump, and when I look up, I immediately crouch back down, swallowing the scream I want to let out. Because Tabby is standing across the creek, on the other side, staring into the water, hood over her head, which is impossible, but here she is. I have no idea if she saw me but I know what she's capable of doing to someone she supposedly loved, so I don't want to know what she's capable of doing to someone she doesn't like at all.

Did I miss something? Did she escape juvie? Was there a breaking news story since we've been in the woods that I didn't see? I whip out my phone, remembering Tabby's excuse that hers was out of power, and that's why she didn't call for help. I'm getting full reception and my battery is charged, but no Google alerts come up about Tabby's case.

I watch through the reeds as Tabby's hood comes down and I realize it isn't her at all. Duh. There's no tumble of black hair, the hair she obviously dyed from a box to get that dark. No, this girl isn't Tabby, but someone wearing her sweatshirt. Someone wearing Mark's Princeton sweatshirt. It's Elle Ross.

I put my hand over my mouth when I realize what it means. The girl walking into the clinic with her hood pulled up wasn't Tabby either. It was Elle. I mean, I should have figured it out sooner. I lend my clothes to my girlfriends all the time, and some of those bitches never give them back. Elle had the sweatshirt. Elle got an abortion. I started a rumor about the wrong girl.

And Tabby let me.

I have no idea what all this means. What it means that Elle is here, across the creek, staring into the water, like she wants something to emerge from it. I mean, how well does she know her way around these woods?

Part of me wants to ask her. I mean, wouldn't you? But there's a creek between us, and besides, I know what these woods are capable of hiding, and what the girls who go into them are capable of doing. So I stay hidden. On my hands and knees, I creep back through the tall grass and weeds until not just my shoes are soaked but pretty much everything from the waist up. And when I'm far enough away, I start to run, just like Tabby apparently did that night.

"Hey," Keegan says. "Hey, slow down. What's going on? You're going the wrong way."

I don't tell him about Elle. I don't ask him why he knows his way through the woods, why everyone but me seems to be able to find their way out.

Excerpt from Tabby's Diary

August 13, 2019

Mark wants to go on a hike. I don't really know why. For some reason, the thought of being alone in the woods with him is kind of scary. Not that he'd ever do anything to me. I guess I'm just afraid of what he wants to say that he needs to take me that far into the woods to hear.

34

BRIDGET

I TELL MY PARENTS I'm going to Laurel's, because they have no reason to believe otherwise. They think we're having a sleepover, that we'll stay up watching movies and eating popcorn, because they still see me as a little girl.

But tonight, I'm someone else.

I'm dressed in a skirt and low-cut tank top I grabbed from Tabby's closet. I'm teetering in a pair of her wedge heels. I'm wearing her red lipstick and my eyes are sooty with her makeup, bordered with the eyeliner she rarely went without. It doesn't look half bad, thanks to the power of YouTube tutorials. I expected to look in the mirror and see someone ridiculous. An imposter. But instead, I see a girl who could seize the world in her clenched fist and mold it into whatever shape she wants.

I changed at Laurel's. She stares at me with wide eyes and it's like I'm older than her all of a sudden, older and wiser, and she's far away, in the safety of my shadow, trembling in the shade. Maybe that's how Tabby felt around me. Maybe that's how she felt around everyone.

"Are you sure this is a good idea?" she says. "I mean, I should come with you."

"No." I shake my head. My newly straightened hair bounces, the ends almost grazing my shoulders. "I need to do this alone."

I told Laurel I was meeting someone who might have information about my sister, and I am, but it's not exactly like that. I'm meeting someone who knew Mark better than anyone, and I'm going to wring the truth out of him. Because that's the secret

Tabby wanted me to keep. Her voice in my ear, low and measured. *They should be looking at Keegan. He didn't love Mark as much as everyone thinks.*

He works at the Stop & Shop. He has scanned our groceries more than once, me in line with my parents, Mom always forgetting to bring in the reusable bags that live in the trunk of her car. He looks perpetually bored and always shoves too much into every bag so that by the time we get home, cereal box corners poke through and peaches roll onto the counter.

Today, I buy one thing. A card. SORRY FOR YOUR LOSS it reads in loopy cursive. He looks at me as he picks it up off the conveyor belt and maybe he sees the resemblance, maybe not. Maybe it doesn't matter. Pretty girls all look the same to him.

"Five ninety-six," he says, pretending he doesn't know who I am. "Cash, credit, or debit?"

"When's your break?" I try to make my voice deeper, more breathy. Something changes on his face. I don't know boys. I don't know if the change means he's interested or doesn't care.

"Uh, I don't have one. But I'm done with my shift in half an hour. Why, what do you want?"

"I'm Tabby's sister," I say. "Bridget."

"Yeah. I know. So what do you want from me?"

"I want to talk about what my sister did to Mark."

He gapes at me, openmouthed. I fight the urge to squirm.

"Okay," he says. "Yeah, I guess so. It's not very busy. We can just talk now."

"No," I say. "This can't be in public. Can we go back to your place?" It's a question, but I make it sound like an order.

His eyes dart down the front of my shirt, to where a Victoria's Secret bra has managed to pinch together my nonexistent cleavage. "Okay, fine. As long as you don't mind hanging around here until we close."

I stare at my knees. I've always hated them—they're too big for my legs. But maybe Keegan doesn't care. Everything my parents ever told me screams in my head. *Don't talk to strangers. Never go on a date that isn't in a public place. Never go on a date, period.*

"That's fine," I say.

This is for Tabby. For answers. I don't care about the rest.

I don't even have to get into a car with him, because his place is right around the corner. It's a shitty little walk-up, and I trail him up the stairs and down a skinny hall that smells like takeout and cat piss. I try to picture Tabby making this walk—maybe with Mark, maybe without—and somehow know she never did. Not my sister.

Boy crazy, Mom called her—I heard her say it the other night to Dad. "She got too involved with these boys and lost herself." Those were her exact words, dramatic and tear-soaked. I know Mom has been reading all of the articles because she leaves her computer open sometimes without closing her internet tabs. Tabby isn't home and her own mother is replacing her with the girl in those articles. The Blue-Eyed Boyfriend Killer, reduced to body parts.

"Sorry, it's a mess in here," Keegan says as he opens his door. When we're both inside, I'm very aware that we're both inside, and he could do something to me, if he wanted, and everybody would be powerless to stop it. Including me.

"It's okay. You should see my room." My face heats as I say it.

"So what couldn't you say in the store about Tabby and Mark? What did she do to him?" He sits down on a corduroy couch and I sit beside him, drumming my legs. His eyes keep flicking to them. *You have the best legs*, Tabby once told me. I never saw *best* the same way she did. I wanted them to be strong and capable for running. Tabby's version of *best* was something that made everyone else stare.

264

The way they're staring at her now.

I shift uncomfortably, then launch into the speech I prepared. "I think there was someone else, and she was planning on breaking up with Mark that day."

It's a betrayal to my sister, talking about her like this, but not as much of a betrayal as I thought it would be.

Keegan shakes his head ever so slightly. "She told you that? Who did she say the other guy was?"

"I—she didn't say." It's the way he asked—not *did she say*, but the *who* in front of it. My little speech, my fiction, sounds like something he has heard before. "Why, do you know who it was?"

He rubs the stubble on his chin. "I don't know, but probably that Beck asshole. Did you want a drink?"

I shake my head. He walks over to the fridge and comes back with a bottle of beer. For some reason I think about Mark, how all summer he apparently didn't drink, then had alcohol in his blood during the hike. What a hypocrite. He wanted the cloudiness in his head to deal with what he was about to do to my sister.

And we'll never know what that was, because only one person did, and he's buried in Coldcliff Heights Cemetery right now.

"I don't really get why you're here, Bridget. I mean, you made it pretty clear what you thought about Mark that day at the beach. I probably shouldn't even be talking to you. I'm testifying at your sister's trial."

I want to get up and leave, but I remind myself why I'm here. For Tabby.

Although maybe I'm here just as much for me. To fill the spaces she left blank.

"You didn't," I say firmly. "You didn't make it clear what you thought about Mark. But you were jealous, weren't you?"

He takes a swig of beer, his face still composed. "I don't know what she told you, but don't believe it. She has so many people brainwashed. It's wild. She gets into people's heads and just infests

265

them. So she's all they think about. She makes them think she cares, but the only person she cares about is herself."

He makes my sister sound like a flesh-eating virus. I glance around his apartment, at what he calls a life. There are clothes everywhere. A laundry basket full of them, plus jackets covering a loveseat, and a girl's bra sticking out. I know he has a girlfriend, because her Instagram is public, and she posts pictures of them almost as much as she posts pictures of herself.

"You really hate her," I say. "For taking Mark away. But it was a bit of a relief, too, wasn't it? I saw how you watched him. You were jealous."

His knuckles are white around his beer bottle. "Mark was my guy. I wasn't jealous. I was just looking out for him. He has this pattern, with letting girls use him."

"You wish they used you instead." I know I'm right. That day at the beach, I saw things the others didn't, because I paid attention when they all tried to talk over each other. I saw Keegan's gaze pinball between Mark and Tabby. I couldn't figure out who he hated more.

I cross my legs. Keegan's eyes flicker over them again. And in this moment, I get it. I understand it. The power Tabby felt every day. The power of her looks. It's heady, reducing people. Maybe it's the only thing she thought she could control.

I'm not my sister. I have different powers. I don't want hers. I shouldn't be here at all.

"What are you trying to say?" he asks. I meet his gaze—I misread him before. He's not just a guy from the grocery store who lost his best friend. He's smarter than he shows people. He and Tabby have that in common.

"I don't know. Why don't you tell me what you want to say? I bet nobody asks you that. They asked Mark instead. He got all the attention, not you. I can understand that. It's the same with

266

me and Tabby." It might be the first time I've said this bit of truth out loud.

"You're in over your head," he says. "She did it. I have no doubt that she did it. She has this dark side, you know. She didn't want people to know about it, but I saw it. And you see it, too."

I almost defend her—almost—because it's what I've been doing this entire time. Because she's my sister, my blood. Then I realize what Keegan said is true. My sister does have a dark side. It's her own little monster, maybe her version of the pet we weren't allowed to have growing up, alternately quiet and sneaky, loud and brash. And the things she did—the things she did that she got in trouble for—were always to defend someone else. The people she loves. Me. Elle.

How dark would she get to defend herself?

"I should go," I say, standing up. It's not like Keegan has made me feel unsafe, exactly. But there's something about him. A darkness, maybe like the one Tabby has herself.

"She isn't who you think she is," he says. I freeze midstep on my way to the door, because part of me wants to know his version of Tabby. The part that keeps walking is afraid to.

"Do something for me," he calls after me when I'm at the door. "Give her a message. Tell her I'm not sorry at all."

When I'm in the hall, I take off the heels I can't walk in and start to run. I run until I get to Coldcliff Park, where I sometimes do chin-ups on the monkey bars after practice. I run until the drumbeat of his words becomes a full roar.

I'm not sorry at all.

Tabby has said that before. And she's not the only one.

35

KEEGAN

IT'S HARD TO EXPLAIN. I know the trial is coming up, and the truth will be revealed or whatever, and Mark will be brought to justice. But I just have this feeling, like it isn't even close to being over. That yeah, something really bad already happened, but Tabby has something else planned. Something bigger. I'm afraid to be around for it.

36

LOU

I'M ABOUT TO RECYCLE the map Keegan gave me. I mean, it's not like I'll ever need it again, right? I'm not planning to pull another Veronica Mars–in-the-woods stint again anytime soon. Plus, holding on to it seems super creepy, like one of those *Outwit the Split* freaks.

It's only when I unfold it and almost send it to the shredder in my mom's office that I notice something really strange about it. And I'm not sure exactly what that means.

37

BRIDGET

TABBY TELLS ME KEEGAN doesn't like her. "He wanted it to just be him and Mark, single for the summer." She rolls her eyes and stares at her fingernails, dark purple today.

"I went to see him," I say. "Keegan. He said he has a message for you."

The arch of her left eyebrow is so small I almost miss it. Almost.

"Oh, really? Why would you go to see him? Stay away from him, Bridge. He's not a good guy."

"I don't need to be protected. He wanted me to tell you he's not sorry at all."

She smiles. "Yeah, I bet he's not."

"What was he even talking about, Tabby?"

She leans forward, so close our foreheads are almost touching. Her summer freckles have all but faded. "You'll see."

Blue-Eyed Boyfriend Killer trial to commence
By Julie Kerr

The trial of Tabitha Cousins, the 17-year-old accused of first-degree murder after the hiking death of her boyfriend, Princeton student Mark Forrester, will commence Monday morning at El Paso County Courthouse in Colorado Springs. Cousins has already entered a not guilty plea, and is being represented by powerhouse attorney Marnie Deveraux, who has told the press that the evidence is irrefutable that her client is innocent.

"The truth will come out," Deveraux said in an exclusive statement last week. "You can be sure of that."

District Attorney Anthony Paxton said justice will be served for Forrester's family.

COMMENTS

SkeletonKrew: this bitch is gonna walk!!!

TabbyCats4ever: Finally, she gets her turn to speak.

38

ELLE

I TRY TO VISIT TABBY once a week. I bring her the things she can't live without. Nail polish, lipstick, fake eyelashes, magazines. Mom always wants to go with me, but I tell her not to come. I know if she were here, she'd be hovering over my shoulder, wanting to do all the talking.

I figured Tabby would look her worst today, with the trial coming up. But she has no tears. She's in a beige prison uniform, socks with slide-on sandals. Her hair is done and she's wearing makeup.

The real difference is in her eyes. They aren't blue anymore but a muddy brown.

"Your eyes." I can't help it—*why are they brown?*

She rolls them. "Yeah. I wear color contacts. Someone stole my last pair. Bridge is bringing more tomorrow. I'm not myself without them."

Everything about her is different without her blue eyes. Her skin duller, her eyes smaller, like they've completely changed shape. She doesn't look like a girl everyone is talking about. She looks like a girl you might pass on the street and never think about again. She looks like me.

"I never knew," I say. "Why didn't you tell me?"

She folds her hands in her lap. "I guess we can't tell each other everything."

I dig my fingernails into my jeans. "Where were you going? The night you were arrested? You packed a bag."

It's the one question I told myself I wouldn't ask her, but I need to know. We talked that day on the phone. *I'm so bored*, she said after calling from the landline. *If I watch one more hour of the* Real Housewives, *I'm going to fry whatever brain cells I have left.* She told me she had already painted her toenails and reorganized her closet.

"Hang in there," I had said. "I'll come visit tomorrow."

That night, they came for her. She had a packed bag. That was when they pulled her in, maybe even when they decided she was guilty. Because she must have been running for a reason.

"It was reckless," she says. "I shouldn't have done it. I just couldn't stay in that house another second. Everyone thinks I did it, Elle. Do you even know what that feels like? To have nobody believe you?"

"I believe you," I say. "So do your parents. And my parents. And Bridget. And—" Except I can't think of anyone else to add to the list.

"I just saw my life, like, stalling right before me. I don't even know where I was going. It wasn't like I planned to leave for good. I just needed to get out of that house." She scuffs her sandal on the ground.

Why the bag? I want to ask, but I stop myself.

"Now you're stuck here, though," I say.

"Just until the trial. Then I'll be free." She sounds so sure of herself. "What are they saying about me now? Tell me everything."

"I stopped reading it," I lie. "It's so pointless. They don't even know you. I wish I could stop them from saying anything."

She pulls on her hair, sweeps it over one shoulder in a thick black cord. "Why? Let them talk."

"They think you're some kind of monster. It's just not fair."

She leans forward. It's disarming, seeing her up close without the eyes I've spent so much time staring at, wanting for myself, like looking at a funhouse mirror.

"We're girls, Elle. We make one wrong move, and we're villains. There's no in between. We've never had it both ways."

Then our time is up, even though I just got here. I tell Tabby there's a care package from my mom at the desk, with the guards. "You're going to be fine," I say as she's escorted back to wherever she came from, wherever she spends her days.

She turns around and smiles. "I know."

39

KEEGAN

"TELL ME SOMETHING about yourself," Kyla says. She's sprawled on my couch like she lives here and her feet are in my lap, and I wish it felt normal between us but there's nothing remotely normal about it. We're both just pretending, going through the motions.

"I'm not very interesting," I say.

"That's not true." She wiggles closer. She's wearing one of my shirts, a Metallica one that used to be my dad's. She always puts on my clothes when she's here, as if that will make us into something we're not. "Tell me something about yourself that nobody else knows. That maybe you're afraid to tell anyone else."

It's too hot in here. My shirt is sticking to my back and Kyla is smothering—not actually, but like there's not enough air for both of us to breathe.

"I have no secrets, trust me," I say. "I'm an open book." *Take the hint. Stop asking.*

She flops back against the couch cushion and sighs. "I'm giving you the chance to talk to me, Keegan. I really think you should talk to me."

Something inside me bristles up. "What the hell is that supposed to mean?"

She looks right at me. I have no idea what game she's playing, and I don't know the fucking rules.

"You know exactly what it means. I'm giving you tonight to—"

Then there's a knock on the door, which is weird, because

275

I'm not expecting anyone. I don't really care, because I want out of this conversation by any means necessary.

I jump up and look through the peephole, hoping it's not Stewart, with more questions I've already answered. Every time I see the guy lately I feel like he thinks of me as a goddamn criminal, like he knows every shitty thing I ever did. Stupid shit he couldn't possibly know, like cutting this chick's ponytail off in kindergarten. Like borrowing my stepdad's car without asking and scratching it in a parking garage, then leaving it in our driveway like nothing happened. Like all the girls I've promised stuff to then ghosted or ditched after a one-night stand. Maybe he does know all that stuff. He probably has a file on me as gigantic as that *Lord of the Rings* book Mark tried to get me to read back in high school.

It's not Stewart. It's Lou, and she looks cold and pissed off. I open the door. She's wearing this little skirt but she's all wet, her hair kind of stuck to her head.

"What do you want?" I say. "I mean, sorry—I just didn't expect you to show up."

From the couch, Kyla turns her head around like an owl. "Who are you?" She stares from Lou to me. "You told me you weren't seeing anyone else."

"I'm not," I say. "But I never said that anyway."

She gets up and I'm afraid she's going to throw something or start crying, and I don't know which is worse, sad girls or angry girls. Usually sad girls turn into angry girls, and angry girls, well, they just eat you alive.

"You're an asshole," she says. "I gave you the chance to tell me. Just remember that you didn't take it." Then she grabs her purse and storms past us, slamming the door shut.

"What the hell was that all about?" says Lou.

"Nothing. She just gets jealous," I say. "We'll work everything out. We'll be fine." Maybe I'm saying it more to convince myself.

Because part of me wants to run out of here after her and tell her all the things she wants to hear, even though I'm not feeling them, because I'm kind of afraid of what will happen if I don't.

"Sorry to just barge in," Lou says, stepping out of her boots. "Do you have a towel or something? I'm soaked."

I rub my forehead. "Sure. Yeah. Just a minute." My towels are all sitting on my bed, over a bunch of clothes. I remember when I told my mom I was moving out, she got me a bunch of cleaning shit, like a Dirt Devil and laundry detergent and even a feather duster, but I can't keep on top of it. She said people wouldn't want to come over if I lived in a pigsty, but it hasn't stopped anyone.

I throw a towel to Lou. She stands over my kitchen sink, wringing out her hair. "So why are you here?" I say. "What do you want? I have no idea how you even found out where I live."

She shrugs. "Instagram. It's easy to find out just about anything."

It's such a Tabby thing to say that I almost want to shake her. She's in my kitchen, soaking wet, wearing barely any clothes, talking like Tabby, and I have no idea what her whole agenda is, only that she has one.

"I've been thinking," she says. "Since we went into the woods. About the hike being Tabby's idea. She had that map, right? The cops found it when they searched her house. But why would she be careless enough to leave it there? You'd think she would have found some way to get rid of it. There are, like, a thousand ways to destroy a piece of paper."

I cross my arms. "I don't know. She's sloppy."

"Did Mark ever print a copy of the map?" she says. "Did he ever do anything like that when you were hanging out?"

"No," I say. "I mean, I doubt he even looked it up. Guys hate asking for directions." She doesn't laugh. "I only printed that copy out because I wanted to make sure you and I didn't get lost."

"So you printed it after I asked if you'd come."

"Yeah." There's this awkward silence. "I mean, why else would I need it?"

"I guess you wouldn't." She rubs her arms. She's shivering.

"I'll get you a sweatshirt or something," I say. She doesn't stop me.

I don't take long—like, maybe a few minutes, just long enough to find a shirt that's actually clean. But when I get back out, she's gone. Almost like something scared her away. Or someone.

So excited for today. See you soon ;)

Text message from Tabitha Cousins to Mark Forrester,
August 16, 2018, 1:01 p.m.

40

BRIDGET

TWO DAYS BEFORE TABBY'S TRIAL, I bolt upright in bed.

I know why I can't stop thinking about the Nikes.

I turn over and look at my corkboard on the wall. There are photos of me and Tabby in a photo booth from last summer. We had driven to Boulder for back-to-school shopping and she dragged me into the photo booth at the mall, forced me to make goofy faces with her. I stare at that girl, tongue stuck out, and wonder if I know her better than anyone, or if I don't know her at all.

There are a lot of things I don't understand.

I don't know what it means that I found the map I drew Tabby, hours after she left for the hike. It was on her desk, in the same place I had left it months ago, not folded in her backpack like it should have been.

And I don't know what it means that the picnic food she and Elle made that morning was still in the fridge that night, but the Gatorade was gone.

I don't know what it means that she wanted to take a shower right away when she got home, how she said she needed hot water, how she went into the tub, huddled in a shivering little ball. I'll never know what that water washed away.

I don't know what it means that her phone was, in fact, not battery-dead, because it beeped when she came in the door, dirty and disheveled.

I don't know what it means that her shoes were wet when she came home. I noticed, because I knew the woods weren't wet that day, because I had been running earlier, willing the trees to swallow me up.

Here's what I figured out about the shoes.

I usually need new ones every six months. I can tell by the tread on the bottom. But this time, I replaced them after four. Not the ones I lent Tabby that day, but my regular pair.

I haven't been running any more often than usual. I do my fifty miles a week, same as always. But maybe someone else has been running, too. In my shoes. And there's really only one other person that could be. And now I keep thinking back to the time I took her with me in the woods, how she seemed to know her way around, almost like she had been there before.

Maybe it's just because of all the articles, always in my face, even when I try to ignore them. How can I help but read every single one? And it's like other people knew a side of my sister I never did. The things they're saying about her—that's not the Tabby I know, the one who French-braids my hair before track meets and makes me a banana cake from scratch for my birthday, because she knows it's the only kind I like. They know another girl, except she has my sister's face.

It's so twisted that maybe she only asked for that map because she knew I was watching, not because she needed it at all.

And just for a second, before I fall back to sleep, I wish I wouldn't have told the police that the Nike footprint was mine.

41

KYLA DOVE

I'M SO STUPID. I mean, I knew the whole time, on some level, but I let myself believe the things I wanted to believe, because it was easier that way. Or maybe because I saw my own happy ending, as fucked up as that is. I've been called dumb my entire life. By my asshole stepfather, by boys who told me things I wanted to hear to get me to do things, by girls in high school locker rooms. I've been called dumb so many times that I was convinced they were right and I was hopeless.

But I'm not hopeless. I'm furious. Furious at everyone who has underestimated me, and furious at him. This time, I did something with my anger. They know my story now, and it's going to change everything.

PART III

And Jill came tumbling

Step right up, folks
By Oberon Halton

Everyone is talking about Tabby Cousins's trial, which starts tomorrow morning. I'll be tweeting any updates at @sharpedgescrime, so be sure to follow along. Be honest—how many of you have made a drinking game out of this, or have money riding on the verdict? I might have made a couple bets myself. I also made a T-shirt. Team Tabby. Because something tells me that innocent or not, she's going to walk.

COMMENTS

MangoSmoothie: Ten bucks says this guy created the stupid Tabby Cats in the first place

DisasterZone: Ten bucks says it's a girl writing this.

TalkNerdyToMe: Twenty bucks says this girl gets rich after she walks

YOU

A COURTROOM, like the ones you see on TV, lit up with camera flashes, circled with news vans parked at haphazard angles, stretching down the streets like scarabs. Her fans—yes, *fans*—are the ones with cat ears and glittery signs, chanting loudly. Reporters huddle outside, eager to get a glimpse of her. They're paparazzi and they're waiting on their star.

There's a roar outside but a buzz inside, where it's too hot, people fanning their faces with their hands. Everyone sits in rows. She hasn't arrived yet. There are Mark's parents; and his older brother, back from Australia; and there's Keegan; all lined up in a row near the front. The Forresters have District Attorney Anthony Paxton on their side. You'd recognize his face from the news. You've probably heard about his near-perfect conviction rate. He's supposed to be a pit bull, relentless with questions. Tabby will crack and admit what she did.

Her defense attorney is the woman in black, the one with her blond hair swirled on top of her head in a butterscotch bun. Marnie Deveraux. She graduated top of her class from Harvard, and behind her back, her classmates called her Law School Barbie. But she's smart. Maybe she's perfect for Tabby Cousins, because she might just know what it's like to be that girl, the one everyone hates.

Paxton and Deveraux came prepared to give you clashing versions of the same girl, and that very girl is about to go head-to-head with Mark's ghost and all the people vouching for him. But Tabby has people willing to speak up for her, too. Maybe not just the expected ones, but other allies in her corner.

There she is now, the girl of the hour. She's being led out in her handcuffs, but there are those blue eyes, that hair, that hint of a smile. She has been beaten up in the news over that smile, what one outlet called "Satan's smirk," but the truth is, it's just the shape of her mouth. Her lips naturally curl up that way, like they're doing now.

She takes her seat, turns around to see who is behind her. Her parents, of course, and Bridget, and Elle, and maybe a few rows back, someone else who she looks surprised to see, if she even notices her at all.

Everyone is here. You can sit down in the back, if you can find a spot.

Let the circus begin.

1

BRIDGET

SHE TURNS AND LOOKS at me every time she sits down. She knows where to find me — nestled safely between Mom and Dad. But there's nothing safe about being here.

It's hard to explain, unless you have a sister, but you just know when her world has been tilted. And now it's like she can see the slant of mine. I wish she'd get out of my head. I used to want to open it up like a coconut so we could share all of the same thoughts.

I don't want to anymore. Not only because I'm afraid of what I'll find in her head, but because I'm scared of what she might see in mine.

2

ELLE

THE POLICE EVIDENCE is presented first, and I have to admit, it doesn't look good for Tabby. They have photos of Mark's caved-in head. Strands of Tabby's hair. Half a footprint. The angry text messages. Tabby's erratic behavior, her jealousy and possessiveness. The map. And worst of all, the backpack, the rock-filled one Mark went over the edge wearing.

He wasn't dead when he hit the water, Paxton says, but considering what happened next, he wished he was. His lungs filled up, and he probably died slowly. A forensic expert Paxton calls as a witness confirms it.

That detail makes my body quake. I hear Tabby sob, just a little sound, more like a squeak. She used to make that noise if we watched a horror movie and an animal got hurt. Tabby doesn't have the stomach for any of this.

"If Ms. Cousins watched Mr. Forrester fall, and it was all one big accident, this doesn't explain why she didn't go down to the creek to see if he was still alive. Instead, she fled the scene, although a disputable footprint was left behind." Paxton gesticulates for the jury like an actor.

During cross-examination, Tabby's lawyer fights back. "My client was sure Mark was deceased and that there was nothing she could do, and she couldn't see in the dark. She thought the best course of action was running for help. Which she did. The footprint is no longer evidence, as it belonged to her sister, who wore the same shoes on a run earlier that day."

Bridget is within arm's reach of me, but when I look over, her eyes are fixed firmly on her lap. Since when did the shoe print belong to her?

"Mr. Forrester's time of death was marked as nine thirty-six p.m. Ms. Cousins didn't get out of the woods until after midnight, at least according to what she told police, a story her sister corroborated. My expert confirmed the time of death was correct based on the state of Mr. Forrester's body. It couldn't have taken Ms. Cousins three hours to get home, even if she was walking slowly."

They're dueling sharks, both trying to find blood in the water. And there's plenty of it.

"My client was lost," Deveraux says. "The sun set at seven fifty-nine on that date. She wasn't familiar with the woods. She ran in circles trying to get out." She turns to the forensic expert. "Dr. Sims, can you confirm with certainty that the footprint was made by Tabitha Cousins?"

Bridget shifts. She looks like she wants to say something, but she bites her lip, like she's struggling to keep the words inside. The world inside. I know the feeling, but not now. All I want to shout is that Tabby didn't do it. That she isn't perfect, but she isn't a killer.

"No," says Dr. Sims. "The footprint belonged to a wearer of size seven-and-a-half Nike shoes. We can't confirm anything beyond that."

Paxton interjects. He keeps doing that, even when it's not his turn. Typical man. "Dr. Sims confirmed that the hair at the crime scene belonged to Ms. Cousins."

Deveraux touches her own hair. "One hundred strands, Mr. Paxton. That's the average number of hairs a woman loses per day, with long hair being even more noticeable."

With each witness, they go over the itinerary for the hike. That's what they call it. An *itinerary*. Like it was some kind of vacation. Paxton argues that Tabby planned the hike, and

Deveraux maintains that it was Mark's idea. I guess there aren't any text messages to prove anything. It was a verbal agreement, the kind of plan regular couples make, like going out for dinner or to see a movie.

I'm getting called to the stand as a character witness but not today, probably not anytime soon, because this trial could go on for days, weeks. It's a nauseating game of back-and-forth. The prosecution goes first. Paxton gets to call his witnesses, then Deveraux can cross-examine them. I learned all of this from Google. I wanted to be prepared, but I'm not prepared for Tabby up there, sitting so close to me, but still so far away. I wonder who did her hair, how she managed to put makeup on. Maybe Deveraux did it for her. She seems like the kind of woman who understands us.

I zone out. I stare at Keegan, across the aisle, and a twisted part of me sucks in a bubble of laughter, because this is like a really fucked-up wedding where he's on the other side. I wonder what would have happened with Tabby and Mark if he hadn't died. Maybe they would have gotten married someday, and I would have been the maid of honor. Probably not.

Mostly I just watch Tabby. She keeps stealing glances at Keegan, or maybe she's looking at someone else in his row. Mark's brother, who I remember seeing once at a party over Christmas break and thinking he was cute. Mark's parents, who Tabby never even met while they were dating, because Mark tried to keep them apart, feeding her some line about how he liked to keep the different areas of his life separate. As if his life was a closet with dividers, shirts on one side and pants on the other and Tabby on a third, secret side, a flap he could open up when he felt horny and in need of validation.

I'm scared of what Keegan is going to say. He always hated Tabby. It's like he wanted Mark all to himself.

I'm scared of the jury, the twelve people sitting and watching, some of them taking notes. They're people I might have passed on the street, at the mall, in the Stop & Shop, and now they're deciding if Tabby did it. I can already see one of the women—middle-aged and scowling—jotting something down. Women like that hate girls like Tabby. There's a man beside her who looks like he could be softer, more willing to believe a girl over all this noise. I guess Deveraux thought it was best to have Tabby tried as an adult because a jury would be more sympathetic. That's what Tabby told me, methodically, one of the last times I visited her.

"I trust her, but it's, like, Russian roulette," she said. "My whole future is in the hands of a bunch of people I don't know. If even one hates me, it's all over." She cocked a finger to her head.

I have it planned, what I'm going to say. But it feels like it's not enough. It doesn't feel like proof, but speculation. Because the truth is, I don't have any proof that Mark did anything bad to Tabby. I only have the story of my best friend, the girl who turned into a ghost while she dated him. I have a grainy video that Paxton will undoubtedly tear apart. I don't have dates or times, just memories of Tabby's tear-streaked face and the dull thud of her "nothing" when I asked what was wrong.

Since Tabby's being tried as an adult, she's facing life in prison. Paxton wants to lock her away. His big bellowing voice, all the gesturing he does with his hands. He's supposed to have this reputation for ripping witnesses apart during cross-examination, and I'm terrified of him.

If I'm this scared, I have no idea how Tabby feels.

3

LOU

IT'S THE THIRD DAY of the trial and they're still calling the witnesses for the prosecution. So far they've called the forensic guy and someone who saw Tabby stuffing rocks into a picnic basket at the beach the day before Mark died, but of course, he has no proof. He didn't take a picture or anything, so Tabby's lawyer pretty much shreds him to pieces.

Today they call up some guy who works at REI (he's kind of hot, actually, in a lumberjack way), who says Tabby came in and asked questions about different outdoor stuff, which Tabby's lawyer says proves nothing, only that she was in the store, which was normal for a girl going on a hike, out of her element. Paxton had led with the fact that Tabby went to the store back in May, way before the hike was even supposedly discussed.

"She said she was planning a hike with her boyfriend," Hot Outdoorsy Guy mumbles. "I didn't ask her when."

But she left without buying anything anyway. Tabby's lawyer asks him a bunch of questions and figures out that he apparently went to high school with Mark's older brother, so duh, of course he's going to make up a story.

"The only thing this proves," Tabby's lawyer says, "is that my client was at the store, looking at products. Cameras show that she was in the store, but not what was discussed."

Keegan is up soon. I was so wrong about him. And I mean, there's a reason I left his apartment that night, and a reason I wake up every night freaked out that I was alone in the woods with him.

I take out my phone and start tweeting. I don't think I hate Tabby anymore.

I don't think she wanted to take anything of mine after all.

4

KEEGAN

I'M THE LAST CHARACTER WITNESS. I have to follow up this douchebag from Tabby's past who claims she got him drunk and convinced him to give her a ride home. Lawyer lady Deveraux has already punched a bunch of holes in his statement and mentioned that it has nothing to do with this, but he argues it did. "Mark was drunk, too," he says. "He's not here to say what happened, but maybe whatever she did to me, she did to him."

I put on a tie this morning and it's strangling me, like some kind of noose. I want to rip it off, but I try to sit still, like I did at high school graduation, my shiny black shoes tapping the floor, wanting it to be over with. I don't look at Tabby, even though I know she's looking at me. She asked for all this. I'm not going to say anything she can't already expect.

When Paxton summons me, I walk up to the stand. My armpits are sweating through my shirt. I bet that makes me look guilty. I don't need to feel guilty. I have the text message, the last one Mark ever sent.

"Did Mr. Forrester—Mark—did Mark tell you he was planning on breaking up with Ms. Cousins on the hike?"

I'm stone-faced. "Yes. He did. Said he'd been wanting to do it for a while, but was afraid of her."

"Afraid of her how?" His hair looks plastered on. There's never a piece out of place. That must take real effort.

"Her temper. She'd go off on him. She threw a sandwich at him one day while we were eating."

"I was aiming for the garbage."

I gape at Tabby. I'm pretty sure everyone does. A couple people laugh, a couple more gasp. She knows she's not supposed to talk. She sat through everything else, through everyone else shitting on her, but a fucking sandwich reminds her she has vocal cords after all.

Paxton clears his throat while the judge reminds Tabby that this isn't her turn to speak. I swear, Tabby winks, but maybe it's just the light in here.

"Continuing," Paxton says. "Mark confided in you that he was threatened by Beck Rutherford."

"He didn't have to," I say. "I was there the night it happened."

So I tell the whole story again. How we were in Elle's backyard. How nobody knew who invited Beck, and nobody would fess up to being the one who did it. How Beck got in Mark's face, then hit him, and told him to stay away from Tabby.

I tell them the other part, too. How Tabby enjoyed it. She watched it like it was some dramatic moment on a reality TV show. Her arms crossed, pushing her boobs up. Her hand over her mouth, probably covering up the smile she can't get rid of. If you know Tabby, you know she wears everything in that smirk, and in those eyes.

"And you encouraged Mark to break off the relationship," Paxton says.

"Yeah. I did. And I have to live with that. Because listening to me might've been what killed him."

Someone coughs. It makes me jump.

"Describe your relationship with Ms. Cousins prior to Mark's death."

I wipe my forehead. "We didn't have one. She was Mark's girlfriend. I had my own shit going on. I mean, stuff. Sorry. I didn't pay that much attention to her. Then when he went back to school, he started complaining about how insecure she was. How she freaked out whenever she saw pictures of him with other girls in them. I told him he should cut it off. She was in high school. He didn't need that, on top of everything else he was dealing with."

"By that, you mean his competitive swimming. His grades. The scholarship he needed to maintain to remain at Princeton."

"Yeah. All that. And I mean, his grades were slipping. His training was still going well, I thought. Until—"

Paxton knows what I'm going to say, but he won't say it for me. "Until?"

"Until he found out about the abortion."

There's a buzz in the courtroom, even though everyone has already heard all this. Tabby remains silent this time. I'm kind of surprised she doesn't jump up to protest that it wasn't her. I guess she's already done enough of that.

"Would you say that Mark went into a downward spiral after that?"

I shrug. "We didn't talk as much for the last couple months of his school year. He was busy with exams and stuff, and I was busy with work." What a joke. Busy bagging groceries. "Then he came home for summer break."

"How would you categorize Mark's temperament at the start of the summer?" Paxton paces in front of me. I swear, this guy never stops moving. He would be annoying to live with.

"I don't know. Normal, I guess. But he got kind of distant. I think Tabby was behind that."

"She had a birthday party for Mark and didn't invite you, is that correct?"

My mouth is dry. "Yeah. That's right."

"Why do you think she wanted to keep you away?"

I know exactly why that girl wanted to keep me away. "Maybe because she didn't want me to talk to Mark. Get in his head. Tell him to dump her."

"So you believe that Ms. Cousins had been planning the murder for several months, and taking calculated actions to keep Mark distanced from those he knew best."

"Yeah. Yes. I do." Hearing it put like that—murder—it's brutal. Hits me in the stomach and it's like I'm going to be sick. It's easier to think *Mark fell. Mark drowned.* Not *Mark was murdered.*

"I have no further questions," Paxton says.

But Deveraux does. I can't leave yet because she has to cross-examine me. I hate that word. It's all clinical, like she's got a scalpel and is about to cut me open, move my organs around a bit. She even looks like she should be a surgeon, not a lawyer. Yeah, she's hot, but in this sterile way. If she has a boyfriend, or a husband, I'm afraid for him.

"Mr. Leach. Keegan, if I may." She clasps her hands together. "You stated that you didn't have a relationship with Tabby. That she was solely Mark's girlfriend."

I gulp. "Well, yeah. She was."

"And you never saw her outside of that friendship."

"Only when she came into the Stop & Shop where I work. Which she did, sometimes. It's the only place to get groceries in town."

"So my client was never at your apartment. She never left anything there."

Now the sweat isn't just in my armpits. It's everywhere, drenching my back, just like it did that day, my T-shirt stuck to it.

"No, she never came over. My place is messy. I barely have anyone over." I try to laugh, but now my forehead is all wet, and when I wipe it with the back of my hand, my skin comes away all shiny. I look fucking guilty.

"When Mark went back to Princeton, he asked you to keep an eye on Tabitha for him, didn't he?"

I nod. "Yeah. He did. But not in a creepy way. Just to make sure she was okay. Kind of like a big brother or something."

Deveraux pauses. "But you didn't think of Tabby as a little sister, did you, Keegan?"

She brings a picture of something up to the judge. "We'd like to present this new evidence. It's a hair tie belonging to my client, found in Keegan Leach's apartment." She holds up her hand to her mouth, almost like she's asking me to *shh*. "Before you try to say it isn't hers, you might want to save it. Her DNA is all over it."

I backpedal. "Well, Mark had a key. Maybe they came over when I wasn't around, to be alone. You know."

"A neighbor confirms Tabitha entered your apartment last fall. And several times after. Mark wasn't with her, but you were, weren't you?"

I swear, you can hear a pin drop in this place, and that's the scariest part of all. Suddenly I know exactly what Tabby's doing. Exactly what she must have been planning this whole time.

"Tell me where you were the night Mark died," Deveraux continues. She's gaining steam. Look at her face, all flushed. I bet she gets off more from this than sex.

"I was with my girlfriend," I say. "Kyla. I told the cops already. So did she."

"I know we have a witness who claims that after she woke up, you were gone, and when you came back, you were wet."

"Yeah. I got up to take a shower. I do that sometimes."

"But she never heard the shower running."

Fuck. *Fuck*. "I mean, I don't know. She had a lot to drink."

"And there's something else, isn't there, Keegan? A fight you had with Mark that one of my witnesses was the only one to hear. Are you going to tell the court what the fight was about?"

I shake my head. "There was no fight. She's making it up."

Deveraux raises her eyebrow, which makes her look evil. "She?"

Fuck.

"You left your shift at the Stop & Shop twenty minutes early on August sixteenth."

I scratch my head. "I don't remember. I guess it makes sense if I was meeting Kyla."

"But you didn't meet Kyla until eight. And you slipped out that night, didn't you? What were you doing while you thought she was asleep?"

I feel like I'm about to explode. It's not like I kept a fucking log of my time. "I don't know, okay? Maybe I went to jerk off. Or take a shit. I don't remember every moment of my life." That gets a few laughs, but mostly people are deadly silent. I make the mistake of looking at Alex, whose eyes are basically lasering holes into my skin.

I make the mistake of looking at Tabby again, and she's enjoying this.

I made the mistake of looking at Tabby over a year ago. Girls should wear signs, or at least different-colored T-shirts. Red means I'm going to ruin your life.

She batted those blue eyes like a Disney character.

"No further questions at this time," Deveraux says, and I'm terrified about what she means by that. Because *at this time* generally means there's going to be a next time, and I don't want to be around for that.

Sharpedgescrime
@sharpedgescrime

@sharpedgescrime: The courtroom is packed and #TabbyCousins looks like she wants to say something really badly. #TabbysTrial

@sharpedgescrime: The DNA stuff is pretty hard to explain. #TabbysTrial

@sharpedgescrime: Well. Didn't see that one coming. #TabbysTrial

@sharpedgescrime: Tomorrow should be interesting. #TabbysTrial

@sharpedgescrime: Looks like somebody is going to be guilty—but maybe not who we thought. #TabbysTrial

5

KYLA DOVE

KEEGAN AND I HAD HOOKED UP a few times and I was on this high, you know? When you really like someone, and think they really like you. So I figured I'd surprise him. I went over to his place with my cutest lingerie on underneath my dress. Maybe you think that's tacky, but that's what I do when I like a guy.

I walked up the stairs and was all ready to knock on his door when I heard him inside, talking to someone. At first I thought it was another girl, and I was ready to turn around and leave, because I've been there, done that, not interested in doing it again, but then I heard Mark's voice. Definitely Mark. And I heard every single word they said. The walls in Keegan's building are pretty much paper-thin.

"She's my girlfriend," Mark said. "My girlfriend. Not yours. You don't get to tell me what's best for her."

Keegan, laughing. "You don't know that girl at all. The things she's done behind your back. You told me to look out for her, right? Because you were worried?"

"Because I was worried about her. But I should have been worried about you instead. That you'd look a little too closely. Am I right here?"

I waited for Keegan to say something, anything. He hated Tabby. He made it clear. We had talked about her. Actually, the first conversation we ever had was about her. I saw her at a party in the shortest skirt ever and made a comment that she looked desperate for attention. Then Keegan appeared out of nowhere and laughed. Told me she *was* desperate for attention, that she didn't just look that way.

"Girls like that pretty much want one thing," I said.

"Try telling my best friend that," he said, and the whole story came out, about Mark and Tabby and their turbulent little relationship. Keegan and I went home together that night, which I maybe second-guessed the next day, giving up everything so soon. I made fun of Tabby for wanting one thing, but we all wanted the same thing. Not even sex, necessarily. Just feeling desired, needed.

"You need to move on," Mark said, and by this point, my ear was pressed right up against the door. "If that's what this is about. You need to forget about my girlfriend, because she's mine. I'm never leaving that girl. She's the one. So get over it, and I'll act like this never happened."

When the door swung open, it pretty much hit me in the face. I tried to hide behind it, but Mark saw me there and just kind of shook his head, like he felt sorry for me, then kept walking. Keegan was standing inside, pushing his hair off his face, and he saw me, too. I half expected him to slam the door and tell me to go away, but instead, he left it open and walked in the direction of his bedroom.

It was an invitation, and I was spineless enough to take it.

We never talked about what I heard. We never talked about a lot of things. You know that old saying, keep your friends close and your enemies closer? Well, I think that's what Keegan was doing the whole time. With Mark and maybe even with me.

Then there's the night Mark died. It was only, like, a month after that fight took place. Keegan made all these plans with me, which was weird, because usually he just texted me and I'd show up at his door. Looking back, it's so obvious I was a glorified booty call. But we were supposed to meet at this Italian place, and he texted me and said he'd be late, *so sorry*, and all that. (I showed those texts to the cops a few days ago. Better late than never.) I waited around for him, had a glass of wine by myself. Then another one. Then I felt like an idiot and was about to leave, when he showed up, all sweaty and out of breath.

But he was acting different. Like a gentleman. He kept talking about *our future*, and he ordered a bottle of wine for us and kept refilling my glass, and he encouraged me to order a dessert, and held my hand across the table.

Later, we went back to his place. He opened another bottle of wine. My favorite kind, Chardonnay—which was so sweet of him. Except I started feeling pretty wasted and had to lie down. Then he covered me up with his duvet and kissed my forehead, such a boyfriend thing to do. I even whispered that. *Are you my boyfriend?* So pathetic, right? I kind of hoped I didn't say it out loud, but I remember him saying one word back. Not mean or anything, just matter-of-fact. *No.*

My eyelids fluttered open at one point. I have no idea what time it was, but he wasn't there, and I wasn't awake long enough to figure out where he was. I could tell I was going to have a hangover, but it was too late to do anything about it.

I was with him the next day when he got the call about Mark. He was sleeping, facing away—Keegan hates cuddling, at least with me. So he gets this call and his voice is all sharp. *What? What happened? Holy shit.*

I didn't see his face until a bit later. Until I sat up in bed and saw him staring into the mirror over his dresser. He looked totally fine, until he caught me watching him. Then his whole face crumpled.

"Mark," he said. "He, um, died last night. I guess they think he drowned."

If he hadn't said that last part, I might still believe that he had nothing to do with it. But they didn't find out he drowned until the autopsy, which was a couple weeks later. Everyone thought the fall killed him.

I'm sure Keegan doesn't remember saying it. Just like he doesn't remember that scrunchie I found at his place. At first he said we weren't exclusive anyway, then he argued it was mine. As if I would wear a fucking *scrunchie*. I almost talked myself out of giving it to the cops, but the truth needs to come out.

I know the police questioned Keegan a bunch of times, but never once did they question me. I thought about telling them he wasn't actually there that night, at least not the whole time. But I didn't know what it meant, or if anyone would even believe me.

After Tabby got arrested, he sucked up to me a bit. He even mentioned that night a couple times, how he was glad we were together. Like he didn't think I'd remember that he specifically said we weren't a couple.

And it felt good, for a while. Like he was actually into me. He even brought me flowers once, blue and purple orchids. Even though I'm pretty sure they came from the Stop & Shop. Whatever. It's the thought that counts. When you're used to being treated like a glorified ATM by guys—insert part here—your standards for a romantic gesture get pretty low.

I guess I knew the whole time that Keegan didn't love me, but it took a while for me to figure out that he loved somebody else.

I don't know that he killed Mark. I do know he wasn't with me all night. Now I'm telling my version of the truth, and honestly, I don't know what Keegan is capable of. I just know that love has a way of turning people into the worst versions of themselves.

It's always the boyfriend's jealous friend
By Oberon Halton

An inside source tells me there was a huge bombshell dropped in the courtroom yesterday, and if you've been following along with my live tweets, I teased about something huge. Well, it looks like Mark's best friend, Keegan Leach, may have hated Tabby a little less than he let on in the bitter little soundbites he has given to the press. (For the record, he never responded to my request for an interview about Tabby.)

I didn't see this one coming! I usually pride myself on my excellent instincts, but this case got the better of me. Every story needs a villain, and it looks like the villain in this story may have been the guy right under our noses the whole time.

> ### COMMENTS
>
> **KeyzPlz:** This guy??? Pretty sure he works at the grocery store near my house
>
> **Melodious:** Called it from the start! I bet she was juggling Mark, Beck, and this Keegan guy the entire time. Girls like her are excellent multitaskers!

6

KEEGAN

I HAVE TO GET OUT OF HERE.

I can't go back there tomorrow morning so here I am, shoving stuff in a gym bag, only the shit I think I'll need. I know it'll make me look guilty taking off, but I know what she's doing and I can't be here when she does it. I'm the guy who didn't realize he was playing this game of cat and mouse, or maybe knew, but didn't think he was the goddamn mouse.

Paxton told me I had to show up. Not to let Deveraux get under my skin, that he has questions for her witnesses and for Tabby herself that will answer a lot of people's questions. But I'm not gonna be around for that.

They have nothing on me. *They have nothing on me*. They can't possibly. Nobody's going to believe Kyla over me.

The only person who would've stuck up for me isn't here anymore. Mark stood up for me when we first became friends, when he could have easily ratted me out for smoking at recess, except he said the cigarettes were his. Mark stood up for me in high school when I got accused of cheating off him on a test. (Truthfully—not that I ever told him this—I was cheating off him, not because I hadn't studied but because he always knew more than me, no matter what I did.) Mark tried to plead my case when this chick Lorena, who I had a thing for, wanted him instead—I still remember every detail about that pathetic night, all of us in the backyard at her dad's place, Mark being like, "You know my friend Keegan, he's such a great guy."

But I'm not a great fucking guy. And when it comes down to it, neither was Mark. He ended up banging Lorena a week later.

I toss more shirts into my bag, even ones I haven't worn in ages. I have no idea where the hell I'm going, but I can't stay here. Maybe I'll take off to Mexico and disappear on a beach. Maybe I'll buy a boat and live in the middle of the ocean where I won't ever meet another girl.

I'm literally on my way out the door when I see him standing in front of it. My buddy Stewart, wearing a shit-eating grin.

"Keegan Leach," he says. "Some of my colleagues did a bit of digging yesterday, and we found something very interesting that belongs to you."

There's no way they could have found anything.

But I know they did.

Mark, we really need to talk. If you want to make things right between us, please call me when you get this.

You sounded so weird earlier. Just know I love you, okay? I want us to work out, but it doesn't sound like you do anymore.

7

BRIDGET

SHE NEVER GOT MARK'S MESSAGE. That's the other thing I did, the thing that might have been worse than lying about the shoes. She texted him—we were sitting in the living room, and I could tell she was obsessing about something. Then she put the phone down in a huff and said she was going for a walk.

I doubt she forgot the phone. She was pissed off at whatever she had just read on it, or the lack thereof. I waited until she was gone and picked it up. I knew her passcode—she never changed it. It was 1313, her unlucky number.

I saw her message to Mark. He hadn't written back. And as I was staring at it, the phone rang. It was Mark, calling her, just like she asked him to do.

I answered. I have no idea why I did it. I wasn't planning to, and I wasn't planning on doing what I did next. I wasn't planning to be Tabby.

"Hello?"

I was sure he would know it wasn't her. We sound extremely similar—Dad used to get us confused when he'd call the land-line from the office to talk to Mom. But if Mark really knew Tabby, he would know he wasn't talking to my sister.

He didn't.

"Tabs, I know I fucked up, but can't we fix it? You know you're the only girl who means anything to me."

"I don't believe you." My voice, ice-cold. "All you ever do is hurt me."

"Come on. We've been through too much to just throw it all away because of one night."

I wanted to scream. I wanted to ask, *What night? What did you do?* But I couldn't, because if I was Tabby, I would know already.

"If you love me so much, prove it," I said. "Prove it, or let me go."

"I'll prove it," he said. He sounded so pathetic, in that moment, that I almost felt sorry for him. If I hadn't known anything about their relationship—if I hadn't seen my tearstained sister—maybe I would have felt bad for him. But instead, I was disgusted. With him, for reducing my sister into a girl he could carry in his pocket. Tabby, for letting it happen. Me, for stooping this low, for invading her privacy.

I hung up without saying goodbye. Then his text message came in. I deleted it, and I deleted his call from her call history, and I hoped he never mentioned it again.

I don't know if what I did played a role in what happened in the woods. Maybe Tabby figured it out. Maybe Mark knew all along. But things might have been different if she had seen that message. If I hadn't answered the phone. I guess none of us will ever know. And it looks like Keegan is going down for his role, but part of me wonders if they got the wrong person.

8

KEEGAN

YOU WANT MY VERSION of the story? Well, I'm on my way to the courthouse to tell it, but whatever. I'll give you a sneak peek. I swear, I've been honest with you the whole time. I never killed anybody. And if Mark didn't need to literally have everything he wanted, he might still be around.

"She's hot," I told him. She wasn't dressed for mini golf. She had barely anything on, just this tiny skirt and a top that showed her boobs. And she kept looking over at us. Not smiling exactly, but kind of smirking.

"She's too young," Mark said. We were one hole behind them. I wanted to catch up, but of course he wanted to do everything by the rules. Each stroke had to be recorded, even though it was just a group of us guys, me and Mark and a couple high school friends we had more or less lost touch with. It was supposed to be for fun, but Mark was like the stern dad, right down to the obnoxious little pencil behind his ear.

"Suit yourself," I said.

But she started kicking the ball in with her foot, and when I went to take a leak, he took it upon himself to give her commentary on her form. By the time I got back, they were flirting. Two hours later, they were making out. It was like he knew I was going to make a move if he didn't. Mark not only wanted the things he wanted, but he wanted the things everyone else did, too.

You know he only took up swimming because of me? Because

my mom was bugging me to do a sport, and I sucked at all the usual team shit, so I joined the swim team. And Mark joined with me. He said he had always been interested in it, but I think he couldn't possibly let me have something that he wasn't part of.

You know how that ended. How he ended up being the best. How he got all the glory, all the medals, the records, the scholarship. And the girls—always ones he knew I was into.

I asked him about Tabby, the day after they met. She was already texting him nonstop, and I could tell when he was messaging her back, because he had this goofy grin on his face. Already in the goddamned honeymoon period.

"I said she was hot," I said after a few beers on my shitty little apartment balcony. "Then you went after her."

He had the nerve to act shocked. "Dude, I thought you meant her friend. Actually, you and Elle would be a good couple. I'll make sure she's there next time we all hang out."

It was only when he left that I said to the door, "I didn't mean her friend, and you fucking knew it."

Maybe everything that happened next was as much my fault as his. I never really stood up to the guy. I think because I knew he'd argue his way out of it, do that thing he did where he made me feel like I was making shit up in my head. I heard him do it to Tabby, too, when they fought. Make her seem like the crazy one. He would have been a good lawyer.

I mean, I'm not innocent. I did stuff. I put ideas in her head about Mark having girls at Princeton. She'd see a picture on Instagram and flash it at me in the grocery store, demanding to know who it was, and I'd make up some story, just because I knew she was already jealous. She was an easy fire to feed.

Just remember, though. He knew I saw her first, and he didn't care. And I think that was the moment he stopped being my friend. Most people just see the surface. But there was another side of Mark. A monster who never got full, no matter how much food you gave it. Kind of like how his swimming diet made him eat a ton of calories every day. His appetite for everything else was just as hard to fill.

9

ELLE

IT ALL MAKES SENSE NOW. Me and Keegan in the front seat of Mark's car that night. I wish I never would have taken the Groupon from my dad. I wish Tabby and I would have gone to a movie, like I really wanted to.

But it all makes sense because—and I never told this to anyone—I tried to kiss Keegan. I was a bit tipsy from the raspberry vodka Tabby snuck inside her purse, and he was cute, and he was there. I figured he'd kiss me back for the same reasons, but he just stared ahead, through the windshield, like there were lasers in his eyes.

"No," he said. "Not you."

Not me, because he wanted her. I still remember how his jaw looked like steel, the kind of tension that makes you less person and more machine. That's what not getting what you want does to a person. I coiled up like that around Beck whenever we were at school, my shoulders migrating up to my ears.

I tried turning on the music, because it was awkward in the car, hearing Tabby and Mark make out and paw at each other in the back seat. But Keegan pushed my hand away.

After that, I just thought he was an asshole. I still think that, of course, but there's more to it than that. Not only the obvious, that he's probably the one who killed Mark. I think he's a cautionary tale. He's what you turn into when you're so used to falling short that it becomes a science. He could have been me.

10

KEEGAN

DEVERAUX LOVES THIS. She has this annoying, dramatic pause thing she does right before asking a question, like she wants you to freak out over what might come out of her mouth. And it's working.

"Tell me what happened the weekend of homecoming," she says.

"Nothing," I say. It's a lie.

The whole weekend was just a reminder of everything that went to shit after I flunked out of college. If I had tried harder, not let girls derail me, I would have been like Mark. Parading back into town, going to the parties, girls falling all over me. Instead, I was the guy who sold them their candy and tampons and told them to have a nice day.

The weekend had sucked. I didn't even get Mark to myself. It was all Tabby, all the time. He even invited her with us to the homecoming game. She rode shotgun in his car with blue numbers painted on her face and legs, even though I'm sure she never watched a football game in her life. I stared at her ponytail, bobbing along to the shitty pop music Mark had let her pick out, and had this sick thought that it was long enough to wrap around her neck and strangle her with.

"Did you come on to Tabitha the night of the homecoming game?" Deveraux asks now.

"No," I practically shout. "I mean, no. If anything, she came on to me."

I kept my hands to myself. I sat on Tabby's other side at the game, rolled my eyes when she asked Mark a thousand questions about football, the dumbest shit you've ever heard. It was like I wasn't even there. Until Mark got up to get the popcorn Tabby had seen other people eating and kept saying she wanted some. She leaned over and put her hand on my leg and said, "Don't worry. I haven't forgotten about you."

I had no idea what that meant, but I looked at her, actually looked at her, and realized maybe she didn't hate me at all.

"Tell us what you mean by that. Did Tabitha flirt with you?"

"Yeah. It was definitely flirting. She was—" She was playing me. I can't bring myself to say it out loud.

"What did she do, exactly, to make you think she was interested in you?"

I squint at Deveraux, like the answer is hidden in her Botoxed face. Tabby was all over me without being on me at all. It's like she knew this would happen. That we'd end up here. Because every rebuttal that comes into my head sounds flimsy as hell.

"It was just how she acted," I settle on. "It's hard to explain."

"It's important to explain, Mr. Leach."

So I do.

Mark dropped Tabby off first after the game, which I could tell she hated, but I could also tell she was trying to keep her cool, so she let it slide, blowing him a kiss from her front lawn. Then on the way to my apartment, he dropped this bomb.

"I think I need to break up with her. You were right about her getting clingy. It's suffocating me."

I was relieved to hear it, but also felt this validation. That Mark was as big a phony as the rest of us. He sat there all day cheering for the home team with his arm around his girlfriend, rubbing circles on her back. He was an asshole, keeping up a charade. Girls liked to shit on me for leading them on, but Mark did it, too. Everyone uses each other.

"You should do it," I said. "Do it before you go back to school. That way you can have some freedom for the rest of the year."

Mark laughed. His hands were at ten and two. His shirt was buttoned right. Everything Mark did was just *right*. "It's not about being with other girls. I just want to be with *the* girl. You know?"

Yeah, I know, I wanted to say. But I couldn't tell the guy that all the girls he deemed worthy were ones I saw first. Mark always said he didn't have a type, but he did. Mine.

"I don't think she's right for you," I said instead. "It's good to break things off before it gets too serious."

When he dropped me off, I went up to my place to take a shower. When someone knocked on my door, I knew it was Mark. I put some sweatpants on and got two beers out of the fridge.

It wasn't Mark. It was Tabby. Still wearing that shit she had on earlier, with the neon bra.

"Mark's not here," I said through gritted teeth. Tabby and I had never been alone together. Unless you counted the times at the Stop & Shop, but we were never really alone there either. This was just the two of us, and it freaked me out.

"Good," she said, letting herself pass me, grabbing a beer off the counter. "We should get to know each other, don't you think? We're the two closest people to him, and I feel like you don't like me."

Deveraux nods when I'm done talking. Her skin is stretched so tight that I have no idea what's going on behind it. "So you're saying Tabitha tried to make peace with you because she sensed your animosity."

"No—it wasn't like that." Sweat clings to my back, just like it did that night. Deveraux is trying to make it sound like Tabby was just being nice. It was a hell of a lot more than that.

"Did you have any sexual contact with Tabitha that night?"

"Well, no," I say.

"Did she try to initiate anything?"

"Uh, I guess not."

I swear, I can hear the entire courtroom judging me. But it wasn't like that. She would have hooked up with me, if I had made a move. She was waiting for it. But I didn't.

"What do you want?" I asked her, then followed it with, "I think you should go."

She took a drink of beer. The paint from the football game was still on her face. "What do *you* want, Keegan? Because I have a feeling nobody ever asks you that, do they?"

They didn't. Ever. Other kids got asked what they wanted for Christmas. I got whatever my mom felt like shelling out for—my mom, not Santa, because she was too lazy to keep up the charade. I never got what I wanted, but Mark did. There was Mark the day after Christmas, bringing over whatever he got, which just so happened to be exactly what I had wanted, and of course he'd let me play with it, but he'd bring it home with him at the end of the day, and I was left feeling like I shouldn't have played with it at all, because now I knew what I was missing.

That's how it would be with Tabby, I was sure. I was determined not to play with her.

"I just want to be alone," I said.

Tabby hopped up on my counter, legs dangling. I could see up her skirt. I tried not to look.

"But you're always alone, aren't you? Mark worries about you, you know."

"Does he know you're here?" I asked.

"Does it matter?" she said. "I don't need his permission to have a conversation with you."

"We just talked," I tell Deveraux, because it's like she's waiting for me to say more. "That's it."

There's no point explaining, but it's the truth. We just talked, sure, but it was what Tabby didn't say that showed her real intentions.

"Wait," I say. Deveraux turns around. "Tabby asked me if Mark was going to break up with her."

Shit. I said it wrong. She didn't ask. She's the one who told me.

"He's going to break up with me anyway," she said, all matter-of-fact. "Isn't that right?"

As if she was in the car with us the whole time.

"Yeah," I said. "Probably."

Then she leaned over and I thought she was going to kiss me, but she just drained her beer and hopped off the counter. "I hope you're wrong," she said.

"And what did you tell her?" Deveraux asks.

This time, I sound sure. "The truth."

The truth was, I told her I was tired, and she got kind of pouty, but kissed me on the cheek and left. She wanted more. I knew she wanted more. But I didn't trust her yet.

The next day, I texted Mark. *Did you break up with her?*

He didn't respond for a few hours, and when he did, it was a selfie of the two of them, tongues sticking out at the camera, almost like they were making fun of me. *Nope. Changed my mind!* ☻

And it was just like every shitty Christmas morning all over again, except a thousand times worse, and I realized the ache in my gut was because I could love her, and Mark never would, but he had her anyway.

11

BRIDGET

AFTER EVERYTHING THAT happened with Keegan on the stand, the cops go to his apartment, get a warrant to search his computer. They find all this in his search history from before Mark's death: the Mayflower Trail, the height from the Split to the creek, and the likelihood that a person would survive the fall.

There's his credit card statement. The flowers he bought my sister. The picnic basket he ordered online. The motel room he booked the same night Tabby tried to run. It all paints a story, an obsession. A girl he couldn't have, but wanted anyway, and all the ways he manipulated her into wanting him back.

It all fits together, and still, there's a piece missing. Maybe it's because I know my sister, and I know she isn't a pawn. Whatever Keegan did to Mark in the woods, she must have known it was happening, and still didn't do anything to stop it.

Maybe it's the map. The fact that she had one before Keegan ever did.

I need Tabby herself to tell me she didn't have anything to do with it. But I guess she'll get her turn to tell everyone that soon enough.

12

KEEGAN

I TRY TO TELL DEVERAUX about how Tabby started showing up at the Stop & Shop when she knew I was working.

"Correct me if I'm wrong," she says, "but did you not say yourself that the Stop & Shop is the only grocery store in town? I don't suppose Tabitha had any other options. Presumably, she didn't go there just to see you."

"But—" It's impossible to explain. Tabby waited in my line, even when it was busy. One time, she was eating a Popsicle she didn't even pay for and she wasn't wearing a bra.

"Do you have any proof that Tabitha was there to see you?"

"She told me she loves a man in uniform," I say, and I swear, the entire courtroom holds in a laugh, and I don't blame them. It sounds ridiculous, like I'm grasping for an excuse that doesn't exist.

The one person I can't look at is Tabby. I have to pretend she doesn't exist. I should have done that from the start.

13

LOU

I MEAN, AFTER EVERYTHING, it's a fucking piece of paper that makes me take Tabby Cousins's side. Makes me want to laugh. It's ridiculous, right?

The map Keegan brought with us the day we went into the woods. The one he said he just printed. He left it with me—I guess he got careless. Then I just so happened to notice the date at the bottom of the page, beside the website name. He printed it back in May.

I ended up giving the map to the police, but maybe it wouldn't have mattered, because of all the stuff they found on his computer. And Kyla, Keegan's ex-girlfriend or whatever, had plenty on him. I guess she had been stewing with it the whole time. You know the feeling—what it's like to pretend something isn't happening, or didn't happen, because it's easier that way.

I'm not even sure what all this means. Tabby was maybe doing something behind Mark's back with Keegan. But she wasn't doing anything behind my back with my boyfriend.

Here's my truth—I just don't think Tabby killed Mark any-more. I saw her as this threat the whole time, this shadow I was somehow eclipsed by, but it's like when you look under your bed and realize there aren't any monsters there after all, just some old socks. I guess that makes Tabby the old socks. I kind of feel sorry for her, because maybe she really did love Mark, and Keegan did something to him.

In fact, when Tabby gets found not guilty—and I'm pretty sure she will, because I've been watching the jury and I'm good

322

at reading people—I might even ask her to hang out sometime. Maybe there really was a redheaded scout in the audience that night, and everything between us has been a huge misunder-standing. I'm willing to give her the benefit of the doubt. I'm just that kind of girl.

14

KEEGAN

"YOU AND TABITHA formed a friendship," Deveraux says. She makes *friendship* sound like some sort of disease. Tabby's the goddamn disease.

"I guess so," I say. I swear, the more questions she asks, the fewer syllables I can manage.

"She confided in you," Deveraux says. "She trusted you."

This time, I'm struck silent. *She used me*, I want to scream, but Tabby has already used up all my words along with the rest of me.

She came into the Stop & Shop and told me she was going to break up with Mark that night. I told her to come over after for a beer, but she never showed up, so I figured it was going badly. I realized I didn't even have her phone number to text her and ask.

She wanted it that way.

Here's what happened next, and it's the truth. She came over two nights later, marched right in and sat on my shitty corduroy couch. "He won't let me break up with him. He talked me out of it."

Mark never even mentioned it. Whenever we talked, things were golden with him and Tabby. He was so full of shit. So determined to remain the goddamn golden boy for the rest of his life.

"I just wish he was more like you sometimes." She bit her bottom lip. "He's condescending and doesn't listen. You're the best guy. You'd make an amazing boyfriend."

"Uh—" I had no idea what to say. She was full-on hitting on

me. She even slipped out of her sweater, and was just wearing this tiny shirt underneath. I wanted her so damn badly.

"He's going to be difficult to get rid of," she said, staring at her fingernails.

I swear, those were her words. As if he was something terminal, like cancer.

"Get rid of?" I echoed, sitting down beside her. I pushed a piece of hair off her face. She let me.

"Maybe you can help me with that."

"Help you how?"

"You know him the best." She put her head on my shoulder, which made me practically stop breathing. "And besides, you're smart."

Nobody ever called me smart. She fed me like that, in these little bites, like she knew exactly what I needed to hear. We were made for each other, I decided, because nobody got me like she did. She fell asleep on my couch that night, in my arms. It was more intimate than sex.

She was wrong about me being smart. She was the mastermind the whole time.

15

ELLE

I FIND BECK at school today. He's actually there, and today he just looks like a boy, a mortal, somebody pretending to be tougher than he is. He's chewing gum, walking away from Principal Stanton's office. Probably another detention.

"Hey," I say. "Did you hear what happened with Tabby's trial?"

"No," he says. "Fill me in."

He's lying. He's always lying. Maybe he and Tabby have that in common.

I thought she and Beck still loved each other. I was sure of it, more sure than I've ever been of anything, but I guess my brain is good at making me believe things that never happened.

All the times Tabby said to me: "I love him so much, Elle. I'd do anything for him. I love him so much it scares me."

Anything, Elle. Like, anything at all.

It never occurred to me she wasn't talking about Mark, and she wasn't talking about Beck either.

16

KEEGAN

DEVERAUX'S QUESTIONS feel less like bullets and more like paper cuts. I don't know if it's good or bad that my skin is getting used to her form of shredding.

"You say Tabitha shared with you her fears about Mark. That he wasn't the person he pretended to be."

"Yeah," I say. And it's in this moment when I know there's no way out of this that ends well for me, so I might as well start dropping bombs. "Mark started treating her like shit. He wasn't the *gentleman* everyone thought he was."

"He's such an asshole," Tabby had complained. "He blames me for everything. Just because his swimming isn't going well. And I guess his grades suck. He's getting all paranoid."

"Yeah," I said, even though I didn't know that about his swimming, or his grades. I just assumed everything in Mark's life was chugging along perfectly, like it always did. "You know, he asked me to keep tabs on you. When he first went back, at the end of the summer. Like he didn't trust you."

She touched my arm. "You didn't do a very good job. You're letting me get into all kinds of trouble."

I explain it to Deveraux and quote Tabby, word for word. Of course Tabby doesn't look at me. She knows it's true, though.

"And you encouraged Tabitha to break things off. You were the driving force."

"No. She was—it was all her idea. I was just there for moral support."

"Moral support," Deveraux echoes. "Did you insist repeatedly that Tabitha break up with Mark?"

I shake my head. I mean, yeah, I remember what I said, but if I were to tell her, she'd rip up my words like confetti.

Me and Tabby, having beers in my apartment. I liked that she didn't complain that I only bought cheap shit. We watched a movie on my laptop and she was drifting off, her head on my shoulder. "You should just end things with him. Break up with him. He'll get over it."

"Why?" she said. "Is there a better guy for me?"

"Yeah," I said. My lips touched her hair. "There is."

"I told you," she whispered. "I tried. If we want him out of the picture, we'll have to do something else."

She was so dark. Sometimes I had no idea if she was kidding or serious. But I glommed on to *we*. She wanted me as badly as I wanted her, but we both knew Mark had to be dealt with first.

A few minutes later, when I thought she'd fallen asleep, she said something else.

"He can't know this is coming."

17

ELLE

THINGS WOULD HAVE BEEN DIFFERENT, maybe, if I hadn't said what I said. If I hadn't planted the seed in Tabby's head, hadn't told her exactly what Keegan wanted me to say. *This is his pattern. I saw him with another girl. It was dark. I couldn't tell if they were kissing but their heads were really close—*

Back then, I thought Keegan and I had a similar interest. Making sure two people who had no business being together weren't.

But he had a different agenda the whole time, and I practically sent her into the woods myself. A girl, a boy, and a monster lurking in wait. Only two came back out.

Do you see what I mean, about how I had something to do with this? I told Tabby about the other girl, the one who probably doesn't exist. I told Beck about Tabby's kiss with Sawyer. And I told Beck that Mark wasn't a good guy. Now I'm not even sure which were truths and which were lies, but I do know that everything could have had a better outcome if I had just not said anything.

18

KEEGAN

IT WAS A GAME TO HER. I can see that now, even though I couldn't see it then. Mark came home for the summer and she went to meet him right away, and I hated her and wanted her to hurt. That night when we all went for dinner, I could tell Tabby knew what I was doing under the table to Elle and I could tell it made her upset.

"You haven't been in Stop & Shop," I told her when we all left the restaurant.

"I guess I have all the groceries I need," she said, all clipped. I almost wanted to tell Mark about us hanging out, but I was afraid if I did, she wouldn't come over anymore. As pathetic as it sounds, she was the only real friend I had. Mark was away at school most of the year and he had his college friends and teammates. I had nobody. Nobody except his girlfriend.

Then Tabby came back to me. She came to my apartment filthy, all sweaty and with dirt on her legs.

"You should come hiking with me," she said. "It's exactly what you need."

We looked it up on my laptop that night. The Split, the Mayflower Trail. She said we'd go sometime soon.

"Maybe tomorrow," I said.

"Not tomorrow," she said. "Mark's training all day."

It was the worst feeling. She didn't mean *we* as in me and her. She meant *we* as in the three of us, this fucked-up triangle I never wanted to be part of.

"Another time, then," I said. "Mark has to be there, too."

330

"Hey," she said. "Look up how far from the Split to the creek. And if someone would die if they fell." She rubbed my shoulders. "I'm just curious."

That's the day I knew she was planning something. I just didn't know what.

19

LOU

SHARP EDGES IS LOSING its mind. Like, seriously flipping out. Some people think it was all Keegan, and some of them think he's just the Clyde to Tabby's Bonnie.

This feels so embarrassing to admit, but I used to want Tabby's life. Like, all the attention she seemed to get everywhere. People noticing her. Now I just feel bad for her. It sucks that girls are either invisible or much too seen.

You never asked what happened to my acting career. Well, I kind of gave it up after the whole Blanche and Stella debacle. (I honestly can't think of acting without seeing Mr. Mancini's wife's surprised face.) I found something I'm better at, something that doesn't involve my looks at all. I'm a journalist. You've probably heard of me. My name's Oberon, and I have a blog you might have read.

Surprised? Why? Because I picked a boy's name? Well, I have news for you. (No pun intended.) When you're a girl, you have to scream to get anybody's attention. And even then, all they want you to do is shut up.

20

KEEGAN

DEVERAUX HAS MOVED on to a new subject. Kyla. Who is apparently one of her witnesses, as if this couldn't get any more fucked up.

"Explain to the court how you met Kyla Dove," she says.

"Tabby set us up," I say. "She told me to go talk to her."

"If Tabitha was secretly in love with you, as you've indicated, why would she encourage you to talk to another woman?"

"It's complicated," I say. They're grinding me down—I don't have the energy to explain anymore. But here's the thing. Tabby practically picked Kyla out.

"The blond girl," Tabby said when we were both drinking from Solo cups at a summer party. "The one with the slutty top and too much eyeliner. She's your type, right?"

I wanted to tell her *she* was my type, but instead, I just shrugged, and pretty soon I was practically being shoved into Kyla.

Deveraux clasps her hands together. "Tabitha knew you were lonely. She knew you were often the third wheel in her outings with Mark. Is it not believable that as your friend, she would want to help you find a girlfriend so you'd have that constant in your life?"

"No—it wasn't like that. Tabby didn't mean it. Kyla was—" She's here in this courtroom, watching me squirm, hearing me confess the worst. "I never felt that way about her."

"And did Tabitha seem jealous of your new relationship?"

Tabby's smiles, the ones she reserved for me. The ones that

stripped me down to nothing. She saw under my skin and what she saw there didn't make her look away.

"Yeah. She did."

I'm not sure if it's true. Tabby wasn't jealous like she was of Mark's Instagram girls. Maybe because she knew Kyla would serve a greater purpose. She told me it would be *good for me* to date someone. She practically insisted on it.

Around the time of Kyla, Tabby stopped coming over at all. When I finally got her alone, I asked her if Mark was pissed about us hanging out.

"Why would he be?" She grabbed my hand and squeezed it briefly before letting go. "We're his two favorite people."

But I could tell by the way she said it that he didn't know about us. And she kept it that way for a reason.

21

BRIDGET

SHE TOOK THE GATORADE with her. Mark had alcohol in his blood, but hers showed no traces. There were two bottles, one for each of them.

What I don't understand is how a third Gatorade bottle with Keegan's DNA was magically found buried near the creek two days ago. How it was underground, then it wasn't. It's like somebody knew where to look the whole time, but was waiting for the right minute to say something. Or it's like somebody was told.

22

KEEGAN

"EXPLAIN AGAIN HOW YOU and Mark spent the morning before the hike," Deveraux asks.

I'm sick of talking about it, but if I don't talk now, I may never get a chance to again.

"Mark showed up at my place, and we went to Rita's for breakfast. It was like he knew something was up, and he was super nice to me all day, even though things hadn't been the same since we had that argument about Tabby. The one Kyla overheard. He ordered a shit ton of food and we didn't talk about Tabby at all, and it felt like the old days, before girls and before things got messed up between us."

I leave out what he said when we paid the bill and left. He said something that changed everything.

"I'm sorry. About that night. I was wrong. I must have been jealous or something, but I feel horrible about it, dude."

He felt horrible for accusing me of something I had been guilty of the whole time. He felt horrible, when I had literally been fantasizing about a world without him in it. I almost started to cry.

"I told him about Tabby," I say. "That she came over sometimes. That we were friends."

"And how did he react to that?" Deveraux asks.

"He was cool with it," I say. "He said Tabby was a good friend to have."

I leave out the surprised look that took over his face. I leave out what he really said. "I know she was worried about you since you don't really have anyone. I trust you, dude." I leave it out because it was so fucking *patronizing*.

Here's the rest that I can't tell Deveraux. I hung out by the woods, watched them start their hike. I guess I had nothing better to do. Tabby was laughing, and holding Mark's hand, like they were a real couple, like she wasn't constantly bitching about him and plotting to end things for months.

I realized that if she could do that to him, she could do that to me. That maybe she'd been doing it to a long chain of guys. That my allegiance was to the wrong person, but it wasn't too late.

So I went back to Kyla. And yeah, she's saying I wasn't there when she woke up, but I needed some air, and I took a walk. I couldn't sleep, because I knew I fucked up. Yeah, Mark was a golden boy, and yeah, I wanted him tarnished, and yeah, he stole every girl I was ever interested in, but I never wanted him dead. I should have warned him, because if I knew Tabby, I would have known she was capable of going that far. What were her exact words? *He can't know this is coming.*

The weird thing is, Tabby never gave me her phone number, and never asked for mine. We always just got together somehow, her showing up at the grocery store, her showing up at my apartment. I think she knew the whole time that this was going to happen. She got close, but made sure we never crossed a line. That girl covered her tracks. And the stuff that the cops did find—I can guarantee she wanted it that way. I mean, she made me search for that stuff about the trails. Because she wanted *us* to go hiking sometime. That's what she wanted me to think.

Deveraux takes another one of those dramatic pauses I really hate her for, and I'm bracing myself for the next onslaught when she nods. "No further questions."

I can't decide if they're the best or worst three words I've heard.

Before I stand up, I make the mistake of glancing at Tabby. Her eyes are right on me.

And she's smiling.

THE COLDCLIFF TRIBUNE

December 11, 2019

Cousins to take the stand in slain boyfriend case
By Julie Kerr

After revelations that rocked the murder trial of Tabitha Cousins, 17, Cousins herself will finally take the stand tomorrow to tell her version of the story. New evidence linking Keegan Leach, 20, to the murder of Mark Forrester, has upended a trial that was expected to focus solely on Cousins. It's now looking like Cousins herself may have been a victim of Leach's obsessive tendencies, and Forrester may have paid the ultimate price.

HER

HER VOICE SHAKES. "I made a mistake."

Nobody dares to breathe.

"I trusted Keegan Leach. We became friends. But we were nothing more. He was lonely and needed a friend, and we had Mark in common, so we hung out sometimes."

Hands clasped in her lap. Her hair is off her face in a pony-tail, no wisps obscuring the view. "Then he started getting more suggestive, and making comments about us being together. I was going to tell Mark about it, but it was a hard conversation to have. Keegan was his best friend. I didn't know whose side he would take. When we went into the woods that day, there was a sick feeling in my stomach, like something was going to happen.

"We didn't talk very much as we hiked. He kept wanting to go higher, farther, and the farther we got, the more I decided to keep it inside. What I wanted to say. I'd save it for somewhere I felt safe. But then we got up there, to the Split, and he turned around and started accusing me of sleeping around."

She clears her throat, wipes her eyes. Tears are pooling in them.

"I guess Keegan told Mark we'd been hanging out, but made it sound like I came on to him. I denied it, of course, because nothing happened. Mark got mean. He said things like, I should feel lucky to be with him because I would never find anyone else who would put up with me. At that point I fought back a bit. With my words. I asked him how he could be so quick not to trust me, when I believed him when he told me the girls on his Instagram, in all his photos, were just friends."

You can't tell what the jury is thinking, only that they're thinking something. The judge nods periodically, as if maybe she agrees.

"I asked him if he was going to break up with me, and why he had to drag me all the way out here just to do it when he knew I hated hiking. He told me Keegan said it was best to do things in private. That Keegan suggested the hike. That was when I knew that Keegan had a whole other motive. The night he made a pass at me, he made some comment about wishing Mark weren't in the picture. I thought he only said it because he was offended I turned him down, so I didn't tell anyone."

She makes a gesture like she's pushing her hair behind her ears, but there's no hair to push back. She's a girl who isn't used to wearing a ponytail, but maybe today she felt like it was necessary not to obscure her face. She wants them to know she has nothing to hide.

"Mark lunged at me. I didn't realize we were that close to the edge until we were. And I screamed, even though nobody could hear me, and pulled back. He lost his balance and fell." She squeezes her eyes shut. "The sound he made when he fell—I'll have to live with that for the rest of my life."

Now she's steely, determined. "I didn't know anything about the backpack. I didn't ask him what was in it, and I didn't pack it for him. I had the picnic basket. I started running. I just needed to get out of the woods, to get help. Maybe I should have gone down to the creek, but I didn't even know how to get down there. I ran. I fell down the steep part of the trail and cut up my legs and hands. I got lost a bunch of times. Then I had to run home from the woods because Mark's car was there and I didn't have his keys, and my phone was dead, which was so dumb, because usually I charge it before leaving the house. There was nobody around, because it was really late. Nobody who could help."

A shuddering breath, shaking hands clasped in a seashell

342

fist. "I didn't know Keegan was waiting for us in the woods. Sometimes I wonder if he planned to get rid of both of us, and I just managed to get away. Mark Forrester didn't deserve to die. And my involvement will haunt me for the rest of my life."

Her fingernails are painted black. They drum on the podium in front of her. "I know Keegan is telling a different story, but this is mine. I can't make you believe me, but I hope you at least heard me."

Then Paxton comes in, asks her so many questions, attempts to flay her open and dissect her, but she remains neatly stitched up. She answers everything. She has nothing to hide. She's not the Blue-Eyed Boyfriend Killer but just a girl, a girl who wants the truth to reign.

The jury takes two hours to deliberate, and when they do, Tabitha Cousins is found not guilty of Mark Forrester's murder.

PART IV

After

Murder charges laid in Blue-Eyed Boyfriend Killer case: Cousins released

By Talia Sims

The trial of Tabitha Cousins, 17, has ended, with a jury unanimously deciding that Cousins is innocent of all charges in the hiking death of her former boyfriend, Princeton swimming champion Mark Forrester, 20. New evidence proved that Forrester's friend Keegan Leach, 20, was more than likely the one who initiated the murder, using Cousins as a pawn to get Forrester into the woods.

"I had no idea he was such a bad guy," a source close to Leach tells *People.* "He just seemed like the kind of guy whose life had lost direction. I guess he really resented Mark for having everything he didn't."

A trial for Leach will be scheduled in the coming weeks, but reports from inside the courtroom at Cousins's trial paint the portrait of a troubled young man with more than enough motive. According to insiders, Leach had been obsessed with Cousins for months, and was looking for revenge after she turned down one of his advances. A Gatorade bottle retrieved from underground at the crime scene included DNA from both Leach and Forrester, and Leach's computer search history revealed he had looked up a way to make Forrester's death appear accidental.

"I noticed his behavior was erratic in the weeks leading up to Mark's death," says a former coworker of Leach's, who wishes to remain unidentified. "Plus, he didn't even take any time off after. He seemed unaffected by the whole thing."

Cousins has been the subject of a media hailstorm since her release, and could not be reached for comment. Multiple sources claim that a bidding war is underway for her first televised interview, and there has already been talk of a tell-all book revealing her experiences being judged as guilty until proven innocent.

COMMENTS HAVE BEEN DISABLED

Accused teen's memoir to be published after bidding war

By Harriet Best

Eighteen-year-old Tabitha Cousins, the girl behind a media frenzy that took the country by storm last year when she was accused of murdering her boyfriend on a hike, will publish a memoir after an eight-house auction among major publishing houses. Cousins will purportedly write the book herself, recounting her harrowing experience in the woods, and her treatment as a monster in the weeks leading up to her trial.

"It's truly a fascinating story," says Addison Lowe, senior editor at Hartley Books, the winning house, which has a celebrated history of best-selling celebrity memoirs. "Readers will finally be able to learn everything about Tabitha, a girl who has piqued the curiosity of a nation."

Publication of the memoir is tentatively scheduled for next winter.

1

BECK

SEE? I TOLD YOU she didn't do anything wrong. Take that and shove it up your ass, Officer Old Man.

And yeah, no comment on anything else. I think I've been asked enough questions already, sweetheart.

2

ELLE

WE'RE SPLITTING UP, me and Tabby. We talked about
going to the University of Denver together but she didn't even
apply—at first she said it was because she missed too much
school, that she would never be able to catch up. But we both
know that's not true. She's staying home, working on the book.
Which I don't really understand, since it's the last place I'd want
to be after everything.

After everything. After Keegan got sentenced, after Tabby
stopped being infamous and started to become famous instead.
The girl, misunderstood, whose life almost got taken away
because she befriended a sad loner who wanted more than she
was willing to give. Keegan still hasn't admitted he did it—I can't
help but still follow everything happening with him. But the evidence says otherwise. More like, it screams otherwise.

Tabby is coming over to help me pack. We spent the summer together, just like old times, watching bad reality TV and
taking long walks and eating all the snacks Mom tried to force
on us. We never talked about Mark, or what Tabby had gone
through. I waited for her to bring it up, but she never did. Maybe
she had talked about it enough. Our friendship has somehow
become more about me, like Tabby wants a way to step out of
her spotlight.

I hear her ring the doorbell. In the distance, somebody is
riding a motorcycle, which always makes me think of Beck. I
haven't seen him all summer, and I heard he's staying in Coldcliff
to work at a bike shop. I don't care anyway. Dallas and I are back

together—well, sort of. We're figuring out what we are, if we can be anything. He'll be in Coldcliff another year, so we're not that far away. Maybe we have a chance.

"I'm glad you're staying in town," Mom says to Tabby. When I'm on the landing, I can see them downstairs, Mom's arms wrapped around Tabby.

"Me too," Tabby says. "All my memories are here. The good ones and bad ones. I don't think I'm ready to leave it all behind yet."

That Day in the Woods. That's the name of her memoir, the one Tabby is writing with the help of some woman named Aria, an author from New York who she has long Skype calls with. Of course there was going to be a book. I'm just surprised Tabby is the one writing it. She says she needs to tell her whole story, not let somebody else do it and get it wrong. She wants people to understand her. She wants the media circus to end.

That is what she calls it. The circus. She's still a regular on websites, even big ones, like *People* and the *Enquirer*. I wonder how they always know where she is. When we went shopping in Boulder a few weeks after her trial, there was a picture of the two of us with Starbucks cups, me a blurry figure beside her, half of my face cut out. *Tabitha Cousins and Friend.*

"I wish they'd just leave her alone," Mom keeps saying. "That girl has been through so much already."

There's going to be a movie, too, about Tabby's life and the case and everything she went through. I have no idea who's going to play her, or if there's going to be some actress playing me. I don't like the idea of other people acting it all out, stepping into our skin. When I asked Tabby how she could let it happen, she just shrugged.

"People are going to talk about it regardless of whether I let them," she said. "You don't know what it's like, for the entire world to be talking about you. It's like you're shaking a snow globe full of bullshit and the truth never lands."

I don't know what it's like, and I doubt I ever will. Drama follows Tabby. Mom asked her last week if she was dating anyone, if there were any special boys. Tabby rolled her eyes and kind of smiled. She gets tons of "fan mail" from people around the world, people claiming they always knew she was innocent. Marriage proposals. Invitations to take a ride on their luxury yachts. She reads every single one, sometimes out loud to me.

"Hey," she says now, thumping up the stairs. "College girl. We'd better get you packed."

Tabby is merciless at dividing what she calls "the crap" from the stuff I should actually bring with me. She shakes her head when I stuff a pair of platform boots into my suitcase, calling them "ancient." She starts pulling things out of my drawers, tossing them into piles. She and Mom read that Marie Kondo book about how decluttering is supposed to enhance your life, as if how much stuff you have in a room really matters.

"This is kind of exciting," she says. "You can pick and choose your baggage. I kind of wish I was going with you."

"I wish you were coming, too." I sit on the edge of my bed. "We could have been roommates, like we talked about. It won't be the same without you."

It won't be the same without her. But maybe that's a good thing. We can finally stop dueling for the same sun, the same one that seems to perpetually shine down on Tabby. Maybe ours is a friendship that will get stronger with distance.

"I just need time," Tabby says. "My publisher wants this draft done by the end of next month. I think I can have it finished by then, but I can't imagine dealing with college at the same time. And there's all this publicity stuff. Plus, they're flying me out to LA to meet with the movie people in a few weeks. I keep telling myself that college will always be there."

I nod, and I try to understand why she's doing all this. It's like everything that happened cleaved Tabby into two different versions of herself. The girl I knew, the one who walked around like a zombie in the days after Mark died, the one who screamed when she got arrested, teary when I visited her in juvie. *I didn't do it.* She's so much harder now, like a shell has formed around whatever soft underbelly she might have had. I have to say something especially sharp for her to even hear it.

"I guess we can probably say goodbye to this one," Tabby says, holding up a blur of orange, and all the breath goes out of me when I realize what it is. Mark's sweatshirt. The Princeton one that I wore to the clinic. She never asked for it back.

"I don't want it," I say. "I don't need another memory of . . . that."

Tabby lays the sweatshirt on my bed with its arms outstretched, as if it's a person and it's telling us to stop. "Same. I don't need another memory either."

I don't know if she's talking about my abortion and the rumors, or about Mark's death, or her relationship with Mark, or all of it, a tangled mess. Despite the heat—our air conditioner is broken again, yet another thing Dad says he'll fix—goose bumps cover my arms when she pulls me in for a hug.

"I'm going to miss you," she says, her embrace hard, her arms like strong wires across my back. "Sometimes I think you're the only person who knows who I really am."

"I'll Snap you every day," I say. "Pictures of shitty cafeteria food and my dorm room." Tabby has a new phone number now, because her old number was blowing up with calls and messages.

"You better," she says. "But you're not even far away. I'm gonna be up there visiting pretty much every weekend. You can't get rid of me so easily."

"I don't want to." I'm lucky to have Tabby. We're lucky to have each other. I'm lucky my secrets haven't surfaced and we can build over them without crushing our foundation.

Her phone goes off, and she smiles at it. "Look, I've gotta go. I think you're good to finish this on your own, right?"

"Sure," I say. "But I thought you were staying for dinner. My mom's making beef Stroganoff."

"I know," she says. "But there'll be plenty of days I can eat beef Stroganoff with Maggie. There's just somewhere I need to be."

"Okay," I say. "I guess this is goodbye, then."

"For now," she says, pulling me in for another hug. "I love you, Elle, no matter what."

"I love you, too."

Then she's gone, with Mark's sweatshirt over her arm, and I realize she didn't help me pack at all. She just took clothes out of drawers and tossed them into a pile of *nos* on the floor. I barely have anything she deemed worthy of taking.

That's when I hear it. That sound. That motorcycle. I run across the hall into my parents' room, which overlooks the street, and look down. Beck is in front of the house, just like I used to fantasize about. For a second—just the tiniest sliver of time—I think he's here for me, and the old feelings bubble back up. *He did feel the same way.*

But then I see an orange blur hop on the back of the bike. He hands her a helmet. Before they speed away, I swear she looks up, even though she has no way of knowing I'm standing here.

I swear she looks up and smiles.

3

BRIDGET

TABBY'S BACK HOME, back in her room. She sleeps a lot, wears the same makeup, eats the same food. She spends more time with me than she used to, because she cleared away some of that mess. There aren't boys anymore, or so she claims. She reads and writes and takes long walks without telling anyone where she's going. And my parents let her, because they know they're never going to be able to rein her in anyway.

Things are normal with us, or as normal as they can be. I guess in a way, our family is in a better place now. My parents weren't thrilled when Tabby told them she wanted to defer college—they accused her of wasting an opportunity—but she pacified them. "College will always be there," she said, all calm and collected—Tabby is always calm and collected now. It's like she left her temper back in juvie. "I have to take this opportunity."

This opportunity—her book. Tabby did tell me she wanted to be a writer, once. I think she was thirteen and I was eleven, and we were new to Coldcliff, and she said something like, *I'll have stories to tell someday. Just wait.* My little eleven-year-old body couldn't begin to comprehend all the messiness that it was about to go through.

I'm in the book, of course. I let Tabby and Aria "interview" me, Aria with her exaggeratedly round Harry Potter glasses that I'm pretty sure are just for display, to make her look cool. I see the glances she and Tabby share and I wonder if Aria has replaced Elle, has replaced me.

I'm in the book but I don't want to read it.

Tabby hugged me fiercely when she was released after the trial. Her body on mine, pulsing and electric. I couldn't remember when she got that strong, or maybe she had always been strong, and I just noticed other things about her first. That's what I've realized, through all of this. The world sees what it wants, and makes sure everyone else sees it, too. If you want to know the truth, you really have to burrow. And most people don't have the energy for that.

"Thank you," Tabby said. She knew about the shoes.

Sometimes when I can't sleep, I think about the shoes. If it would have made a difference if I had told the truth, or if I would have wanted it to. *They weren't mine*, I imagine myself saying. *I never got that close to the creek*.

Sometimes I wonder if the worst things people thought about my sister weren't even the worst things she's capable of.

I wear Sauconys now. And I run faster than ever. Most of the time, my thoughts can't keep up.

4

LOU

MY MOM'S COMPUTER is password protected now, but that doesn't stop me from trying to guess the password every time she's in the shower or at the gym or getting coffee with a girlfriend. I'm not even sure why I care so much about hacking into her computer. It's not like I'm expecting to find something about Tabby. I guess I'm just bored, and bored girls usually have very interesting appetites.

You can't really blame me. I mean, yes, Keegan did it, and I have no idea why I didn't see that he was a psycho sooner. (I was alone in the woods with him! Honestly, I'm never doing that again.) He knew where he was going, and he had that map, and he lied to me about when he printed it. Plus, there was the Gatorade bottle with some of his DNA on it, buried by the creek, and all that stuff on his internet search history. I thought he was kind of a sad loser, but he's so much creepier than I ever thought. He keeps saying he didn't do it.

It's not like I believe him. It's just, something he said in his last interview kind of got to me. It feels like he was trying to talk directly to me. *I had nothing to do with Mark Forrester's death. I know somebody out there must believe me. Yeah, I made mistakes, but Tabby was the mastermind. She pulled it off. There has to be proof somewhere.*

There has to be proof somewhere. And I'm maybe the only one who can find it. I don't owe it to Keegan, or Beck (God, I have no idea what I ever saw in him—we are so over!), or even my readers at Sharp Edges. I owe it to myself, because the truth is what really keeps me warm at night in a way no boy ever will.

There are a few holes in Keegan's story, but I keep coming back to the Gatorade. Why not take the bottle with him? Why leave it there? People are saying it was some kind of trophy, but Keegan seems smarter than that. Pretty much it's assumed that he panicked and had nowhere to put it—there aren't many garbage cans in the woods, and he was meeting Kyla and didn't want to take any evidence with him.

He claims he didn't even drink Gatorade that day. He says Tabby must have taken an empty bottle from his apartment and had Mark drink out of it, too, because that explains how both their DNA ended up on it. I'm not sure what I believe, but, like, he's pretty fucked, excuse my language. The odds are most definitely not in his favor.

I got coffee with Tabby once during the summer, at the Starbucks downtown. It was like having a celebrity friend—well, what I imagined it would be like. People stopped to talk to her, to tell her they always knew she was innocent. A couple girls wanted her autograph and asked about her book. She was so patient with everyone, the smile never leaving her face. I wondered how she did it.

"Everyone is so nice," she said when it was just the two of us, iced coffees sweating on the table between us. "When you're not a threat anymore."

It was a weird thing to say. But who am I to judge? I mean, I've never been in juvie. I'm sure it messes you up. There were a lot of things I wanted to say to Tabby, about being sorry for being a bitch and stuff, but I never said a single one. Maybe because I wasn't, and I'm not. Maybe because she hasn't apologized for taking Blanche and messing with my head about the scout.

That night was when I thought of a place that Keegan's

somewhere might be. My mom's computer. I have no idea if my mom still sees Tabby or not, but she got to meet one-on-one with her. She must have some kind of opinion.

I've tried every combination of password. My mom's middle name, her maiden name, her favorite wine, all the place names she talks about wanting to visit. Today, I'm just about ready to give up when I try a name I haven't yet. Mine. *Louisa.*

And just like that, I'm in. Kind of embarrassing that it took me that long, right? Don't tell my Sharp Edges readers.

My mom is out for a run, which means I probably don't have much time left. Luckily, she has file folders for each patient labeled with their last name. I click on *Cousins* and see the same document I saw before—same format—but totally different content. This doesn't even sound like the same girl.

Speaks about her paranoia and has nightmares. Trouble sleeping, feelings of isolation and guilt. Afraid to admit to anyone that she thinks her sister played a role in Mark Forrester's death. Scared her sister isn't who she says she is.

I pause on the last line, then scroll back up to the top. The file isn't about Tabby at all. It's about *B. Cousins.* Bridget. I don't see the other file at all and now I'm wondering if I misread the name, or if my mom sees both Cousins girls.

That doesn't matter. What does is that Tabby's own sister thinks she did it.

I'm dizzy, slumping against the back of my mom's chair. The sun shines in hard from the street, slanting into her office window and making yellow pools on her desk. A familiar laugh makes me jerk up—she's back from her run, chatting with our neighbor. I click out of Bridget's folder and watch my mother, in her spandex tights, put a hand on Mr. Roth's shoulder. Maybe he's the one from the bar. Or maybe he's the one now, and there will always be a one.

I close her laptop and slink out of her office, leaving everything exactly where she left it. I think about visiting Bridget Cousins, about somehow finding a way to ask her everything. But Tabby lives there, too, under the same roof, guarding her sister like a dragon. Maybe Bridget is just troubled, just confused. Or maybe she's the only one close enough to understand what we all missed.

5

KEEGAN

I KNOW WHAT EVERYONE THOUGHT about me when I hung out with Mark. That I was his charity case, the stray dog taken in by the Good Samaritan. Turns out, it's that way even when he's not around. Except I'm not stray anymore. I'm the exact opposite. Caged.

Don't bother asking me if I did it. I told the truth, what happened between Tabby and me. If you didn't believe it then, you never will. Not after she went up there and fucking lied in front of everyone. I hated that girl, then I loved her, and now I hate her all over again, and I don't even know what was real for her.

I know what she told me. I guess that's what I'm stuck holding on to for the rest of my goddamn life.

Just take my advice—don't talk to her, don't listen to her, don't even look at her for too long. That's what did me in. No fucking comment on everything else.

Hello America: Anne Leon Interviews Tabitha Cousins
Tuesday, January 5, 2021

The camera loves her. It hits her black hair, raven-shiny, zooms in on her face, because it's a face so easy to get close to. She wouldn't be this famous, nowhere near this known, if she wasn't pretty to back it up. Girls get wronged every day of their lives, but sometimes pretty girls get to make it right.

Today she's on *Hello America*, talking about her book. The movie. Her life, since *That Day in the Woods*. She's sitting down with Anne Leon. Rumor has it, she'd been offered sit-down interviews with just about every television news station in America, but she specifically wanted *Hello America*, wanted Anne. Rumor has it they paid six figures for her.

"Sometimes it feels like it happened last night," she says, staring straight into the camera. "I wake up sweating, thinking I'm still out there, lost in the woods, trying to find my way out. Sometimes I still wear his sweatshirt, because it's all I have left of him." Even her tears, when they fall onto her cheeks, are pretty.

"You've become a role model for a lot of girls," Anne says. "About being strong in the face of adversity. The storm you weathered last year—that wasn't easy. How did this affect your relationships with family and friends?"

Tabby sighs, a quick little intake of air. "It really let me know who my real friends are, and who really cares. And those people will be in my life forever." She cocks her head at the camera. "You know, sometimes you find out people are lying to you, and the only thing you can do is cut them from your life, and realize you're better off without them."

"Wise words," says Anne. "Especially when so many girls feel the need to be people pleasers. Tabitha, we've already talked about your book and what it means to you. Now there's going to be a movie based on your life. Instead of retreating, you've really put yourself out there. Do you think there's a reason why?"

"Oh, absolutely." Her hands rest in her lap, unmoving. She knows exactly what she's going to say. "They expected me to retreat. But stories like mine need to be told. I lost months of my life being accused of something I didn't do. I missed my senior year, because I couldn't go back after the trial, with everyone talking about me. I missed having a prom. I know they seem like silly little things, but they're the moments that make up a life. Putting myself and my story out there are ways of getting that life back."

Anne smiles sagely. She knows millions of people are watching this show. She knows this interview is headlining every website. "Tabitha, we've talked a lot about forgiveness, and about learning to move on. To leave it all behind, to quote your book. You said something so memorable in that searing first chapter. 'When all eyes are on you, there's nowhere else to look but in. I saw a girl there, young and scared. She's not there anymore, but I am.' What do you have to say to the people who didn't believe you? All the people who had a role in changing your life and perception of yourself?"

Tabby smiles at Anne, then stares directly at the screen, to the millions of viewers in America and beyond, at the legions of people who either believed her or didn't. It takes a minute before she speaks. Maybe she doesn't know what to say. Or maybe she has been waiting to address them all this time.

"I'd tell them not to believe everything they hear," she says, her voice measured. "I'd tell them I'm just a girl, just like some of them." The corners of her mouth turn up, her signature smirk. "And I'd say that unless they were me, they'll never possibly know the whole story."

6

TABBY

NEVER FORGET WHOSE STORY THIS IS.

You've either been waiting to hear from me, or you don't even care what I have to say, because you've already made up your mind about me. And if you're in that second camp? Congratulations, you're everybody who perpetuates what every girl already thinks about herself. That people look at us and judge before we can even open our mouths.

Let me just say this: the boys are still in my head. They're shacked up in there, almost like they're Ken dolls, playing house, except they're boys, and nobody wants to cook or clean. They all expect someone else to clean up their messes.

If you've been waiting for me the whole time, well, that's sweet. Except really, it's not, because you're expecting me to spill. You want me to unzip myself and take out all my secrets, one by one, polish them and put them on a shelf and explain them. Maybe Exhibit One would be the Nikes, the footprint left behind. Exhibit Two, the map. Exhibit Three, the rock-filled backpack, which nobody has really been able to explain very well, have they? And good old Exhibit Four, the fact that someone saw me packing a picnic basket full of rocks the day before it happened. I know people online are talking about all that, even urging the police to keep investigating, because there's something they missed.

I mean, if you really want the whole story, you'll buy my book, right? Did you know it's always been a dream of mine to have a *New York Times* bestseller before I hit twenty? Why twenty, you ask? Well, because life puts girls in a pressure cooker, and everybody wants the teenage sensation. I always knew I could write. Well, now the world knows it, too. (Yes, Aria helped, but I did the heavy lifting. Like I said, never forget whose story this is.)

I'm going to assume you've already bought my book, or are going to buy it, so okay, I'll give you some bonus content. I'll tell you a story about a girl who loved not just one boy, but more than one. She liked how they looked at her, how they touched her, how powerful she felt when they worshipped her body. Is that so wrong? If you're nodding your head, well, nobody's making you keep reading.

But let's say that something got in the way of every single boy. That the first one you really loved made you promises, then went back to his girlfriend, every time, then got drunk and crashed into a tree and blamed you when his football career was over, so everyone else did, too. That the next one found out about one thoughtless kiss that meant nothing and broke your heart. That the next one you trusted was just a glorified college playboy, and you trusted the one who came with him, who didn't just throw you under the bus so much as tie you to the road and watch the bus run over you. Again and again.

I spent almost two months in juvie. Maybe you don't think that's a big deal, but have you been there? It's a truly awful place, but it gave me time to think. My brain went to some dark places. Sometimes, when things were really bad, I turned on myself, the same way the rest of the world turned on me. I thought of myself as guilty, even though I had done nothing wrong except trust my heart with the wrong people. I plotted how I would have done it, if I were capable of that kind of thing.

Let's get something straight. I never slept with Keegan Leach. But I trusted him in another way—with my mind. We were friends, or so I thought. I didn't really tell anyone else about the friendship, because I knew what they'd think. *Oh, there's Tabby, screwing her boyfriend's best friend*. It was so not like that. We both missed Mark, and at first I think we were jealous of each other. I was Mark's new shiny thing, and Keegan was Mark's constant.

But Keegan has convinced some people otherwise. That I wanted to break up with Mark to be with him instead. Did you believe him? (If so, really?)

I don't owe you the truth about what happened that day in the woods. But here, I'll humor you a bit. I'll mess with your head the same way everyone else tried to mess with mine and make me think the worst things about myself.

Maybe the hike was my idea. It was as simple as Mark saying something righteous like, *Where is there to hike around here?* And I told him I'd heard of this place called the Mayflower Trail, and that I'd wanted to check it out. With him, of course. Guys are suckers for being the protector. As if I need to be protected from anything.

Okay, okay, so let's just say I already knew those woods well. I didn't tell Mark I'd been there before. I didn't tell him that I knew every single path. I didn't tell him I knew where the ground was hard and where it was soft, that I knew how to practically dance over the roots to avoid a sprained ankle. I let him think it was all his idea. He got all macho, telling me I needed to get hiking boots and proper gear. I let him play the man role, knowing it would be the last time he ever played it.

Shh. This is all hypothetical, remember? It didn't really happen this way, and you've made your mind up about me anyway.

In this scenario—where I'm guilty—I used Keegan, the sad loner who was not-so-secretly in love with me.

We researched everything together—on his computer, of course. He thought we were going on a hike to the Split. He said Mark was afraid of heights and would need a good shove to make it up there. I joked that the shove would be better at the top, because that way I wouldn't have to break up with him and endure the aftermath.

"Anything for you," Keegan said. It had been pitifully easy to get him to fall for me. He was *so* desperate for human contact. "I'll do it, you know."

But we don't actually need boys, do we? We're capable of doing things on our own.

Mark put up a fight. Well, technically, we fought the entire way up to the Split. We argued about last year, about now, about what was going to happen next year. He accused me of being jealous and overbearing. I called him an asshole. I stared at his back—of course I was behind him, exactly where he wanted me—and the backpack there. He'd bitched when I asked him to carry it, of course—don't believe everything you read, folks, because Mark was no gentleman, just your average horny frat bro minus the actual frat house.

Anyway, when Mark asked what was in the backpack, I just said "Stuff we might need. Why, can you not handle it?" And he scowled and put it on his back, because of course the great Mark the Shark, (former) swimming champion, could handle a goddamn backpack.

Mark got way ahead of me, because he was six inches taller and probably also because he was pissed off and wanted to show that he could do that. He could leave me there if he wanted to. The Split loomed in front of us, this big dark mass, and I was basically one giant heartbeat.

When we stood at the top, I realized I was terrified of heights. Mark sensed it, softened toward me. He liked me weak.

"Don't worry," he said. "Nothing will happen to you."

I put the picnic basket down. I stared at the view—we had earned it, right? The trees were everywhere, a green and brown swirl, some of the leaves orange and red at the very tops, like they were getting a sunburn.

Mark sat down. Started to shrug out of the backpack, which wasn't part of the plan. The backpack would make him drop fast, pull him under, kill him quickly. It would be okay, though. When he stood up and put it back on—then I'd do it.

But instead, he opened it. My mouth became an O of shock when I saw his eyebrows come together like they did when he was confused.

"What the—" he said, launching to his feet. "Why are there rocks in here?"

Oh, Mark. Dense to the very end.

I had thought a lot about what my last words to Mark would be, but in that moment, I forgot them all. He still hadn't put it together, and time was slipping past. Any second he would really figure it out, and any second he would move, because he was standing so close to the edge.

"I'm sorry," I said, and I held my arms out. His went out instinctively, too—he thought I was going to hug him, maybe. But instead, my palms made contact with his chest, and he went over the edge, with the backpack slung around one arm.

My scream was louder than his.

I don't know how long it took me to get down—maybe an hour, maybe more—but I ran, I fell, my legs bled. I was a mess, dirty and sweaty, and I realized I had left the picnic basket behind, and that it didn't have any food in it—the sandwiches I'd made were still in the fridge. I would get rid of them when I got home. The key to getting away with it was not being sloppy.

I didn't see Mark at first. It was dark out and I panicked, thinking he managed to get out, that he was staggering through the woods and I would have to hunt him down like a wounded animal. I had to get right up close to the creek—ta-da, the footprint!—and that was when I practically bumped into his body, bobbing there, arms outstretched, like a starfish.

You're wondering if he was dead by then, or if I had to finish him off. And that's one secret I'll never tell. Maybe I only stuck around long enough to see if he would surface. I knew from all his bragging that Mark could hold his breath for just shy of five minutes. I waited ten.

The backpack, though—it was nowhere to be found. I thrashed around for a few minutes, digging under the water for it, before realizing the creek was a lot deeper than I thought. I wasn't going to find it, and I needed to get home.

But not before I planted something of Keegan's where nobody would ever find it, unless they really knew where to look. The Gatorade! That was another brilliant touch. Mark and Keegan both chugged the stuff nonstop. It was so easy to slip some vodka into Mark's bottle, and if he noticed, he didn't say anything. I wanted him just a bit disoriented. Just a bit slow, so that I could pounce right.

I knew I'd end up arrested, but that was okay, because I also knew they didn't have enough to convict me in the end. The diary—did I really believe what I wrote in it, or was it a whole bunch of bullshit, because I knew they'd find it? You decide. Maybe it was my best work, the most brilliant fiction I'll ever create. Maybe it was the truth, from a girl who didn't know any better.

I gambled with my own future, and they say the house always wins. But the house is no match for the teenage girl living in it.

If you were to look at my junior high yearbook, you'd see my hopeful little face, my boobs pushed up to my chin even then, because I had them before everyone else and figured I might as well use them. You'd see my nickname—Tabby Cat, which nobody ever called me, but I was embarrassed to not have an actual nickname. Kennedy just called me "Hottie," but she called everyone "Hottie," probably because she thought it made her sound cool. You'd see my favorite quote—"a prayer for the wild at heart kept in cages"—which I told anyone who asked that it was from my favorite Tennessee Williams play, but it was really stolen from one of Angelina Jolie's tattoos.

You'd see my ambition, the heart of that girl, out there on the page for everyone to see. *Become a best-selling author by age twenty.*

I'm sure they laughed at me behind my back. It was ridiculous, putting so much of myself out there. I should have put something generic like everyone else did. *Get rich* or *be happy*. But if you've followed along, you know I'm not generic, now, am I? Plus, I read somewhere that your chances of achieving something are at least fifty percent higher if you write it down.

I don't know what became of everyone else in that class, if they Got Rich or Became Happy. But me—I'm a girl, nineteen now, and my little life story is about to hit the *New York Times* bestseller list. I guess you could say I got what I wanted, even though I had to do something wild to get there.

Okay, did you actually believe all that?

Because I made it all up. I'm supposed to be modest, but you believe it, because I'm a damn good writer. (Or because you want a reason to hate me, in which case, you're part of the problem.)

I spent so much time in juvie with nothing to do that I've made up a lot of stories in my head. Imaginary friends are great company when you're alone in the dark, and imaginary enemies are even better. I've thought about that day in the woods, all the days leading up to it, so many times that I've been able to construct endless versions of the same thing. I've been able to consider how I would have done it, if I did it at all. I've cast myself as a victim and a villain, but can you honestly tell me you haven't been both in your own life?

Here's what really happened. But I'll warn you, it's not nearly as exciting. Mark's fingers were gripping my arm, tight enough to hurt. *We're going on a hike this weekend. Eight miles. I know you're out of shape, but you can handle it.* (Really nice, right?)

I went along with it because I loved him, and maybe because I wanted to prove something to him. That I could do it.

He bitched and complained the farther we got into the woods. He hated that I brought a picnic basket. He chastised me for wearing shorts instead of long pants. He laughed because I had lipstick on. (Excuse me for wanting to look nice!) And when we made it up to the Split (him a few minutes ahead of me, because he was sick of waiting around), I felt this sense of pride in myself that I had done it. Do you know what he said? He turned around and said, "It took you long enough."

Then he took a drink of Gatorade and laid into me about coming on to Keegan. I started to cry, because that's what I do when someone yells at me. Then he lunged, like he wanted to hurt me. That's when he lost his balance. I'll never forget the look on his face—a mixture of revulsion and shock. I wake up with it burned into my brain, along with a question nobody will ever be able to answer. Would he have hurt me, if he hadn't slipped? Would I have been the one underwater in the creek? Or would he have realized he was being an asshole, apologized, and let me tell my version of the story?

I tried to find my way down, to see if he was okay. But the whole time, I swear, I heard breathing, and the occasional laugh. I know I wasn't alone in those woods. When I told the cops, they told me I had gone through a trauma. They convinced me I was hearing things. I knew they didn't believe me, and wouldn't believe another word I said.

Now, be honest. Ask yourself if you really think I did it. And if the answer is yes, ask yourself why. Why you assumed I was guilty. The answers might be very telling.

I've pretty much said everything I have to say. You can love me or hate me, victimize me or demonize me, but after all this, you're going to remember me, and that goddamn counts for something.

Maybe I'm just a girl who was in the wrong place at the wrong time.

Maybe I'm just a girl who has had to live with all of your eyes on me for too long.

Maybe I'm just a girl.

ACKNOWLEDGMENTS

Making fictional characters feel real is a job that starts in an author's (sometimes disturbed) imagination, but involves so many other smart, passionate people. I have been very lucky indeed to work with the enthusiastic team at Imprint. Thank you to my editors, Erin Stein and Nicole Otto, for your excellent suggestions and the care you took with this manuscript. I had so much fun collaborating and editing with both of you.

To Connie Gabbert and Natalie C. Sousa, thank you for designing such a striking cover that perfectly captures Tabby's infamous gaze. Thanks are also in order for the rest of the Imprint team—Jessica Chung, Carolyn Bull, John Morgan, and Weslie Turner. To Dawn Ryan and Avia Perez in managing editorial, Kerry Johnson for her copyediting magic, and Raymond Ernesto Colón in production. To the Fierce Reads team for your marketing and publicity efforts. To Katy Robitzski and the Macmillan audio team.

Thanks to my magical superagent, Hillary Jacobson, for believing in this book and in all of my writing, and to Josie Freedman and Randie Adler at ICM for their hard work on the film side.

Thank you to Kathleen Rushall for your support, encouragement, and guidance, and to Taryn Fagerness for handling the foreign rights side of things.

Most writers would be nowhere without their writer friends, aka the only people who truly understand the roller coaster that is publishing. So much love is owed to all of mine.

Eternal hugs (and bags of all-dressed chips that hopefully don't explode) to Emily Martin, who is an utterly brilliant critique partner and an even better friend. To Samantha Joyce, for believing that I can do great things and being there for me when I'm down—always with the best advice and panda GIFs. To Marci Lyn Curtis for our hilarious and often questionable DM chats that shall never see the light of day. To Darcy Woods for our marathon phone calls (#bubblesmakeitbetter) and Erika David for both writerly support and SOMA. To the talented, inspiring members of the debut groups Sweet Sixteens and Sixteen to Read—we're still on this ride together four years later, and I respect and adore you all more with each passing year.

To everyone who read early drafts of this book and offered encouragement and support—I love you all.

Being a writer means a lot of time spent alone, which requires an incredibly understanding family. I may be biased, but I have the best one. My parents, Denis and Lucy Burns, knew I was meant to be a writer and never failed to encourage my creativity. Now that I'm a parent, too, I can't thank them enough for all they did to shape me into the person I am now. Thank you, Mom and Dad, for letting me grow up seeing my massive ambitions as balloons—buoyed by hope and optimism—and not as anchors. Dad, I like to think I inherited (some of) your work ethic, and Mom, I know I got my fair share of your fun-loving spirit. (Oh, and I feel like in every book acknowledgments, I have to say a word of thanks for all the leftovers and groceries you guys still bring me.)

My sister, Erin Shakes, is also my BFF, and continually supports me in everything I do. Thanks for the world's longest Messenger conversation (sorry to our husbands), for enabling my purse purchases, and always being up for a Sephora trip or dinner with bottle(s) of wine. Thank you to Jermaine Shakes for being an eternally positive and upbeat presence, and to Fiona for her adorable royal waves.

To all of the Flynns, thanks for reading and recommending my book babies so enthusiastically. To my in-laws, Jim and Doreen, for always being interested in what's happening in book world and celebrating my good news. To my sisters-in-law, Suzanne and Kelly, thank you for making the time to read and tell friends about your book nieces.

Thank you to my extended family—aunts, uncles, cousins—for your support, with special hugs to Aunt Linda, Uncle Tom, and Aunt Pat. And to those no longer with me in person, but there in spirit: I know Grandma Gibb (Honeybee) and Grandma Burns are watching out for me, and I continue to feel their presence in my life.

To my network of girlfriends, both old and new, thank you for being exactly the kind of independent, inspiring women I want to surround myself with. And as always, to the RBF ladies for too many laughs and DC jokes.

To the person who puts up with me on a daily basis and has been there since before I sent my first query—my husband, Steve. Thanks for letting my head live in the clouds part of the time, for making space for my big dreams, and for talking me through lots of mental roadblocks. To my babies, Astrid and Cullen—you're too young to read this book (yet), but your brilliant, effervescent little spirits motivate me every single day. Astrid likes to say "I love our family." I do, too, more than anything.

To coffee, quite simply, for everything. Aside from my husband, you're my greatest love story.

To you—readers, bloggers, teachers, librarians, booksellers—your passion makes the writing community what it is, and I'm endlessly grateful to be part of it.

Lastly, I want to send love to my inspiration: teenage girls.

To the Tabbys, Elles, Bridgets, Lous, and Kylas. To every girl who has ever felt judged, used, or misunderstood; who has ever felt too invisible or too seen. I hear your voices, and for what it's worth, I believe in you and your ability to do great things. I wrote this book, and will continue to write, for you.